BROKEN SHIELD

BROKEN SHIELD

ISABELLA

SAPPHIRE BOOKS

SALINAS, CALIFORNIA

Acknowledgements

Thank you to the beta readers. Lee Fitzsimmons, her nursing skills proved invaluable, as well as the sage advice she gave throughout. Lynette Mae, for her encouragement and her law enforcement expertise. Terry Baker, whose feedback is much appreciated. I can't thank you enough for your suggestions. Finally, Peggy Adams, who made the few catches no ones else could.

To Ilene, the best editor I've ever worked with. Thank you for making me think. Your honest feedback made the book better.

Finally, this is dedicated to all those that put on a badge and put their lives on the line to keep us safe. I am forever in your debt.

My heart, my love, and my world have room for only one woman, Schileen. If I am lucky, the last thing I will see when I take my final breath, will be your beautiful brown eyes. Your lips, the last kiss I taste and your voice, the last song I hear.

Mi Amor, Schileen!

Prologue

Tyler sat cross-legged in the riverbed and looked down at the chrome deliverance cradled in her hands. The smell of honeysuckle drifted through the air. It enveloped Tyler as she contemplated what had brought her to this instance in time. It was ironic that she had picked a river bottom to sit in. Lately, it felt like every step Tyler took was like walking through quicksand. The struggle to move forward only added to her resolve to do what needed to be done today.

Thinking about Jill, tears began streaming down her face falling in little pools on her shirt. Tyler had stopped trying to control the tears weeks ago. They made her feel weak and she had finally just succumbed to the weakness. She had been so strong for so long, never once did she cry. She didn't want to be weak, not when she had been so strong. Remembering the day she lost Jill, Tyler's body curled under the memory.

She and her partner had been dispatched to an officer down call. Everyone in the city responded to the scene, including the fire department. Coming on scene, Tyler and her partner had to wind their way around a dozen police vehicles that were already there. Tyler's focus was clear, get to the victim, assess the situation, and save their life. She had done it a hundred times. This time, a set of hands stopped her progress to the group of officers circling the officer who lay on the ground. Tyler could barely see between their legs as the group shifted to let her partner through. Blood was pooling around the navy uniform, an arm stretched out in the middle of it.

"Tyler, stop. I can't let you go in there," Jill's partner, Kelly said, stopping Tyler's further progress.

"Kelly, I need to get in there. What the fuck are you doing?" Tyler looked down at the hands on her chest and then up at her friend's face. Realization hit her.

"It's Jill, Tyler."

"No," Tyler whispered. Her resolve to get to her wife pushed her past Kelly. "Mike?"

Tyler looked at her partner, watching as he was halfway through his routine. The blood pressure cuff hung from Jill's arm. Pointing to her wife's stomach, he ordered Tyler to apply pressure to the blood soaked gauze under his hand. Tyler's legs felt as if they would buckle any minute so she dropped to her knees on the other side of her wife's body.

The pale color of Jill's skin terrified Tyler as she pushed hard on the blood soaked gauze. Blood oozed between her fingers as she called for more gauze. Slipping her arm under Jill's head, she lowered her head to whisper in Jill's ear.

"Baby, you're gonna be fine."

Jill slowly opened her eyes to look at her lover.

"I love you, Baby," she whispered.

"I love you, too." Tyler tightened her hold on Jill's slight body.

"Be strong."

"I can't."

"You have to. Promise me," Jill said looking up at Tyler.

Tyler could only nod as she gently caressed Jill's face. Bending down and kissing her lips, Tyler savored what looking back now, would be the last time they kissed. Resting her head against Jill's, she felt Jill take one last shuddered breath and relax. The silence around the couple was deafening. No one moved. Tyler gently rocked Jill, refusing to believe her wife was dead.

"Do something, Mike. Don't just sit there," Tyler said, laying Jill down. "Get the paddles." Tyler began chest compressions. "One, two, three …"

Mike stood and pulled Tyler back. "Ty, there's nothing we can do. She's gone."

"No, she's not gone until they call it at the hospital. Now, get back there and do your job, damnit."

"Tyler." Kelly grabbed Tyler's shoulders and pulled her away. "Tyler, you did everything you could."

"No, Kelly…" Tyler whispered in desperation, "I can't lose her."

"I know, Honey." Tears pooled in Kelly's eyes as she held Tyler.

Tragedy would quickly play itself out again in Tyler's life. Two weeks later, a similar scene occurred as she rolled on a motor vehicle accident. This time though, it would be Tyler holding her father as they both stood strong in their grief. Her mother had been hit head-on when a driver feel asleep at the wheel. Molly Jackson was the pillar of the Jackson family. She raised a family of firefighters and carried on the stoic tradition of a woman who accepted tragedy as a part of the firefighter lifestyle. Tyler's mother was her rock when Jill died. She had helped Tyler plan the funeral, held Tyler when she thought she might crumble at Jill's funeral, and waited and watched as Tyler bore her grief silently. Molly's death was the final brick of an already weighty load that pushed Tyler over the edge.

Now, Tyler sat looking down the barrel of what

would bring Jill and her back together. She spun the cylinder, hypnotically watching the silver tips as they made their circular journey to their new location. Tyler had thought she could deal with the pain but she now knew she was wrong. Every morning she woke up and pulled Jill's pillow to her face, breathing in her scent. But she never cried. She was strong, just as she had promised. Today though, Tyler would break that promise. *Would Jill be mad when we see each other again or would she understand?* Tyler wondered.

Tyler put the barrel in her mouth and her fillings tingled. The sight on the end of the barrel hit the roof of Tyler's mouth as she slid the gun back further. Her tongue caressed the smooth barrel as she closed her mouth. Closing her eyes and squeezing them shut, Tyler felt the last of the tears roll down her face. The ridges of the hammer gently bit into her thumb as she clicked it back. The first click rang in Tyler's ears, the second click alerting her that the painful journey through life was almost over.

As she sat there Jill's smiling face flashed in Tyler's mind, her laugh echoed in her ears, and Tyler felt Jill's arms wrap around her body.

"Baby, please be strong," was whispered in Tyler's ear.

I can't, I just can't. I'm sorry. A warm soft breath caressed her neck as Tyler took a deep breath and closed her eyes.

Brinnggg, brinnngg.

Tyler's cell phone went off in her jacket pocket. She didn't want to answer it. Tyler was on a mission and it didn't matter anymore who called. Reaching in, Tyler pulled it out and pushed the end button. Without thinking, Tyler looked down and saw a message from her father. Pulling the gun out of her mouth she tapped the screen.

"Shit."

Tears began streaming down her face again as she read the message.

Happy Birthday, Honey. I know you're going through a tough time, but I just wanted you to know I love you. Don't forget dinner tonight, love Dad

Chapter One

One year later.

Hey, Sarg. What do we have?" Captain Russo asked the police sergeant on the scene. The two story wooden structure was fully engulfed by the time Engine Company Three got to the residence on Harcourt drive.

"Hey, Captain. We might have someone inside the residence," the officer said, quickly jotting down notes for his report.

"No Shit? In that?" Captain Russo pointed to the red-hot structure.

"Well, the neighbor over there called it in about ten minutes ago. He said he heard a popping noise, went to check it out and saw the house smoking. The neighbor looked around and said by the time he got over to it, one of the windows in the back blew out. So he ran back and called 911," the sergeant said. "He said that he thought the parents had left for the weekend, but that there might be one of the teenagers home. He couldn't be sure."

"Thanks," Captain Russo said over his shoulder, as he walked over to a group of firefighters checking their oxygen tanks and helmets. "Ok everyone, we might have people inside, but we're not sure. You three—" pointing to the three closest to him, "You get the job of trying to see if anyone is inside. Remember, everyone goes in alive and you all come out the same way. I don't want anyone taking any unnecessary risks. You got me?" yelled the captain over the fire raging behind him.

"The rest of you, help finish laying down the lines from the street to the pumper and let's get this baby out," he said as the Fire Chief approached.

Captain Russo went about explaining the situation to the chief and discussed the possibility of people inside. Because of the blown out windows, the captain knew the fire was going to accelerate quickly. It was getting the oxygen it needed to burn hotter and quicker. He knew this would put his people at greater risk, but he didn't have a choice. He had to send them in.

So far, the fire looked as though it was limited to the first floor of the house, with smoke starting to billow out through the windows and doors. The flames licked out the windows and doorframes, causing the firefighters that entered the house to drop down to the ground immediately.

"John, I'm gonna take the right side of the downstairs first," said Tyler. She reached up to flick on the mag light taped to her helmet.

"J.J., you start on the right hand side of the upstairs. When we're done we'll join you up there," Tyler directed, kneeling down to start the job of looking for people.

"Okay, I'll take the back end of the house. Then we meet back here and go up to the second floor, together Tyler. Got it?" J.J. breathed into his headset.

"Got it."

Taking a quick survey of the burning left side of the house, they split up, reaching out for anything that might look like a person. The smoke was already so thick that it left only two feet above the floor for the firefighters to maneuver in safely. Since no one had told them what age the occupants might be, the firefighters checked every closet, piece of furniture and cabinet to make sure a child wasn't trying to hide to avoid the smoke.

"Clear on this side, John," Tyler said into her mic.

"Good, clear back there, too," John replied.

Making their way back to the entryway, the firefighters were getting ready to go up the stairs when they heard a huge crash. Looking back into the already engulfed room, they saw the source of the crash. The ceiling had come down and the fire was burning through to the second floor. A bathtub, toilet and sink fell through the floor, barely missing them.

"Shit, John, we gotta hurry. If someone is up there, we might have just lost them," shouted Tyler over the penetrating sound of the flames working up the walls.

Outside, the fire crews worked to control the fire, while the police set up lines to keep the local residents back. This was an older part of the city with wide streets and big wooden houses. The kind of established neighborhood where everyone knew each other and spoke regularly. It wasn't surprising to see all the neighbors, and a few who didn't belong, watching the action.

###

Ashley Henderson knew this neighborhood well. She grew up in the upper middle class neighborhood, so it was difficult to see one of the old homes going up in flames. Her mom lived nearby and had probably heard the sirens. Ashley made a mental note to go over and let her mom know what was going on before she left the scene to write her report. Her mom would probably be surprised to see her, since Ashley usually didn't work this side of town. But she had requested a change in her patrol, and this was her new assignment. She proceeded to finish taping down the scene when Lt. Connors came over.

"Officer Henderson, I want you to make sure the residents stay back. And keep everyone out of the way of the equipment. We still have EMT coming, just in case anyone gets hurt, as well as another engine company since it's now a two alarm," Lt. Connors advised. "Oh, and welcome to your new patrol area. I hear you grew up here?"

"Thanks, yeah just a couple of blocks over. My mom still lives there," she replied, realizing he would eventually wonder why a rich kid like her would want to be a police officer. She recognized the look the officer gave her when her words sank in. Shrugging it off, Ashley went about finishing the barricade. Both officers glanced back at the house when they heard the loud crash come from inside.

"I hope that wasn't one of our guys going down in there," he stated matter-of-factly.

"What would one of our people be doing in there?" Ashley questioned, concerned that a police officer would risk their life in a burning building.

"When I say 'one of our guys' I mean one of our firefighters. We're all public servants. You know—A brotherhood of sorts," Lieutenant Connors said, fondly acknowledging the professional courtesy police and firefighters extended to one another.

"Gotcha," said Ashley.

She'd had few dealings with most of the local firefighters. Ashley worked mostly vice and gangs in her short career, but met a few firefighters when a bust went south and the John got hurt. Her bachelor's degree was in computer science, so her superiors felt that Ashley was more valuable working behind a computer than in a patrol car. She had spent a lot of her time establishing a database for the department of all the gangs and gang members in the city. Her work made it easier to track those members and what they were involved in. The move to vice was a welcome change when it was offered.

Vice, on the other hand, had been fun for her. Ashley worked catching Johns and drug dealers. Her "good looks" made her an easy choice, according to her captain. She didn't disagree outright, but she never really felt attractive. She wouldn't have picked a vice assignment if it hadn't been for one of her peers getting pregnant. The department was desperate to find someone when prostitutes started being assaulted, so she volunteered to help out. Her offer was really made tongue-in-cheek to a friend in the department, but word got back to the brass and the next thing she knew, she was a "working girl". After that assignment though, she was ready for patrol duty.

Looking back at the burning structure, she wondered what type of individual would volunteer to walk into a burning building.

The two-story structure was starting to burn through the exterior on the north side and the captain was starting to worry about the firefighters inside.

"Ok, you three. I want you to start working your way out of that structure. We have the left side of the exterior engulfed and it won't be long before the whole thing is fully engulfed. So get your asses out of there now," he yelled into his headset.

"Roger Captain. I am starting to work my way

out," shouted J.J. into his headset. He had covered the left side of the upstairs and had found nothing. The smoke was starting to choke off his vision and make it more difficult to differentiate things. He was working by feel now and knew that he had little time to get back out of the maze he had worked himself into.

"I am almost done on this side, Captain. How about you Tyler? You ready to rock and roll outta here?" asked John as he felt around for his exit.

"Yeah, I'm workin' on it. Man, the smoke is thick as shit up here. Geez, we had better make short work of this search and get the heck outta here. John, be careful of that big hole on your side. I don't want to have to come save your ass again," joked Tyler, trying to maintain communication with the other firefighters.

"Right, like you've had to do that," he chided.

"Don't make me remind you of that fire over on Hillcrest," she said.

"That's enough. Focus on what you're doing and get your asses out of there now, you three," screamed the captain, listening to the whole exchange between the crew.

"Roger, Captain," the three quipped in unison.

It was clear that the captain was not going to be happy with them when they got out. He hated to send his people in without clear direction but, unfortunately, this was the part of the job that worked his patience and his nerves. Working a fire was dangerous, however sending people into a burning building was worse. One never knew how fast a fire was going to work its way through a structure. A second story made it even more lethal.

"Come on, come on," he thought as he watched the glowing house. So far, he couldn't see any of his people exiting the building. He watched as the firefighters worked the exterior, dousing the flames at their base. But it didn't stop most of the flames from greedily eating away at the wooden structure. The whole left side and center of the house were glowing from the burning timber and he knew it wouldn't be long before the entire property was lost.

"Get your asses out of there now, you three," he yelled into the headset, his frustration evident in his voice. "I want to see your asses out here now, do you hear me?"

"J.J., where are you?" John asked.

"I am coming out of the hallway right now. Can you see me?" he replied, not stopping for an answer.

"Yeah, I got a visual on ya. How about you, Tyler? Where are you?" John asked again.

"I am working my way out of the right side. I'll be right behind you guys. Start moving before the captain comes in here and drags our asses out feet first," Tyler said, knowing the captain just might do that very thing if they didn't get out soon.

The three would-be-rescuers began working their way out of the glowing structure. Each one was relieved that not only did they not find anyone inside, but that they had once again left another burning building intact. John and J.J. reached each other at the top of the stairs and gave each other a high-five and a thumbs-up. They knew they had spent too much time in the house and their oxygen was getting dangerously low. A quick exit was definitely in order.

The captain stood watching the house. He began to see his people exiting the blazing structure. He released a deep breath and felt the tension leave his shoulders. Scanning the group, he did a head count and realized he was one short.

"Shit," he mumbled.

Just then, Ashley came up to the captain. "Sir," she said, interrupting his growing concern. "These are the owners of the home. I think you might want to talk to them about who's home."

"Huh? Right. Sorry about your home. Can you tell me if anyone is inside? Your neighbor thought that one of your children might be home. Is that possible?" he asked, watching the front door of the house.

"Well, we just talked to our son and he left earlier this afternoon. So no, no one should be home," cried the older gentleman, hugging his wife and watching his life going up in flames. Ashley put her arm around the shoulders of the older couple, trying to offer what little comfort she could.

"Okay, then let's get this doused and mopped up before any other structures become involved," yelled the captain.

"Tyler, where the fuck are you? Get your damn ass out here now."

A dark figured started to show itself, slowly growing in the blazing glow of the fire. Finally stopping a few yards away from the group, she dropped to her knees.

"Shit," yelled someone from the group, the captain, J.J. and John all running to her.

"Are you alright, Tyler?

Tyler lurched forward putting her hands out in front of her to steady herself as she gulped for much needed air. When she did, the package that she was protecting fell out of her jacket and onto the lawn. She had run out of air minutes before exiting the house and it was all she could do to make it outside before passing out. Her head was spinning from the lack of oxygen and she knew she was in bad shape.

"Capt …" was all she could get out before passing out and landing just next to the reason she had risked her life in the first place.

"Kittens? You risked your life for some stupid cats, Tyler," Captain Russo yelled, bending down to pull off Tyler's mask. "Medic, get over here."

A group of firefighters gathered around Tyler, taking off her helmet, air-tank harness, and turnout jacket. Two paramedics reached Tyler's side. One started oxygen while the other peered into each eye with a flashlight.

Rubbing a knuckle across Tyler's chest, one of the paramedics called her name, "Tyler, Tyler, wake-up. Can you hear me?"

Ashley watched while the paramedics went through their resuscitation routine. Tyler's soot covered face couldn't hide how beautiful she was. A small ring around her face, where the mask had protected it, showed high cheekbones and a straight nose. *She could be a model*, thought Ashley, as she continued her assessment of the firefighter. Suspenders framed the white tank top she had on, the outline of her bra showing through the tightness. Her turnout pants rested just below the firm breasts.

When there was no response, one of the paramedics started an I.V. Looking up at the captain, he raised his eyebrows as if to ask, *what now?*

"Shit. Get her on the bus and let's get her to the hospital," Captain Russo said as he shook his head and rubbed his mustache.

Chapter Two

Tyler rode her motorcycle like a woman possessed. The bike ate up the highway, each stripe on the road becoming a blur whizzing past her. Her short hospital stay had produced no ill effects and she had gotten the number of a cute RN for her troubles. All in all, a wash, thought Tyler, remembering the ass chewing she had gotten from the captain afterwards. The warm breeze caressed her chest and bare arms. The goose bumps were a result of the tingle that etched through her body when she rode this fast. Her headphones thumped in her ears, the music an indulgence she enjoyed when she rode. The sultry voice of the blues singer made her smile when she thought about the last time she danced to the song. It had been their song, Jill and Tyler's, and they played it every time they danced together. But that had been over a year ago and now Tyler's gut clenched at the memory.

The smile evaporated and she punched the MP3 player that was attached to the handlebars to the next song, wishing she had remembered to take the song off the darn thing. Memories weren't a friend she invited over anymore. She'd had her one shot at happiness and it had ended badly. Now, all she needed was a fast bike, a faster woman and a shot of good tequila. Then, the pain could join the rest of their friends tucked away in the back of her mind where they belonged. Weaving between the now slowing traffic, she wished she had left earlier to ride. Her days off were few and far between sometimes. Switching shifts with other firefighters who needed a day or two more for vacation or more time for a family event gave her the diversion she needed. Besides, what would she do with all the free time? Working only nine days out of the month was starting to drive her crazy.

The traffic was starting to let up as she passed the reason for the slowdown. A stranded motorist with a cop car behind it had caused all the rubber-neckers to slow down and watch the drama, obviously hoping it was something more. Tyler gunned the bike when the traffic dispersed more, weaving in and out of the nosey crowd. Looking down at the clock in her fairing she calculated it would take her a good half an hour more because of the traffic before she met the guys over the hill at the Look Out. The restaurant was a magnet for bikers. Street racers loved the curves up to the restaurant and cruisers liked the easy ride through the mountains. Who would have guessed both saw the same ride so differently. Leaning back Tyler stretched herself, propping her long legs on her highway bar pegs. Getting comfortable, she rolled the throttle a little more until the baritone of the pipes smoothed out. She didn't need to worry about being side swiped now that she was out of city traffic, so she let the rumble roll out a bit softer.

Ashley heard the bike as it passed her location. The stranded motorist was frantic and swore she had filled the car with gas the night before.

"Is it possible you have a hole in the tank,

Ma'am?" Ashley inquired, watching the motorcycle as it crept past her location. *Illegal pipes,* she thought before responding to the answer she received to her question.

"I know I filled it. I have the receipt right here," said the motorist, shoving the paper at Ashley. "I want to file a robbery report. Someone has obviously stolen my gas."

"Ma'am, I'm not sure we'll find whoever stole your gas. Besides, unless you saw them, I'm pretty sure we won't catch 'em." Ashley smiled at the older woman, wishing for one short second she had stayed in vice. "I'll be happy to send an officer to your house later and he can look around and see if he can find anything."

"What about fingerprints? Why don't you take some fingerprints right now?" The woman's persistence was wearing on Ashley.

"Ma'am, we're right in the middle of traffic and that wouldn't be safe for either of us. Besides, I work patrol and you would need to see someone from the burglary division to write a report. Okay?" Ashley knew she was placating the woman, but she was hoping the woman would see reason. She wished the day was already over and she had just started her shift. "Why don't you call a tow service to come out and bring you a gallon of gas so you can get where you're going. I can wait here until they arrive."

Crossing her arms indignantly, the older woman said, "I don't own a cell phone. I don't want brain cancer getting me just because someone wants to talk to me right now. They can wait until I get home and call me then."

Dropping her head in defeat, Ashley pulled her cell phone from her belt and handed it to the woman. "Please, tell me you have towing."

"Of course. We've been auto club members since they started forty years ago." Looking inside her huge purse, the woman started rummaging around. "Now if I can just remember what I did with that card."

Keying the mic on her shoulder, Ashley let dispatch know she was going to be at her present location until the tow truck arrived. *Unless, of course, I'm hit by a bus,* she wished, continuing to watch junk fly out of the small carry-on the woman called a purse.

Chapter Three

Tyler stretched in the chair and listened to the conversations swirling around her. She picked bits and pieces of one or another, yet didn't commit any to memory. She was letting the last beer she had over an hour ago work its way through her system. The ride back would be slow and relaxing, hopefully. The talk around the table turned to women, everyone's favorite topic of late. The guys she hung with were all single and serial daters. Few of them had steady girlfriends, a reflection of their firefighter lifestyle. Women loved men in uniform and lesbians were no exception. Tyler never lacked for female companionship, ever, and the best part of it all was that she didn't have friends with benefits. She didn't need friends. She needed diversions that kept her body stimulated and her mind engaged in the moment.

"Yeah, did you see that hottie working the Hawthorne fire the other night?" J.J. asked, taking another pull from his beer.

"No, I was too busy saving Sparky over here," one of the paramedics said, slapping Tyler's thigh.

Tyler heard someone let out a meow and everyone started laughing. Tyler blushed as she looked around the table. Her buddies were like family. But she didn't take shit from her family, so she wasn't about to take shit from these guys either.

"Very funny, ya bunch of dick heads." Tyler

slapped at the hand that briefly rested on her thigh. "Keep it there and you might lose it. Then what will you tell your penis when it wants a date?"

"That you're available." The smirk that greeted Tyler made her laugh. It had taken a long time for her to become one of the 'guys' and she had appreciated their support when she lost Jill.

Tyler jumped up and sat in the paramedic's lap with a thud, wrapping her arms around his neck. Planting a kiss on his lips, she devilishly smiled at her buddy.

"Last time I checked, I didn't bat for your team. So unless you're switching sides," Tyler said, looking at his flat chest, "you're dreaming." Leaning in, she gently slapped his cheek. "Wake up honey. You're having a bad dream." Her face rubbed against the rough bristle of the young man's face.

The raucous laughter worked its way around the table as she hugged the paramedic closer. Tyler knew she was making the paramedic blush but she didn't care. If he was going to give, he better be willing to receive.

"Big strong men like you make my heart flutter," Tyler said, batting her eyes at the now visibly embarrassed paramedic. "Eww, I love your scruff, too, ya big bear." Tyler ran her hand over the chest hair that peaked out from his shirt.

The paramedic tried to toss Tyler off his lap, but she just hugged him tighter. "Geez, Tyler. I can't understand why you're still single, bein' such a sweet talker and all."

"Anyway, what were we talking about?" Tyler wiggled her eyebrows at the men sitting at the table. "Women?"

"Come on Tyler, are you saying you didn't notice

Officer Henderson the other night?" J.J. asked, throwing Tyler a skeptical look. J.J. knew Tyler better than anyone at the table so she just shrugged her shoulders and went back to stroking the furry chest. Tyler didn't remember much after dropping the kittens on the ground. The next memory she had was the voice of her captain yelling at her as the ambulance closed its doors and raced to the hospital. This time she had been admitted to the hospital overnight, the scorching pain in her chest a testament to the careless way she treated her life. Sitting back down in her seat, she tried to remember if she had seen anyone new at the fire scene, but drew a blank.

"Guess not, buddy. I actually don't remember much except the Captain chewing me a new ass before the bus took me to the hospital." Tyler smiled at J.J. and shrugged again. "Nice, huh?"

"Nice? This chick is hot, man, and there is no way she bats for your team. No way," J.J. said, a few others echoing his proclamation. Tyler laughed as the men started making bets on who would get her number first.

"Well you know what they say guys, two drinks away ..." Tyler raised her empty glass and smirked. The men grumbled around her with comments of "bullshit" and "no way, she's too hot" or "we didn't get the gay vibe off her".

Smiling, Tyler raised her hands in defeat and said, "Okay, I'm just saying."

Chapter Four

The bar started to get crowded as Tyler looked at each and every woman that walked through the door. Soon, seating would fill up and Tyler would have her pick of any of a number of beautiful women. Surveying the room, she picked out one or two as possible options for when she was ready to leave. Until then, she would work the room as she always did, chatting them up, dancing, and then slowing cruising around the room until she decided.

"Hey Max, the usual," Tyler said, tapping the bar with her wallet.

"Sure thing, Stud." Max winked and pulled the tap.

"Knock it off," Tyler said, as she remembered the last time she and Max hooked up.

"What?"

"Truce," Tyler said, as she lifted the glass in salute to Max.

"Look Tyler, it was nice and all, but I wouldn't call it earth shattering. Okay?" Max said, filling another order.

"What? You mean I didn't rock your world?" Tyler laughed, as she winked at Max.

"I know you could do better than that if your heart was in it. So let's just leave it at that." Max smiled and moved down the bar.

Tyler pondered what Max said for a few moments before raising her glass again. She liked her life, one woman at a time, two if she was lucky, and work. What more could a woman ask for? *Oh well, you can't please 'em all the time,* thought Tyler, scouring the room for a future replacement.

Tyler relaxed into the beat of the music and watched the games begin. She was definitely a people watcher. It came from her years in the military as a medic.

"Sit around and wait for the wounded to come to you," her sergeant told her one day when she was ready to jump out of her skin. *"Don't worry. It won't stay quiet for long."*

He was right. Ten minutes later, they were jumping through their asses when a platoon was hit by an IED. Luckily, it was mostly shrapnel wounds, but she had seen busted arms and legs cause by IEDs. Moving fast, she helped triage the wounded and worked on the worst soldiers first. That was four years ago and old habits died hard.

Looking up from her beer, Tyler was amazed to see a red haired goddess standing right next to her. How could Tyler have missed her walking in, let alone walking up to the bar right next to her? Smiling, Tyler positioned her body closer to the beautiful woman, so close that her perfume enveloped Tyler—sweet, citrus and arousing. As Tyler looked at the stunning woman, she noticed something familiar about her, but she just couldn't place it.

"Max," Tyler said, nodding her head in the woman's direction, "it's on me."

"Hi, Max," Ashley said, as she looked at the bartender. "I can buy my own drinks, thanks."

"Okay, what'll it be then?"

"Rum and cola and a pale ale," Ashley said, tossing bills on the bar.

Sticking her hand out, Tyler said, "Hi, I don't think we've met yet. I'm—"

"I know who you are, Tyler," Ashley said, trying not to look at Tyler.

"Have we met before?"

"No, but I know all about you, so you're just wasting your time," Ashley said, smiling back at Max. "Thanks."

Not missing the look, a sudden realization hit Tyler. "Oh, you're with Max. Sorry, I didn't know," she said, throwing her hands up as if to block something.

"No," Ashley chuckled. "I'm not with Max. Sorry Max." She smiled at the bartender, who winked back.

"Maybe next time though," Max said as she sauntered off.

"Okay, I'm confused. How do you know me?"

"Let's just say your reputation precedes you," Ashley said, sipping from the ale.

"What reputation would that be?" Tyler's tone became chilly.

"You're a player. Everyone knows it and I'm not interested in being a notch on your bed."

"Aren't you being just a bit presumptuous?"

"Hmm, well were you just about to buy me a drink and chat me up?"

"Well," Tyler stumbled, not sure what to say next. She had never had her motives questioned and it was irritating her.

"Well?" Ashley asked back.

"What's wrong with buying a beautiful woman a drink?"

"Nothing, as long as that's all it is," Ashley said as she grabbed both drinks and started to leave.

"Wait, *who* told you about me?"

Tossing her head towards the dance floor, Ashley said, "She did. She said she's a good friend of yours."

Tyler looked and saw Kelly, *her* best friend, waving at her.

"Shit, how do you know Kelly?" Tyler asked, waving back at her friend.

"She's my partner."

"You're on the force?"

"Yep, and she told me all about you. Night," Ashley said, walking towards Kelly.

"Shit," Tyler said, slapping her hand on the bar.

"What's wrong, Stud? Get shot down?" Max snickered again.

"Fuck you, Max."

"Sorry, Honey, not tonight. Maybe next time." With that, Max was at the other end of the bar chatting with a sexy blonde.

Aggravated, Tyler pushed her way to the back of the club and leaned on the pool table. She was rarely turned down. It had been a long time since someone had rejected her bed. Well, the conversation hadn't gotten that far, but Tyler had hoped it would, considering how beautiful the woman was. Sulking, she watched as women danced against each other. The sexual energy in the room was rising with each song. She searched for the two prospects she had pegged earlier, but couldn't find them. It was turning out to be a crappy night and she hated being alone when she wanted company. A pair of hands reached around her stomach and pulled her close.

"Hey sexy," a voice whispered, caressing her ear.

"Hey Kell," Tyler said, as she pulled on the arms, prying them from her. "What gives with that gal?"

"Oh, you mean Ashley?" Kelly said, looking over

her shoulder at Ashley.

"Is that her name? I guess I didn't get a chance to ask her, since she already knew so much about me." Tyler sat on the corner of the pool table and palmed a ball.

"Look, Tyler, I can explain. She's my partner and when she started going all gaga over you after the fire, I needed to set her straight. She's a nice gal and I don't want to see her hurt."

"What are you talking about, Kell? She's an adult who can make her own decisions, right?"

"Yeah, and you're a player, Tyler, plain and simple. You use women like placeholders for Jill. Well, news flash, Jill isn't coming back. So let her go and move on."

"What are you talking about? I know Jill is gone. I was there when she died, remember? I held her in my arms and watched her die, remember?" Tyler became agitated as she relived that day.

"Look Tyler, it's been over a year since Jill died and you live like you don't expect to see tomorrow," Kelly said, biting her lip. "The motorcycles, going back to being a firefighter, the fast cars and even faster women. I'm surprised you haven't caught a disease or two. You haven't, have you?"

"Screw you, Kell." Tyler reached in her pocket and pulled out her keys. She didn't need this and she wasn't about to stand around and listen to Kelly talk about Jill. "If you haven't noticed, I'm not sitting around feeling sorry for myself. I know Jill is gone and I don't need you to remind me."

"I'm sorry, Tyler. I know you think you're fine. But watching from the outside, I see it differently," Kelly said, grabbing Tyler's arm to stop her from leaving.

"Take your hand off me." Tyler's tone became menacing as she stared Kelly down. "I don't need someone rating my dating habits. Now, if you will excuse me."

"Tyler, I'm sorry. I know you think I'm out of line, but I've known you for a long time. I've never seen you like this and I'm really worried about you."

"Well don't worry. I can take care of myself. I've been doing it for years."

Tyler tossed the cue ball down the table and started to walk off.

"See you Sunday," Kelly said to the retreating back.

"Sunday?

"Michael's birthday," Kelly reminded Tyler. "He wants to see his god-mother's motorcycle."

"You got a bike," Tyler said without turning back.

"Yeah, but mine is for work. It doesn't have flames and skulls like yours."

"What time Sunday?"

"One o'clock is good."

"Fine."

"Tyler? One more thing." Tyler felt Kelly put a hand on her shoulder and knead the muscle underneath. "Could you make sure to cover your tank? I don't want any of the mothers mad at me because their son saw a naked lady."

Tyler had painted her motorcycle two years ago in memory of Jill. A nude angel, in Jill's likeness, sat on the top of her gas tank and flames and skulls framed the sides. Tyler told everyone it signified the hell she was going through without Jill. The truth was Tyler didn't want to be without Jill, no matter where she was.

"Whatever."

"Sorry. I hope I didn't cause you any problems with Tyler," Ashley said, wiping the sweat from her glass.

"Naw, Tyler's cool. She doesn't like to have the reality check cashed. Her dad handles her with kid gloves and women just throw themselves at her, so I get to do the heavy lifting when it comes to dealing with her."

"I don't understand." Ashley looked at Kelly and wondered what she was trying to say. Throwing up her hands, Ashley said, "You know what, it isn't any of my business. Forget I said anything, 'kay?"

"It's probably better that way. Besides, it'll give you and Tyler something to talk about next time you see her," Kelly said, taking another pull from her beer.

"I thought you warned me off her. I'm confused."

"If you think that was the last time you'll see Tyler, think again. When she wants something, she goes after it. Besides, you turned her down. You're a challenge now." Kelly smiled at Ashley and wiped the foam from her lip.

"Okay, so …?" Ashley said, searching Kelly's face for an answer.

"Go with your gut when it comes to Tyler. She's a great gal, she just doesn't know it."

"But you just said earlier she knows how good she is." Ashley was completely confused now.

"She knows she's good in bed. She just doesn't know what a great catch she is. She's too busy running from herself to get caught."

Ashley took a deep breath and closed her eyes. She was confused and starting to feel like she was in a Laurel and Hardy movie and she didn't know who was on first. She was attracted to Tyler the first time she saw her at the fire, but Kelly had warned her about

Tyler. In fact, Tyler had quite a history with more than one woman in the department. She was known as the female Casanova of Precinct One. Tyler "started fires and left 'em burnin'," was how one female officer had said it. Another said that Tyler had given her "third degree burns in all the right spots". Ashley figured she had heard every fire metaphor when it came to Tyler.

"I don't understand."

"Tyler was married to the only female officer killed in the line of duty. It happened two years ago and, ever since then, she's been meeting the devil head on. She takes risks she shouldn't take, and does things she would never do if Jill were still alive."

There were a few who talked about the other Tyler, too. She had heard the stories of Tyler being in love with a fellow officer named Jill Sherman, who had died in the line of duty. Jill's picture hung on the "wall of the fallen" and it had been the first thing Ashley had seen when she came to the precinct. Her beautiful face made Ashley choke up when she realized where Jill's picture was. Jill was young, too young to be hanging on a wall with just a few other older male officers. But it was a fact of life for officers on the force and no one was exempt from the chance that they could give their life in the line of duty.

"I see. Well I'm not the fix 'em type, if you know what I mean," Ashley said, wishing she hadn't been so harsh with Tyler now that she knew about Jill Sherman.

Chapter Five

Tyler slammed her hands against the steering wheel of her car, cursing. Who cared how she lived her life? She wasn't hurting anyone. She wasn't a drunk and she didn't hide away in a dark apartment, depressed. No, she didn't fall apart after Jill's death. She had kept it together, so whose business was it who she slept with?

Losing both her mother and her lover in the same month nearly killed her. She sure as hell didn't owe Kelly an explanation about her behavior and she didn't need to explain her life to anyone, including the beautiful redhead, Ashley. Tyler flicked the lights on and gunned the fastback. Every muscle in her body was strung tight, on the verge of snapping as she watched the speedometer click past eighty. The deserted road was no match for her fastback as it ate up the pavement. Thoughts of Jill flashed before her as each mile brought her closer to her lover.

Stop, Tyler. No good can come from this. Jill's voice echoed in Tyler's head as she stomped on the accelerator. Jerking on the wheel, the car made a quick right on to a dirt road. Dust kicking up in her wake made her invisible to anyone stupid enough to follow. Weaving between scrub brush, she pushed the car faster, burying the needle past one hundred ten miles per hour.

Stop this now, Tyler. Jill's voice thrummed in her head now as she kept her foot on the gas. She was starting to outrun her headlights, the car running over small patches of brush in her race to outrun the voice. Suddenly, Tyler stomped on the brakes with both feet, feeling the car start to slide sideways, coming up just short of hitting a massive oak tree. Her head throbbed as adrenaline pumped through her. Her body started to shake as she looked at the massive oak filling up her side window. Getting out of the car, Tyler fell to the ground and started pounding it with her fists.

"Get out of my head, damn it." Tyler choked on the dust billowing up around her. "Damn it, Jill. Why couldn't it have been me instead? Why? Why you?"

Sitting back on her heels, Tyler felt her body sag with defeat. She hadn't had a moment like this in years, so why now? She was sick of the innuendos, the looks of sympathy she still got from some of the police officers and the pity that always followed. Her life had stood still, captured by bookend tragedies that now framed the way she lived. Moving on wasn't the issue. Dealing with the pain she tried to outrun was. She and her father had faced the tragedies together. One solid and unwavering as it overshadowed her life, the other devastated from the loss of the woman he had been married to for thirty-five years.

Had her years in combat changed her so much that outwardly she couldn't grieve? For Tyler, to grieve would show a weakness she didn't want anyone to see, least of all her fellow firefighters or Jill's fellow officers. They lived with risks and no one complained. As firefighters, they faced death nearly every day. Tyler had even faced her own mortality on the battlefield, only to cheat it. Perhaps, that's why death claimed Jill and her mother, because she had eluded it one too many times. Maybe that's why her fellow officers still looked at her with pity, because she hadn't broken down like her father. To be weak would get you killed. Losing your edge would get someone else killed, so she tucked it all away in some dark corner of her mind. But the memories revisited when they wanted and she knew she couldn't control when they came, only when they would leave.

Tyler sat back against her car. Tears etched their way down her dust covered face. A warmth enveloped Tyler as she heard Jill's voice again, *I'm always here with you, my love. But you can't keep doing this to yourself. It's time to move on, to love again.* Then, Tyler felt a soft caress on her cheek. The memories of Jill's touch were fainter and fainter with each passing episode and she was afraid she would lose them completely, so she hung on as long as she could to the moment. Sobs racked Tyler as she lost control. The command left Tyler speechless, her heart breaking at the thought of moving on.

"Don't leave me alone here, Jill. Please," Tyler pleaded, wiping her face as she stood and looked around. "Please don't leave me," she whispered, in desperation.

Chapter Six

Ashley finished the ticket and handed it with a warning to the young driver. "Don't let me catch you horsing around again. Driving is a privilege so you better treat it like one or you'll lose that privilege, understand?"

The driver, barely sixteen, nodded and blew out a deep breath before rolling up his window.

"Damn kids." Ashley slapped her ticket book against her hand as she walked back to her car. As she reached for the door handle, a loud motorcycle blew past her. Even before Ashley looked up she knew it was breaking the speed limit. All she saw when she did finally look up was a white tank top, a black helmet, and a blur of blue.

"Shit. What is it today?" Tossing her hat on the seat next to her, she flipped the lights and siren and waved at the driver still sitting on the side of the road. "Better not let me see you anytime soon, kid," she said as she merged into traffic giving chase to the motorcycle.

She watched as each car cut her a wide path, merging into the right hand lane. Maneuvering past the cars, Ashley accelerated to catch up to the motorcycle. Within a few seconds she was right behind the speeder, who was clearly oblivious to the lights behind him. Ashley keyed her siren on and off. The driver looked down into the mirrors and for the first time acknowledged her presence. The driver watched for an opening between two cars and merged right, but there wasn't enough room for Ashley's cruiser so she picked up the mic to the PA.

"Driver." When the driver on the motorcycle looked back at Ashley, she continued, "Yes, you. Pull over."

Traffic eased back and Ashley merged behind the motorcycle as it pulled off the pavement. Calling dispatch, Ashley requested wants and warrants on the license plate of the motorcycle and waited.

"No wants or warrants on Bravo, India, Tango, Echo, Mike, Echo. The motorcycle is registered to an T.J. Jackson, 1342 West Haven Drive."

"Roger Dispatch."

Ashley grabbed what she referred to as her "smokey" hat and slid it on. She had a "take no prisoners" attitude when dealing with men, especially with men who rode motorcycles. They usually had attitudes as big as their dicks and they let everyone see it. She was sure if they could, they would expose themselves at the drop of a hat just to prove they had the balls to ride that fast. The driver was still seated on the bike and watching her approach as she opened her ticket book.

"License, registration and proof of insurance, Mr. Jackson," Ashley said, as she started to fill in the necessary license plate information for her ticket. As requested, Ashley was handed the documents and a wallet. "Please take the license out of your wallet, Mr. Jackson." Still not looking up, she looked at her watch noting the time and day of the month and adding it to the ticket.

"Uh, hum."

Ashley heard the slight tenor of his voice as Mr. Jackson cleared his throat. Obviously he was pissed at being pulled over, but Ashley didn't care. He had broken the law. A long slender gloved hand tossed a license and other paperwork on her ticket book.

"Let me know if you need any more information, Officer." The last word hung like a slap across the face.

Ashley watched the slender man sit back down on his motorcycle, turn on the radio and prop his feet onto the handlebars. Leaning against his backrest, he reached up and laced his fingers behind his head, clearly dismissing Ashley. She could feel her temperature rising at the lack of respect displayed for her authority. Obviously, Mr. Jackson wasn't too concerned about breaking the law and his actions showed how patronizing he was. The demonstration only solidified Ashley's opinion of men. Arrogance rolled off the rider and it agitated Ashley. Well she would show the rider his mistake.

"Mr. Jack—"

"Ms. Jackson, Officer ..." Ashley watched as the driver paused, pulling down her shades and looking at Ashley's nametag. "Officer Henderson. Interesting."

Her shades. Ashley thought, immediately realizing her mistake. Looking the rider over she noticed the firm breasts tightly bound in the white tank top and a ponytail peeking out from under the helmet. Great, she had been so preoccupied with the ways she wanted to torture the rider that she completely overlooked the obvious slender figure of a woman. Geez, she said to herself, thinking about the apology she was now going to have to offer.

Ashley watched the woman swing her long legs off the handlebars and plant her feet firmly on the dirt shoulder. Slowly her gaze traveled up from the thick black boots, to the denim clad thighs and rested on firm, full breasts. The woman was tall, athletic and buff. Bare muscular arms ended with gloves so short Ashley thought they looked more like black finger cots attached to a leather pad. Never had Ashley taken such an assessment on a woman and she felt her body tighten at the sight.

"Uh hum."

Ashley's head popped up to look the driver in the eyes.

"My eyes are right here," the rider said, pointing to her face.

"My apologies, Ms. Jackson. I just assumed that you were a man. I don't usually get many speeding females riding motorcycles." Ashley adjusted her hat, wiping the sweat from her brow. Narrowing her eyes she took a second look at the driver. A familiarity swept over her, but she couldn't place it.

"You don't get speeding females?" Tyler questioned.

"No, I get speeding females. Just not ones that look like you, riding motorcycles." Ashley quickly turned and rolled her eyes. *Great, that came out just perfect. Now she's going to think I'm hitting on her.*

Ashley continued going through the paperwork she had been handed and wrote the ticket. Handing the license to the rider, she noticed the shine of a shield as it was slipped into her wallet.

"Excuse me. Are you a police officer?" Ashley inquired, still staring at the wallet.

Tyler flipped the wallet open and showed Ashley the badge next to her city I.D. "No, I'm a firefighter, Officer Henderson."

"Now, I remember. You're the woman from the bar. Shit, why didn't you say something? I could have extended you a professional courtesy and you would have just gotten a warning."

"Really? Thanks, but if I broke the law, I broke the law." Tyler's indifference surprised Ashley.

Many civil servants were quick to flash a badge and remind their brothers and sisters in blue that they were all one big happy family, hoping to get extended a professional courtesy. It often rankled Ashley that they used it as a get out of jail free card. It was treated as a license to speed and it was happening more often than she liked.

Ashley handed the rest of Tyler's documents back to her, giving her time to assess the woman in front of her. It was clear that she spent a lot of time outdoors, the tan muscular arms and shoulders framing the tight white tank top nicely. Snug jeans hung well off her hips and fit like a glove. Ashley couldn't help but notice the firm ass as Tyler bent over to stuff the items into her saddlebag. Clearly, she had a great body and didn't mind sharing it with anyone who wanted to look.

"Nice bike. Been riding long?" Ashley quickly lowered her gaze back to her ticket book and busied herself with finishing the write up. She had already said something she was sure would come back to haunt her, so she wouldn't stoke the fire Tyler always seemed to have burning just under the surface.

"Yeah." Tyler swung her leg over the bike and settled down on it. It was clear to Ashley she wasn't in the mood to talk and, frankly, Ashley wasn't willing to send the wrong signals. But since she was a friend of Kelly's, Ashley knew they would be seeing each other more often now that she and Kelly were partners.

"Look, Tyler, I'm sorry about what happened in the bar the other night." Handing Tyler the ticket, she continued, "I had no business judging you. Can we just start over?" Ashley extended her hand to the sullen woman and waited.

Crossing her arms Tyler looked at the extended hand.

Tyler looked at the officer standing near, her hand extended in some sort of peace offering. Only she wasn't sure she wanted to let the straight-laced woman off so easily. She had caught Officer Henderson cruising her body when she put her paperwork away and now it was her turn to make the officer squirm. Only Tyler's assessment would be brazen and deliberate. Looking at the officer, she got a clear picture of how squared away she really was—starting with the uniform and its razor creases. The uniform fit extremely well considering she was wearing a bulletproof vest. However, the humps on her chest made it obvious she was well endowed. Her slender form and straight back gave her an air of superiority that most officers seemed to have. Tyler wasn't sure if the attitude came with the clothes or if it was inserted anally during their time at the academy. It had taken a few years to rub Jill's pointed edges down to a smooth edge, but it had been worth it to find the diamond that lay underneath.

Officer Henderson also opted for the Smokey hat, rather than the service cap. It made a statement and was often the butt of many jokes. That told Tyler she could take a little heat from civilians if she wore the silly hat. Barely peeking out from under the hat was auburn hair, the color of the sunset on a brilliant rainy day. The kind of sun that peered out between clouds that had deposited their life giving nutrients and then, with one last hurrah, gave a grand exit. Lowering her gaze, she looked at the way Officer Henderson's pants were tailored. To the average person they fit fine, but Tyler recognized what was called a West Point cut to her trousers, with one single break in the front seam and the back of the slacks straight and lowered to the heel, but not touching the ground. *Military service,* thought Tyler. *Seems we do have something in common.* Well-shined shoes completed the uniform. Tyler would almost bet there was a second pair in the trunk, just in case one pair got dirty on the rare occasion she chased a suspect.

The soft make-up Officer Henderson wore was very conservative and accentuated her flawless skin. Eyes the color of a green shamrock stared at Tyler as she finished her assessment. Puckering her lips in a smirk, Tyler reached for Officer Henderson's hand, gave it a firm shake, and then let go.

"Well, if you will excuse me, Officer. Unless there is anything else, I need to be going before I'm late to a very important appointment," Tyler said, slapping her helmet on and buckling it. Strong arms grabbed the handlebars and righted the motorcycle as Tyler started it. The guttural moan from the pipes caused her to smile and look over at Office Henderson. If she wasn't careful she might get a ticket for loud pipes, but she would risk it considering there was little else the officer could site her for.

Peering around Ashley, she watched traffic and eased her bike closer to the pavement. This was often the most dangerous part, getting back on a busy highway. Too many distractions like cell phones, texting, eating, and the occasional hand job, all of which she had witnessed, kept people from paying attention. So, she had to be hyper-vigilant or stop riding and that wasn't an option. Nodding her head in Officer Henderson's direction, she went through the gear pattern pretty quickly and made it to highway speed in no time, disappearing into the heavy traffic.

Chapter Seven

Tyler could hear the children's laughter as she walked up the steps to Kelly's house. It was clear the party was in full swing and the exuberant screams inside made Tyler smile. She had fond memories of her and her brother's birthdays. Her mom had made every effort to make each one special, and they were always filled with laughter, cake, and plenty of presents. Stepping up, she pounded on the front door, making sure Kelly would hear her arrival, just in case she hadn't heard the motorcycle pull up.

"Tyler, Tyler. Can we see your motorcycle?" a cherub faced boy said, reaching his hands up.

He was so enthusiastic that Tyler knew she couldn't deny the birthday boy anything. Tyler bent down and picked up the giggling boy, gently tossing him in the air. Michael wasn't just the apple of his parents' eye, he was also Tyler and Jill's godson and he had been the one thing Tyler could focus on when Jill died. Tyler had spent endless weekends with Michael, offering to baby-sit every chance she got. The distraction was not only welcome, it was something she looked forward to. When Kelly had changed her schedule so she could be home with him more, there was no reason for Tyler to hang around. Besides, Kelly didn't need a third wheel following her around the park, preschool, and all the others things she was doing with Michael.

"Hey, glad you could make it," Kelly said, standing

by the door watching as kids started to marvel at Tyler's motorcycle.

"Yeah, I wouldn't have missed it for the world. Looks like things are just getting started."

"Not really. They've been like this for about an hour." Kelly looked frazzled as she picked up a dumped cup of punch, wiping the sugary drink off the vinyl floor.

"Wait, I thought you told me the party started at one." Tyler reached for the cup, taking it out of Kelly's tired hands. "I would have been here sooner if I had known."

"It's fine, Tyler. I thought more of the mothers were going to stay. Seems they just dropped and ran. Can't blame 'em. I probably would have done the same thing."

Tyler looked around the room, paper and cups everywhere. *How could half a dozen boys demolish a house in an hour?* Tyler shook her head. It was something she would never know now. "Come on. I told them they had to wait to get in the bouncy house until you got here. I need a few more eyes to keep watch. You never know when you might need someone with medical knowledge to help."

"Sure. Okay boys, bouncy house, then cake, then motorcycle. And if you're real good, I'll even start it and let you rev the engine. Deal?" A chorus of "deal" rang out and then Tyler was almost trampled by a stampede of boys making their way to the backyard.

Smiling, Tyler followed her best friend to the backyard and the cacophony of screams. This was a boys only party and the activity was almost more than Tyler could handle. Not one of the boys was still and she watched as the endless streams of energy ran the yard like an obstacle course, finally ending up in the bouncy house.

"God, Kelly, how do you do it?" Tyler looked around the devastation of the yard. A piñata hung from one of the limbs of the tree, ready to take its mandatory beating before pouring its bounty all over the ground. Toys littered every corner, making Tyler wonder how many would survive the day's events.

"Oh it's not that bad Tyler, trust me. I've been through worse at work," Kelly said, always looking on the bright side of things. Walking around the yard she and Tyler picked up the debris left behind by the marauding boys. "It's only once a year so I can manage. It really makes me reconsider more kids, though."

"Yeah, it reminds me why I never want kids—ever." Tyler smiled, knowing she was lying.

"Yeah, well everyone knows you're just a big kid. So whoever took you on would have to raise you, too."

"Funny," Tyler said, then stuck her tongue out at Kelly.

"Adult, Tyler. Really adult," Kelly said, sticking her tongue right back at Tyler.

"Cute. You better be careful, I just might interpret that as the lesbian high sign." Tyler winked and then went back to picking up the last few errant toys. "Where's Mike? I wouldn't think he would want to miss out on all the action, considering he's just a big kid, too."

Mike and Kelly had waited to have kids for years. Being a cop wasn't easy and being married to a cop was even more difficult, as Tyler could attest, but both Kelly and Mike were cops. Making matters worse, they both worked patrol, which left little time to be together. But they made it work and Tyler admired them for it.

"He wanted to be here, but he got called in to work.

You know it's killing him missing Michael's birthday."

"I bet. Well, I'll stand in for him till he gets back." A knock at the door interrupted the conversation.

"Hold that thought. Michael get off Jason. I don't care if he's a pony, you're not to ride him. Get off, now." Kelly looked at Tyler imploringly for help.

"I got it. Go answer the door and I'll watch the young heathens." Tyler laughed as she walked to the bouncy house.

Ashley pulled into Kelly's driveway and parked behind a very familiar motorcycle. Kelly hadn't told her that Tyler would be at the party. It didn't matter. She would have come regardless. She was just assigned to partner-up with Kelly and she wanted to be a good partner so she jumped at the chance to come to Kelly's son's birthday. A few more car doors slammed drawing her attention back to the reason she was there, to help celebrate a young man's birthday. Pulling her hat out and positioning it on her head, she heard someone address her.

"Oh, don't tell me, Officer, that the party is already out of hand?" a giggling woman said patting Ashley's arm. "Hi, I'm Sally, Jacob's mom, and this is Jennifer, Justin's mom," Sally said, pointing to the woman walking up to the group.

"No, I don't think they're quite that bad yet." Cupping her ear, Ashley listened to the laughter coming from the backyard. "We might want to hurry though. It does sound as though they might need some help." Ashley smiled at the women as they rushed to the door. "Mothers."

The women buzzed around her, talking about their sons, school, and other assorted items related to their nearby sons. The women didn't seem to notice that the door still hadn't opened after several knocks, so she excused herself and stepped between the women. Pulling her nightstick she rapped harder on the door, a few scuff marks her reward for being so aggressive. Looking back at the now silent women, she flashed them a smile and shrugged her shoulders.

"I don't think she heard us."

"Well, she has now, obviously," whispered one of the mothers.

"I'm sure she has," Ashley said, sliding her nightstick back in its holder.

"Ladies, Officer Henderson. I'm so glad you made it," Kelly said, looking at the group.

"We come bringing gifts, Kelly," said one of the women as she squeezed her way through the small crowd. Thrusting a cup holder at Kelly she continued, "We figured you could use a break and some adult nourishment."

"Oh, you're a saint, Sally." Kelly pushed the door open wider and stepped aside so the gaggle of women could enter.

"Officer Henderson? Really?" Ashley flashed Kelly a smile.

"Sorry, I figured it was you who practically pounded the door down. These moms are as meek and mild as deer. It's not their style."

"So I noticed." Ashley stuck a finger in her ear, ringing it around.

"Oh stop. You'll be fine. Come on in. Tyler's in the backyard corralling kids."

"Oh, good thing I brought my gun for the OK

corral. I would hate to see four year olds get the better of Tyler, but somehow I think she can fend for herself."

"Yeah, well these aren't women, they're kids and they're used to getting their way. So, Tyler might be out of her league."

Kelly laughed when she saw Tyler on all fours with two kids riding her back. "See? She's already giving horsey rides."

Ashley watched as Tyler rolled to her side and began tickling the first boy she could get her hands on. Screaming, the boy squirmed and called to his friends who immediately ran and jumped on Tyler. A game of dog pile broke out and Tyler was desperately trying to protect the young lad she had been tickling.

Chapter Eight

Tyler lay pinned under the screaming boys, trying to protect her godson who had started off as her tickling victim, but now found himself pinned with her at the bottom of a pile. Ashley's spit shined boots and Kelly's canvas low tops walked into Tyler's line of sight.

"Having fun, Tyler?" Kelly tapped her foot in front of Tyler's face. "Okay boys, off."

Tyler looked, sliding up the uniformed legs, and found Ashley smiling down at her, eyebrows raised. Kelly stood next to her, arms crossed, with a smirk.

"Hey."

"Hey."

"What are you doing?" Kelly asked, reaching down to help Tyler up. "I can't leave you for one minute before it turns into a free for all. You're just one big kid yourself, Tyler."

Dusting the grass off, Tyler just shrugged. She loved being one of the guys, but one of the boys? She laughed at the thought, Yep, I would've made a great mom.

"Hello, Officer Henderson. Twice in one day. Who would have thought?" Tyler said, walking towards the house.

Tyler wasn't about to stand around and make nice to the officer who had just ticketed her. She wouldn't be disrespectful, but she wouldn't pretend that the officer who had shot her down in the bar, and then wrote her a ticket, was anything other than that, a police officer. She watched as Ashley and Kelly talked. Tyler noticed that Ashley gestured when she talked. Small, little hand gestures that gave Ashley that "girly" look Tyler liked. Her slight frame and gestures would have been more at home, literally, at home. She could easily see Ashley as a housewife with a pack of kids around her. Tyler had to admit she wore the uniform of a police officer with confidence, strength, and bearing, so being a housewife was probably out of the picture for someone like Ashley. Tyler found Ashley's quiet confidence sexy as hell, not like those officers who mistook cockiness for confidence. No, she had something about her that, under different circumstances, Tyler would want to explore. Looking away, Tyler knew that Ashley was officially off limits. She had made it clear at the bar and Tyler wasn't about to get kicked twice.

Tyler tried to divert her attention to the boys, who were playing with the marshmallow shooters Tyler had brought for them. Tyler figured they were harmless since they had to blow a miniature marshmallow through a blowgun. Soon, marshmallows were flying everywhere including at Tyler. Kelly's laughter caught Tyler's attention as she tried dodging an errant marshmallow that succeeded in hitting her on the side of the face. Glaring at the boy who shot her, she made tracks to the other side of the yard where the rest of the boys were playing. Turning her attention back to Kelly and Ashley, Tyler caught Kelly looking at her with raised eyebrows and a smirk. Tyler felt trapped as she watched Ashley walking towards her, smiling.

"Can I get you something to drink Tyler?"

Ashley's perfume engulfed her as she turned to

answer. Tongue tied, she just shook her head and walked towards Kelly.

"What's so funny?" Tyler asked, wiping marshmallow from her face.

"Nothing. Ashley just told me what happened today." Kelly attempted to wipe the sticky mess from Tyler's face with a napkin she was holding, but Tyler brushed her hand away.

"Nothing happened today, Kell. What did she tell you?"

"She told me about giving you a speeding ticket and how sorry she was that she didn't know it was you."

"Yeah, right. She has eyes. She could have seen it was me, but she was too busy getting ready to bust some guy's," Tyler made air quotes, "'balls' that she wasn't paying attention. It's not a big deal. Trust me, it isn't my first ticket and it won't be my last."

"She said you were speeding, Tyler. How fast were you going?"

"What are you, my mom?"

"No, just someone who cares about you. Why do you have to make such a fuss about people who care about you? Look, maybe I was wrong warning Ashley to stay away from you. She's a big girl and can take care of herself. You, on the other hand. Well, let's just say you need someone watching your back." Kelly slipped her arm around Tyler's waist and hugged her. "She's kinda cute huh?" Kelly said, looking at Ashley talking to one of the mothers.

"You were right to warn her away from me, Kelly. Besides, she's probably one of those women who keeps a diary. No, wait, she's an adult now. She keeps a daily journal and writes in it every night. She probably writes down all her hopes and dreams for the future. How she wants to get married and have two point three kids and live in a house with a white picket fence around it." Tyler closed her hands as if they were a book and then batted her eyes at Kelly.

"That is so ridiculous, Tyler. I'm sure she doesn't keep a journal. Besides, with all the paperwork we have to do, who has the time or the desire to write anymore when our day is over?" Kelly rolled her eyes at the silly implication.

"Oh, come on Kelly. Don't tell me she isn't so 'dreamy' that she hasn't sat around a time or two and written out her name with that of her girlfriends and said 'Gee, I wonder?'" Tyler said, using her finger as a pen, writing in the palm of her hand.

"Tyler, where are you getting all of this? Are you so jaded, you expect everyone to have a heart of steel like yours?"

"No, the exact opposite. I see Ashley as a good soul who sees the good in everyone and everything and thinks that life is like an Ozzie and Harriet show. Only in this version, it's Harriet and Helen and they have kids, a house and everything is wonderful. Well life doesn't work out that way now, does it, Kell?" Tyler asked, stuffing her hands deep into her pockets.

Tyler felt her jaw clenching as she tried to control the anger seething to the top. Why was she mad? Ashley hadn't done anything to her, and here she was making judgment calls about someone she didn't even know. That was the problem. She didn't know Ashley and she wanted to, but Ashley had made it clear that Tyler would never get that chance. Well, Tyler knew she had sealed her own fate long before she met Ashley and Ashley's rejection of her at the bar was just an outcome of that behavior. So she had no one to blame and no one to get pissed at but herself. She had to accept responsibility for that behavior and now she faced the very real consequences of not getting to know a nice woman like Ashley because of it. Regret replaced the anger as Tyler took a deep breath and sighed.

"I'm gonna go, Kell." Tyler kissed Kelly on the check and gave her a hug. "Tell the birthday boy bye for me. I hope he likes his birthday gift." Tyler smiled and waved at Michael.

"Tyler, you don't need to go. It's fine, really. No harm, no foul. Besides, you haven't had any cake yet." Kelly said, tugging on Tyler's elbow.

Patting her stomach, Tyler said, "save me a piece. Besides, I gotta watch my girlish figure ya know." Tyler smiled and kissed Kelly on the check. "I'll talk to ya later."

"Later then."

"Later."

Tyler maneuvered through the maze of toys, boys and moms, saying her good-byes to all as she walked through the backyard and into the house.

Ashley handed Kelly a drink and asked, "Tyler leaving already? I didn't get a chance to apologize."

"Yeah, she said she's tired and needs to get ready for work tomorrow," Kelly lied. She didn't want to discuss Tyler with Ashley. She had done enough damage for now. "You don't happen to keep a journal do you?" Kelly asked, raising her glass to her lips.

"Yeah. Why?" Ashley responded, giving Kelly a puzzled look.

"Oh, no reason. I was just wondering."

###

Tyler pulled her head out from under the sheet, whipping the sweat-matted hair from her face.

"Oh, that was nice, Baby," a silky voice said from under the covers, pulling Tyler back under.

"You like that, huh?" Tyler said, her voice raspy from sex. "Well, I'm not done with you yet, so you better settle in for the long haul." Tyler settled between the slender legs, kissing the soft skin under her.

The smell of sex in the room filled Tyler's nostrils as she took a deep breath, relishing the intoxicating aroma. Tyler picked up the sexy brunette on the way home from Kelly's quite by accident. A stop at the gym to work out her aggressions and the next thing she knew, she was following the beautiful aerobics teacher to her house. Tyler licked one salty nipple, her tongue leaving a trail around it, then moved to the other, biting the tip. Blowing on the erect nub, she could feel Cindy's pussy clinch on her finger. Again, she sucked the nipple into her mouth and swirled her tongue around the hard nipple.

Tyler felt a hand on her head pushing her down the hard body to the triangle of hair where her fingers were buried. A soft moan made Tyler smile as she worked her fingers faster in the wet pussy.

"Wait." Cindy grabbed Tyler's wrist stopping her progress. "I want you to take me from behind."

"Okay, you're the boss." Tyler said, watching Cindy flip on to her stomach and lift her ass in the air. Cindy spread her knees and waited for Tyler.

"Lick me first, Baby. It makes me so hot thinking of you taking me from behind."

The request wasn't as weird as others Tyler had participated in, and she was always happy to oblige a sexy woman's fantasy. Tyler slid her tongue between the silky lips that had opened when Cindy spread her legs. While Tyler couldn't quite reach Cindy's clit, that didn't seem to be an issue for Cindy. Slowly, Cindy started rubbing her clit with a vigor Tyler thought would hurt the woman.

"Fuck me, Baby." The command came out as a barely audible whisper.

Tyler wet her fingers and slid one, then two fingers into the wet opening. Before she could do anything else, Cindy began to rock back and forth on Tyler's hand. The slow rock started to speed up as Tyler pumped into the wet pussy. Reaching around, she rolled a hard nipple between her fingers, then squeezed and gently pulled on the hard nub. Each time she squeezed, Cindy's pussy clamped down on her fingers. Tyler found her g-spot and rubbed the engorged area until she felt Cindy's muscles begin to spasm, announcing the impending orgasm. Tyler felt Cindy push harder on her fingers, her orgasm spreading throughout her body, giving Cindy goose bumps everywhere.

Cindy slipped off Tyler's wet hand and fell limp on the bed. Tyler lay down next to the sweaty body and wrapped her arms around her. Burying her nose in Cindy's hair, she took a long, deep breath and relaxed. She didn't need to come to be satisfied. In fact, there were times when Tyler didn't want to be touched sexually, she just needed to touch someone else. A soft thigh draped across Tyler's hips, as if taking possession of her body. Tyler had seen this type of behavior before and she knew she would end it like she always did, promising to call, promising she would see her lover again and then never doing either. She was a cad and she knew it. What surprised her was that most women didn't know how detached she was emotionally. But then again, she was good at her job and she threw herself into it heart and soul, never letting on they wouldn't be getting what they wanted. At least that's what she told herself every time this happened.

"Hmm, Cindy, I—"

"Cynthia. My boyfriend calls me Cindy and I hate it," Cynthia said, snuggling closer.

"Boyfriend?" Tyler said, suddenly feeling like someone had just punched her in the stomach as she gasped.

"Yeah, I thought you knew."

"No, if I had known I would have used protection." Tyler scrubbed her face. "I'm assuming since you're not monogamous that your boyfriend isn't either. Right?" Tyler closed her eyes as she waited for the answer she knew was coming.

"Well…" Cynthia said, picking at a lint ball on the blanket.

"Great."

"Wait, you didn't think this was going to lead to something did you? I mean, you weren't planning on us dating or something, were you?"

The words had a sting to them that Tyler hadn't expected. Cynthia was at least ten years Tyler's junior, but that hadn't stopped her from taking what was offered. No, she was pissed that Cynthia was using her own lines on her and it smarted.

"Trust me. A long term relationship was the farthest thing from my mind," Tyler said, sitting up.

"Oh good. I thought maybe you were going to ask me out. That would be awkward, you know?" Cynthia said, stretching then yawning.

"Yes, that would be awkward now, wouldn't it?" Tyler rolled her eyes as she grabbed her jeans. *Clearly, the young woman lived life without a care for her partners. The least she could have done was tell me she had a boyfriend, but no.* Tyler shook her head as she realized she was getting mad at the woman for doing what she did all the time.

How does it feel, Tyler, when the shoe's on the other foot? Tyler thought as she slipped her bra and shirt on. Turnabout was fair play, but she felt stupid that she didn't know the woman had a boyfriend. Looking around the room, the telltale signs were everywhere. Pictures of the couple, men's clothes tossed on a chair, and the faint smell of cologne all assaulted Tyler's senses. All were lost in the throes of passion as Tyler was more worried about getting the woman's clothes off than where she was. She would have to be more careful in the future. She didn't want to accidentally face a pissed off boyfriend or husband.

After tying her boots, she went to say something to her bedmate, but was met with snores. Tyler didn't know what was worse, the sleeping woman or the indifference she showed Tyler. There she was again, getting mad for being treated the same way she often treated other women. A taste of her own medicine was making her sick, but she knew eventually this day would come. *But did it have to come from someone with that body?* Tyler thought. She could have easily made another date with the sex-starved woman. It was obvious her boyfriend wasn't giving her what she wanted. That didn't matter now. Tyler had been bested at her own game.

Locking the door as she left, Tyler grabbed her cell phone and scrolled through her contacts.

"Drs. Smith, Hartsock and Wilson, Ob-Gyn, can I help you?"

"Hi, I need to make an appointment?

Chapter Nine

Ashley lay on her bed, the covers tossed off. The heat in her bedroom was stifling. The silk camisole and panties felt like a second skin so she shed them, favoring the cool breeze that gently caressed her skin. The rare heat wave had pushed more than a few people past their breaking point and Ashley had to work overtime that week to handle the overload. Still amped from her shift, she slipped off the bed and headed to the kitchen for something cool to drink. Rummaging through the endless supply of condiments, take-out containers, and pudding packs, she found a single can of root beer and an imported beer. Grabbing both, she placed one on the counter and wiped her forehead with the other. It was hot enough the can sweated immediately, leaving a moist trail everywhere she wiped.

Picking up the bottle of beer, she nearly gagged as she remembered the smell of it on her ex's lips. Her relationship with Leslie had started off beautifully, but it didn't take long for the abusive woman to show her true colors. Ashley berated herself for not seeing through Leslie's lies sooner. Love had clearly shaded her view of the woman and it had taken months to disengage herself from the spiteful bitch. She still got the occasional text from Leslie, but nothing compared to what she received when they broke up. It had gotten so bad that Ashley had to get a restraining order. Being a cop meant nothing to Leslie and in her threats she had made it clear that Ashley would pay for breaking up with her. She never stopped looking over her shoulder and she never stopped worrying that Leslie might pop up unexpectedly.

Rolling her shoulder, Ashley still had a small stabbing pain from the broken collar bone she had gotten in one of their many fights. Ashley felt a fine sheen of sweat break out on her neck, goose bumps covered her arms. The memories still vividly played out in her mind. She tried to quell the rising bile in her throat, but felt herself sicken. Erratic flashes of Leslie's anger started to assault Ashley. Her body readied itself to take a punishing blow she had felt before but now, thankfully, wouldn't come. Covering her head, another memory flashed in her mind. Another slap that never materialized whisked past her. She tensed again as she prepared to fight off Leslie's vicious attack. She had all the signs of post-traumatic stress. Her counselor had told Ashley it would take time to work through the inner turmoil her body felt when she remembered Leslie. Still, she couldn't believe that she had been so stupid as to ignore the warning signs that had started almost from the beginning. The gentle push that morphed into a shove, the slap on the ass that turned into more, or the vicious names that came out of the mouth of someone who supposedly loved her. Two months, two very long and unsettling months was all they lasted, but the repercussions still could be felt as she rubbed her shoulder. Being a police officer taught her how to recognize the signs of someone being abused, but it never dawned on her she would have to recognize those signs in her own life.

The sheer panels in front of the window fluttered

in the cooling breeze. Leaning against the window frame she popped the can of root beer and took a long swallow. Sputtering as the carbonation burned its way down her throat, she rubbed the can between her breasts in an attempt to cool herself. It had taken her a long time to be able to relax in her home again, but new locks, a dog, an alarm and a gun worked wonders on her mental state. The fact she had seen a counselor didn't hurt either. Twisting a strand of hair between her fingers, she enjoyed the quiet as Mongrel, her German Shepherd, rubbed against her leg.

"Can't sleep either, boy?" Squatting down, Ashley scrubbed the dog behind the ear. "Come on, I'll give you something to cool you off and then off to bed with you."

Walking back into the kitchen, she dropped her empty can in the recycler and washed her hands. The cool blast from the freezer felt good on her chest. Grabbing a couple of ice cubes she walked over and dropped them into Mongrel's water bowl.

"There you go, boy. Cool and wet." Mongrel lapped at the floating cubes, trying to catch one with his teeth.

Sleep had evaded Ashley long enough and the trip down nightmare lane did nothing to help her prepare for bed. Her journal lay open on her nightstand. The last entry was from several days before when she had attended the birthday party for Kelly's son. Strange that Kelly would ask her if she kept a journal. Picking it up, Ashley read the entry and smiled.

> Today was like every other day
> I have at work, with one exception. I
> attended my first birthday party for a

five year old. What a wild, crazy party. I don't know how Kelly does it, all those boys, the noise and the non-stop action. My head was spinning by the time I left. God Bless her. She has the patience of a saint. It makes the parties the boys in blue throw look like a baby shower. Hahaha. Then there were all the mothers. I had nothing in common with those women who talked non-stop about preschool, house décor, and the stuff of straight women. Saw Kelly in a whole new light, too. Great Mom!

One big surprise, Tyler Jackson was there, which wouldn't be so bad if I hadn't just given her a ticket half-an-hour before the party. Can you say uncomfortable? Tyler Jackson is a conundrum. She's striking to look at, seems to have a great personality. If it wasn't for the piss on the world attitude, I could definitely give someone like that the time of day, or night. Grrrr!

Ashley remembered watching Tyler play with the boys at the party. She was built for children, Ashley thought to herself. Tyler was a completely different person at the party, playful, funny, and loving. Nothing like the player she presents to the outside world, or the throw-caution-to-the-wind firefighter Ashley had seen at the house fire earlier in the week. *Although, she did save those kittens,* Ashley remembered. *She can't be all bad.*

Ashley closed the journal and stuffed it in the

drawer of the nightstand. Tyler would have to stay a mystery. Ashley had sworn off bad girls after Leslie and Tyler was definitely a bad girl, albeit a handsome bad girl. Life throws all kinds of curve balls, her father used to say. How you handle them is a measure of the person you are. Ashley wondered what kind of person Tyler was before losing Jill. *Well some things will remain a mystery,* Ashley thought turning off the light.

Chapter Ten

Tyler stood in front of the barber shop watching the older men chat. Running her fingers through her long hair, she had made a decision and she wanted to get it over with before she changed her mind. It was time to start putting things in the past, changing what she could and leaving behind any baggage that was starting to weigh her down. A haircut might just be a haircut to some people, but she wanted a new look to help go with her changing attitude. Even during her overseas tour, she had managed to keep the long locks. But now she was tired of the time it took to wash, dry and put it up. Besides, it would make riding her motorcycle easier, she justified. Jill wasn't around anymore to squash her protests about the up-keep and this was part of that "baggage" she wanted to ditch. Nervously, she ran her fingers through her soft locks once more. Jill wasn't baggage, Tyler reasoned, she was a beautiful memory that deserved respect as her wife, but she needed to move on. The last few weeks had taken their toll. Hell, that last year had exacted a price she hadn't realized until just recently.

Tyler couldn't put her finger on it, but she suspected her godson's birthday party had been the spark. His young, naïve face and innocence had touched a place in Tyler that almost made her cry when she was playing with him. That unconditional love a child shares with those around him made Tyler realize she wanted a family. But more importantly, she wanted someone to share that family with. She wanted, no needed to establish roots of something bigger than she was. Funny that something as innocent and simple as a birthday party could make her think of something bigger than herself. Tyler shook her head and smiled briefly. Twisting a lock of hair around her finger, she ran the end of it through her mouth, just as she had when she was a kid. Her mother's voice was ringing in her ear.

"Tyler, stop that. It's not very lady-like, Honey." The gentleness in her mother's voice wasn't condemning, but the exact opposite, loving. "Tyler, Honey ..."

"Tyler?" A gruff voice replaced the loving tenor of her mother's. A firm hand on her shoulder brought her back to reality. "I'm ready when you are."

"Right," Tyler said, standing and shaking off the dusty memory.

The barber shop smelled of aftershave and clipper oil. It was the same shop her dad had brought her to when she was younger. Once a month he had a standing appointment with George, the older man who whisked away the remnants from the last customer.

"So, what'll it be Tyler? Trim the ends?" George positioned the plastic shield around her neck and turned her to face the mirror.

"No ..." Tyler looked at her reflection in the mirror and she knew what she wanted to do. "Cut it all off, George."

"What?'

"You heard me. I want a haircut." Tyler fingered the hair out of her eyes.

"Tyler, you know this ain't no fancy hair salon. If you want some smart up-do then you need to go down to the mall and get it done." George started to pull on the plastic bib around Tyler's neck.

"I don't want a fancy up-do, George. I want a haircut." Tyler stopped his hand before he could pull the Velcro on the bib. "My dad's been coming here since I was a little girl, my brothers come here, and I'm just fine having you cut it. So, George, here's what I want." Tyler explained how short she wanted it and how she wanted her hair cut. A half an hour later, Tyler brushed the last bits of hair from her sleeve and admired her new look in the mirror.

"You're gonna make some child happy with the hair, Tyler," George said, holding the long pony tail in his hand.

"Well, it's made me happy for a long time, but it was time for a change, George." Tyler ran her fingers through her hair for the umpteenth time trying to get used to the shorter style. She looked different, younger and a bit more boyish. Not exactly what she was going for, but it would work for now. Besides, it's only hair, she reasoned.

Stepping out in the sun, Tyler pulled her ball cap from her pocket. She had brought it just in case she didn't like the new look. The lack of hair made the cap practically rest on her ears, so she readjusted it and rolled the bill into the perfect "softball roll", as she liked to call it. Tyler accidentally stepped into the path of a kid walking his bike across the driveway.

"Sorry, Sir."

Tyler stopped dead in her tracks. *"Did he just call me, Sir?"* she thought looking up at the young man.

"Oh. Sorry, Ma'am. I thought with the hat and the short hair you were a ..."

Tyler held up her hand and stopped the young man

from further embarrassing himself. "It's fine. No harm done. Easy mistake," Tyler babbled, just as embarrassed.

Tyler looked in the window and tried to see what would make the young man think she was a guy. She rubbed her fingers along her jaw. A strong jaw is what her mother called it. But, looking now, she saw more of a square face. *Obviously, it was hidden behind all that hair,* she mused. Looking back at her reflection, she realized she looked more like her father now. When she was younger, she was never considered *girly*, whatever that meant, but now she was definitely more handsome than pretty. Letting out a deep breath, she wondered if she had just made the biggest mistake of her life.

"Great. Now I have to walk into a fire station full of brutally honest men. My life is going to suck for the next few shifts," Tyler muttered to herself, walking back to her car. "Screw 'em. I like it."

Chapter Eleven

Ashley sat at her desk finishing up the report on an accident involving a drunk driver and a tree. Lucky for the driver, he had an air bag that saved his life. Not that he was going fast, in fact the exact opposite. Ashley laughed as she remembered driving up on the accident. The driver was leaning, or better yet swaying, against his truck, trying to light a cigarette.

"Sir, is this your truck?" Ashley asked, as she looked in the truck, her flashlight exposing what was left of two deployed air bags. Looking over at Kelly, she shook her head and smiled at the look she got back from her partner. The front of the car rested on the sidewalk and the backend was pitched up in the air, balanced on the bent over tree trunk.

"Nope. I was just walking and I saw the truck like this. I thought I would see if someone needed some help and look, there's no one in there," he said, pointing his cigarette at the ground.

"I see. So this isn't your truck?"

"Nope."

"And you don't know whose it is?"

"Nope."

"And I suppose you don't know how you got a bloody nose?

"Nope." The driver dabbed at his face with the two fingers that held his cigarette. "I got a bloody nose?"

"Yep."

Ashley had a hard time trying to figure out exactly how the truck had ended up on top of the tree. The only thing she could imagine was that the driver had put it in four-wheel drive and practically driven up the young tree, bending it down enough so the truck could climb it.

"Hey. You done with that report?" Ashley felt Kelly tap her shoulder.

"Almost. Why don't you go home? I got this." Ashley typed the last line and hit save on the computer. Ashley hated paperwork, but it was part of the job. Stretching, she looked at Kelly and waited for an answer.

"Why don't we go get a drink?" Kelly asked, thumbing through the stack of folders on her desk.

"After what you saw tonight, you still want a drink?"

"Really? You can't be serious. We see shit all the time that if we let it get to us we wouldn't eat, sleep, or drink anything. So yeah, let's go and get a drink. I'm buying."

"An offer I can't refuse," Ashley said heading to the women's locker room.

Within half an hour both women had showered, changed, and were sitting in Ashley's car.

"So anywhere in particular you want to go?" Ashley asked, pulling out from the station.

"Yeah, let's go to your bar?"

"My bar? I don't have a bar."

"You know what I mean, that lesbian bar you like to go to."

It had been weeks since Ashley had been to the bar. In fact, the last time she was there, was the first and last time she had rebuffed Tyler Jackson.

"Hey speaking of lesbians ..."

"Were we speaking of lesbians?" Kelly asked jokingly.

"Yes, we were speaking of lesbians. Now stop. Have you seen Tyler around lately?" Ashley hoped the question didn't give Kelly the wrong idea.

"Funny you should ask. I haven't seen her since my son's birthday party two weeks ago."

"I thought you girls were pretty close?"

"We are, but sometimes she gets in these moods and hibernates for a few weeks. I just give her space and usually we reconnect when she's ready," Kelly said nonchalantly.

"Oh."

"Why?"

"Oh, no reason. Just trying to make conversation," Ashley said, once again hoping she didn't sound too interested in the missing woman.

"Usually, she's working everyone's shifts, but I asked the guys and they said she's been taking her days off. But something must be going on 'cause one of her buddies asked me if I had seen her lately. Asked him why, and all he said was 'wait till you see her' and then walked off laughing. I'm not sure what that meant, but I'm sure we'll find out sooner or later." Kelly shrugged.

"Hmmm."

Truth was, Ashley had been thinking a lot about Tyler lately. Every time she opened her journal she thought about the gorgeous firefighter. Rereading the passages she had written when she stopped and ticketed Tyler and the birthday entry made her wonder more and more about the dark spirit of the woman.

"So, any new women on the horizon, Ash?"

"No, not really. Not that I'm looking. After Leslie—" Ashley stopped mid-sentence. She hadn't told

Kelly or anyone, about Leslie. Too ashamed to reveal her secret, she had chosen to keep that part of her life separate from everything else. Hopefully, burying the past kept it in the past, until now.

"Leslie?"

Ashley saw the questioning look on Kelly's face, but tried to change the subject. "Hey have you tried that new steak house over on Harbor? I hear they serve a great Margarita."

"Okay. I get it. You don't want to talk about it."

"Not really. It's a part of my life that's been boxed up and put away." Ashley smiled at her partner. She wasn't in the mood for another trip down nightmare lane.

"Did I know Leslie?" Kelly continued.

"Nope, I don't think so." Ashley turned right then left.

"Turn signal."

"What?"

"Turn signal. You didn't use your turn signal. I'd hate to see you get pulled over for not using your turn signal."

"Oh, right." Ashley hated that she couldn't focus even for just a fraction of a second when Leslie's name was mentioned.

"She gets to ya, huh?"

"Who?"

"Leslie, silly."

"No she doesn't get to me anymore, but she did."

"That good, huh?"

"No, that bad."

"Oh, sorry. I didn't know."

Ashley's legs began to shake as she slowed her car down. Afraid she might accidentally hit the gas and not brake in time, she slowed the car even more. She felt

Kelly rub her leg and sigh.

"How would you? I don't talk about her." Ashley covered Kelly's hand and held it. "Careful, I might think you're coming on to me in my moment of weakness," Ashley said, a nervous laugh squeaking out.

"Ash, are you okay, Honey? You're shaking like a leaf." Kelly's concern almost made Ashley cry. It had been a long time since she had shared anything of her personal life with anyone. She just wasn't that type of person, at least not tonight.

"Yeah. Yeah, I'm fine. I think I might need that drink after all." Smiling, she glided into a parking space at Vic's, the local lesbian bar. Looking around, she always looked around now, she tried to see any familiar faces. Only fresh-faced baby dykes hung out at the front door, stubbing out cigarettes and poking at each other as they eyed all the women that entered. *Great! Running the gauntlet,* as she referred to it. Ashley wished she could wear her shield in the hopes of scaring off any potential hopefuls, at least hopeful on their part. Many times women saw the badge before they saw who wore it and were attracted to it like pussycats to cat nip. Instead, she kept her badge tucked in her wallet and put on a smile. It was a glass half full night and she wanted to keep it that way.

"Hey Sam," Kelly waved to the bartender and signaled for two drinks. "So," Kelly said turning towards Ashley, "what's your type? What does Ms. Right look like?"

Ashley looked around the room and made it a point to notice everyone and quickly dismissed most of the gyrating women. Her type, what was her type? Tall, everyone wanted tall, didn't they? Sexy, smart, and drop dead gorgeous didn't hurt.

"Oh, I'd settle for Ms. Right-Now. I guess it depends on the woman." Trying not to sound flippant she continued, "I think I like confidence in a woman. You know the type. She owns the room when she walks in, but isn't arrogant." Taking a sip of her drink, her face twisted briefly. "Hey Sam, could you put a bit more soda in this and a little less courage?"

"Sure thing, Gorgeous." Sam smiled and winked.

"Thanks Muffin," Ashley joked back.

"Maybe Sam's your type, Gorgeous," Kelly said, smiling.

"Ah, that would be a no. But I do like a butch if you must know." Ashley looked around the room still not spotting anything she would consider possible dating material.

"Really?"

"Really."

"I had you pegged as a femme kinda gal." The perplexed look on Kelly's face almost made Ashley blush, but she didn't know why. "Really?"

"Why so surprised?" Ashley liked the softer butches that had a tool belt, a tight, white boy beater and a smile that went along with the attitude.

"I don't know. Guess I had you pegged as a connoisseur of the femme variety."

"Too high maintenance," Ashley said sipping her drink. "Besides, I'm already high maintenance enough for two. More soda, Muffin." Ashley slid her drink towards Sam and winked. Leslie had been a femme, so maybe that had something to do with her choices in women. "Call me old fashion, but I like having doors opened for me and a chair pulled out. I can't have that if we are both checking our make-up and pulling down our dress as we get out of a car. Guess I should have been born straight, huh?"

"I think it's sweet. Just because you're gay doesn't mean you lose those ideas of romance and relationships. Shoot, my dad still opens my mom's door. I think it's great actually. I need to train my husband better."

Ashley laughed at the suggestion. Kelly's husband was a heartbreaker, but he was known to be true blue to his wife. The few times Ashley had met him all he could do was talk about Kelly, when he found out Ashley and Kelly were partners. She wanted what Kelly had, a loving partner, a family, and a life outside the force.

"Was it hard?"

"Was what hard?"

"Your relationship with Leslie?"

A long pause rested between the two women. Ashley hadn't expected Kelly to press her about Leslie and she wasn't sure what to say without seeming standoffish.

"It was abusive and now she's gone. End of story." Ashley smiled at Kelly hoping she had said enough to her persistent partner.

"I'm sorry, Ashley. I should learn to mind my own business, but when I saw your reaction in the car, I knew it had to be something bad. If you ever want to talk about it …" Kelly let the statement hang.

"I'm fine, really. I've been to counseling. I've changed the locks and burned her stuff. It's all good now. Really," Ashley said, trying to sound convincing. She didn't want to explain how she, a trained police officer, had missed all the warning signs of an abusive relationship. What would Kelly think of her then?

"Burned her stuff, huh?"

"Yeah, it was cathartic."

"Did you have a burn permit for that?"

Ashley smiled. It had been cathartic and freeing to burn what few things Leslie left behind. She was sure Leslie would use them as an excuse to come back, but when she told Leslie what she had done, Leslie was furious. Too bad. After what Ashley had been through, Leslie was lucky she wasn't facing assault charges, at a minimum.

Chapter Twelve

Tyler sat in the darkened corner watching the women on the dance floor doing their ritualistic mating dance, as she liked to call it. Usually, she would be right there in the middle of the mélange, skin on skin, hips brushing against each other. But tonight she was just a spectator. Her self-imposed hibernation period had ended when she came into the bar. She had spent her days off cleaning out some of Jill's things, boxing up uniforms, clothes, and other odds and ends. She had sent some of the items to a benefit store where they could help someone else and the rest she stored in a closet. Tyler's emotions had been all over the place as she remembered fingering a blouse Jill wore or a book she had read.

Hunching her shoulders in defeat, Tyler had begun the hard process of taking down pictures of Jill. Her reasoning felt sound at the time, but now she doubted she could finish the project. It was one thing to box up clothes and brick-a-brac, but another to take down the photos. They were of fun times, of milestones in both their lives and meant more to Tyler than a shirt or earrings. She almost melted as each photo brought a memory and a smile. Every time Tyler looked at a picture of Jill, she felt as if a scab had been pulled off a wound. It had taken all day to pack the photos away, but she had done it. With the exception of two, they were all placed in a box in the corner of the living room. Every day she looked at the box a pang of guilt went spiraling through her body. It was almost more than she could bear, so after a week of looking at the box, she finally had the nerve to put it in the closet in the spare room. The walls, like her heart, were bare, but she knew it had to be done. Now she needed a break from the assault her mind had been under. She couldn't think of a better way to forget than to head to Vic's Bar and that's how she had ended up at the lesbian bar sipping a drink.

She hadn't seen Kelly since Michael's birthday and Kelly hadn't seen her new haircut yet. This was a situation that looked like it was going to rectify itself quickly as Tyler watched Kelly and Ashley make their way to the bar. Tyler felt electricity shoot through her when she saw Ashley. She had a thing for red-heads. *Shoot, who didn't?* Tyler thought, looking at Ashley. Tyler noticed that out of uniform Ashley wasn't lean and athletic, she was solid and curvy. From her vantage point she could study Ashley, the way she flipped her hair out of her face, the way she flirted with the bartender, and the way she smiled at Kelly. Tyler watched as Ashley's gaze wandered over every woman in the bar, a slight smile for some and a passing glance for others. When Ashley's gaze finally wandered towards Tyler, Tyler turned away and leaned her butt against the pool table. Had she been thinking, she would have retreated back into the shadows, further disguising her attendance at the bar. Peaking over her shoulder she looked back and saw Ashley's attention had returned to Kelly and it looked like they were in a deep discussion. Ashley's body language was closed off now. Her shoulders were tense and her hands clenched as she dipped her head and said something to Kelly.

"Wonder what that's all about?" Tyler whispered,

suddenly feeling fingers glide across her shoulders.

"What's what all about, Sexy?" A sultry voice whispered in Tyler's ear, causing her to blush. "Oh, I love the new cut, Tyler. It's rather roguish on you."

Tyler turned and once again leaned against the unoccupied pool table, her back to Kelly and Ashley.

"Hello, Cassie. I haven't seen you here in a while," Tyler said as the woman wrapped Tyler's arms around her waist.

"I've been here. I think you're the one who's been MIA," Cassie said, squeezing between Tyler's legs. Sliding closer, Cassie rubbed herself against Tyler's crotch and purred in her ear, "I've missed you." Fingers ran up the back of Tyler's neck and through her short hair, gently scratching her scalp.

For a brief moment Tyler closed her eyes and rubbed her head against the long fingernails. Her heart started to beat a bit faster and her skin had goosebumps from the contact. She felt Cassie rake her nails down her tight t-shirt, which offered no protection from the contact. Tyler knew she would have scratch marks down her back later, but right now she didn't care. Her reaction was instant and visceral, goose bumps sprouted along her arms. Her nipples harden as Cassie ran her tongue along Tyler's ear and then gently blew into it.

"I see you've missed me," Cassie said continuing her assault on Tyler's body.

"Actually—" Tyler began.

"Shh, the body doesn't lie, Sweetie." Cassie covered Tyler's lips with hers and slid her tongue against Tyler's, begging for entrance.

Tyler felt Cassie's tongue flick at her top lip and then pull it between her teeth and gently bite it. Tyler was used to the game Cassie played. They had briefly been lovers a month ago, but it hadn't worked out the way Cassie had hoped. The slow grind Cassie was doing against Tyler's crotch was starting to have an effect though, and if Tyler wasn't careful she knew she would do something impetuous. *A girl can only handle so much,* Tyler thought grabbing Cassie's hips to stop their movement.

Cassie wrapped her arms around Tyler's neck, her hips still rocking back and forth across Tyler's.

"Cassie."

"Hmm?"

"Cassie." Tyler felt lips kissing her neck and begin to suck on a spot Tyler was sure would be her undoing. "Cassie, you need to stop, Honey. This isn't the time or place for this."

"Sure it is. You've never complained before?"

The sensual voice was starting to get to Tyler, so she stood hoping to distance herself from the lusty advances. Cassie held on around Tyler's neck and raised her knees up, putting them on the pool table. Tyler noticed this brought Cassie closer and her breasts practically flush with Tyler's face. *God, why am I being tortured like this,* Tyler thought as she wrapped her arms around Cassie, keeping her from pitching them both forward. The low cut top gave Tyler a perfect view of Cassie's soft breasts and tempted Tyler more than the sweet perfume that wafted off them. Tyler snaked out a tongue and slid it between the soft mounds then instantly regretted the move. Cassie arched her back slowly, pressing her crotch against Tyler's stomach. The movement caused Tyler to cup Cassie's ass, discovering Cassie wasn't wearing underwear beneath her skirt. The proximity of Tyler's hands to Cassie's pussy made Tyler's body clinch at the contact. She wasn't a nun, but she was trying to change, wasn't she? Tyler could feel wetness start to cover her pinkies. Tyler felt Cassie tighten her pussy at the contact and knew she was a goner. Tyler had will power, but this was ridiculous. Cassie wanted her, so why shouldn't she give Cassie what she wanted? A mindless fuck without strings wasn't out of the question, was it?

Ashley looked around the bar. *What was her type*, she wondered. After everything with Leslie, she was shocked she could still consider even having a type. "Life goes on," her mom used to say when something bad happened. The eternal optimist, Ashley called her. It hadn't rubbed off on Ashley or, if it did, it rarely showed itself to her anymore. Jaded? No. Realistic? Yes. Ashley was glad she hadn't introduced Leslie to her mom, even when Leslie insisted she wanted to meet her "future mother-in-law". The relief that Leslie didn't know where her mother lived gave Ashley some comfort. It was clear that Leslie would use whatever leverage she could to try and get her back and her mother would be no exception, Ashley was sure.

Femmes filled the dance floor and dykes stood on the outside like they were lions zeroing in on prey. Each dyke had her own style, her own look. Most of the time Ashley shied away from the hardcore butches. They were … Ashley clenched her fist and looked down.

"Hey, you okay?"

Ashley felt Kelly rub her arm. "Yeah, I'm fine. Thanks." Ashley gave a half-hearted smile and looked back around the room.

"So, what's your type? Point her out and I'll go get

'er." Kelly laughed.

"Yeah, right." Ashley laughed, too.

"No, seriously. Point her out and I'll go chat her up for you. If she passes muster, I'll bring her over. Besides, it isn't like we have the same taste in women." Kelly raised her eyebrows and smiled again. "Right?"

"You're straight right? You're not gay for the stay are you? I mean you aren't one of those who considers bringing a lesbian home to freshen up your marriage, are you?" Apprehension quickly crossed Ashley's face before she reconsidered what she said. She had been hit on just for that purpose once or twice and it pissed her off.

"You're funny." Kelly poked her with her elbow and pointed, "Hey what about her?"

Ashley looked in the direction Kelly was pointing and smiled. The butch woman had a tough look, but a cute smile. Ashley looked at Kelly who was still pointing at her and raised her eyebrows. Ashley quickly turned towards the bar and grabbed her drink.

"Aw, no. She isn't my type," Ashley said, praying the woman wouldn't come over and talk to them.

"Okay, how about—"

"No pointing," Ashley blurted out, before taking another sip of her drink. "More soda, please," Ashley said, pushing her glass across the bar.

"Okay, but look. That woman in the back of the bar, leaning against the pool table." Kelly looked again towards the back of the room and elbowed Ashley. "You can't see her face, but she has a rock solid body. Man, I would do her if I were gay."

"Lesbian."

"I'm sure she is or she wouldn't be here."

"No, I mean 'you would do her if you were a

lesbian'. Guys call themselves gay."

"Oh really? Who knew?" Kelly shrugged her shoulders.

"It's just one of those things I have a pet peeve about. I mean it isn't a hard and fast rule, but it's how I think about things." Ashley took another sip of her drink and looked towards the back of the bar. "It's like calling toilet paper tissue. While they might do the same thing, they just aren't the same."

Ashley turned and took another sip of her drink, looking at the tall woman over her glass. The tight t-shirt was stretched nicely over broad shoulders that weren't too masculine. She could see the softness of the rounded muscles and smiled. The short brown hair wasn't spiky and it hit the woman about mid-neck. Ashley watched as another woman ran her fingers through the brown locks and stroked the woman's arm.

"Looks like she's taken," Ashley said, nonchalantly.

"Well, she's still hot."

"Yeah, she's got a great body, but maybe her face could stop a train, as my mother used to say."

"Gosh, I haven't heard that one in a long time, Ash. Ever the optimist, huh?"

Ashley felt a slap to her arm. Feigning injury she looked at Kelly. "Hey, that's battery."

A yell and then a loud slap reverberated through the bar and both women turned to see the tall, brunette rub her face just as her frisky companion walked towards them.

"No, that's battery," Kelly said, grabbing the woman's arm as she walked past them.

"Hey, what gives? Take your hands off me right now or I'm calling the police," the woman said as she tried to pry her arm from Kelly's grip.

"Well you're in luck," Kelly said as both she and Ashley pulled their wallets from their back pockets. Opening them, they flashed their badges in the angry woman's face. "We are the police. That's considered battery in this state and unless you were protecting yourself from her, you could be under arrest."

"For what? She likes it rough. Besides, she didn't take it personal. I did."

"What do you mean?" Ashley let Kelly continue the line of questioning as she watched the woman in the back of the bar. She debated whether or not to go back and talk to the woman, but decided to wait until she had this woman's side of the story first.

"Look, who wouldn't want a hot chick crawling all over 'em? Besides, we have history. Now let me go," Cassie said still trying to pry Kelly's fingers from her arm. "If that leaves a bruise I'm going to sue you."

Clearly this woman thought she was hotter than she really was and it made Ashley want to puke. Looking the woman over, it was clear she was high maintenance. From her little designer bag to her designer strappy heels, she had player written all over.

"Tyler, get your ass up here and clear this shit up," the angry woman yelled. "Please," she said a little more sweetly. Tears started to form as she looked back at Kelly and Ashley.

"That isn't going to work with us, so try a different tactic," Kelly said, rolling her eyes at Ashley.

"God," Ashley said, looking back towards the back. "Tyler? Did you just call her Tyler?"

"Yeah. Why, you know her?"

"Your Tyler?" Ashley asked, looking at Kelly.

"No, my Tyler has long hair. Besides, she's been hibernating for the past two weeks," Kelly said, rising on her tiptoes to get a better look.

A crowd had gathered around the three women and it was starting to make Ashley uncomfortable. Alcohol, pissed off women, and sexual tension were not mixes for a good cocktail. The mumbling had started and a big butch had pushed her way to the front.

"Problems here, Cassie?" she said, grabbing Cassie's other arm.

Before Cassie could answer, Kelly pulled her closer and pulled out her cuffs. "Unless you want to go with her for interfering with police business, I suggest you walk away." Kelly's voice dropped an octave as she went into police mode. Before she knew it, Sam was over the bar, shouldering her way between Kelly and the butch.

"Back-off, Beatrice. This isn't your business."

"Beatrice?" Kelly whispered just loud enough for the three to hear it.

"It's Bea," the butch said, puffing up her chest.

"Yeah, I got your Bea," Sam said, puffing up her chest. "If you want to keep it, you'll back off or I'll kick ya from the bar, permanently. Got it?"

The near mini riot was starting to dissipate. Ashley took a deep breath and relaxed her shoulders. Bea still stood close enough to worry her, but Sam stood between her and Kelly. Both women mad dogged the other until, finally, Bea sauntered off back to where she had parked her drink. A short blonde femme slinked over and stroked the arm of the butch. Clearly, Bea had scored enough points to win a date tonight.

"Ashley, I'm gonna take her outside and call dispatch to send a car down to pick her up. Can you get that other woman and bring her outside too, so we can figure out what's going on?" Kelly finished cuffing Cassie and pulled her elbow, leading her towards the door.

"Sure. I'll question her in here first and then bring her outside." Ashley walked to the back of the bar, but the woman wasn't there. She had only taken her eyes off her for an instant, obviously enough time for the woman to disappear.

Chapter Thirteen

Splashing cold water on her face, she looked in the mirror at the stinging hand print on her face. She could almost make out the impression of a ring near her eye and the lines of Cassie's palm were clearly visible on the side of her cheek. Tyler moved her jaw back and forth trying to loosen it up. She had been trying to explain why she wouldn't sleep with Cassie when the woman hauled off and slapped her. A pop and a crackle echoed in her ears as she continued to move her chin back and forth. Turning her neck, she saw a bite mark just under her t-shirt collar and her nipple hurt where Cassie had pinched the hell out of it. Tyler liked it rough, but usually she gave it when asked and rarely was she on the receiving end of a spanking. Twisting her neck around, she felt a pop and then another as she dipped her chin down to her chest.

"Excuse me. I'm Officer Henderson. Can I speak to you?"

Tyler froze. She had a feeling they would come looking for her when Tyler saw Kelly cuff Cassie. *Standard procedure*, she thought. Without moving her head, Tyler looked down and turned the water on and answered.

"Sure. Can you give me a minute? I just need to wash my face and then I'll be right out."

Ashley's quick breath assured Tyler she had seen the slap mark on Tyler's face. Tyler needed a minute to calm down before she exposed herself to Ashley's probing questions. What had Cassie said to Kelly and Ashley? She was about to find out. Dabbing at her face, she tossed the paper towel and took a deep breath. Now what? Tell the truth and hope to hell Cassie didn't accuse her of something awful. Pulling open the door, Tyler had to adjust to the darkened club. Searching the room, Tyler heard someone calling her over. Ashley sat on a stool at one of the tall bar tables, pen and paper in hand.

Taking the seat opposite Ashley put the light at her back and shadowed her face. She could see Ashley searching her features before realization hit.

"Tyler? Tyler Jackson?"

Tyler hunched her shoulders and let out sigh.

"You cut your hair. Wow, it looks great. You look so—"

"Boyish," Tyler said, cutting Ashley off.

"Actually, I was going to say different. But okay, boyish if that makes you happy." Ashley wrote something on her pad. "Can you tell me what happened, Tyler?"

Tyler fidgeted with a napkin that had been left behind, tearing it into strips. Twisting her neck around again, she felt another pop, this time catching Ashley's attention.

"Are you hurt?" Ashley wrote something else down on her pad and continued, "Of course you're hurt. Stupid question. Sorry." Ashley smiled nervously.

"Look, I don't know what she told you, but—"

"She hasn't told us anything other than she couldn't believe you would turn down a hot gal like her. Now, she's outside with Kelly and maybe she said something out there, but all I know is what I witnessed. So, wanna tell me what happened?"

Tyler felt Ashley's gaze checking out the reddening

hand print. "I think you might need some ice for that. Let me ask Sam for some. I'll be right back."

Tyler put her hand up to her cheek and felt the heat rolling off it. Ashley was right. She needed to make sure it didn't swell too badly. Hopefully, the ice would help with the black eye she was sure she would get from the ring so close to her eye. She didn't want Cassie to get into any trouble, but she had a feeling it was too late for that. Tyler rubbed her hand across her breasts just as Ashley laid the ice on the table. Embarrassed at being caught, Tyler just looked down and applied the ice to her swelling face.

"Okay, so where were we?" Ashley opened her pad and pulled out her pen. "We heard a yell. Was that you or Cassie?"

"I don't yell."

"Okay, so Cassie yelled. Do you remember what she yelled?"

"No."

"We saw her strike you. Did you strike her?" Ashley methodically asked the questions without looking at Tyler and wrote down her answers.

"I don't hit women. Look, it was a misunderstanding, that's all." Tyler still looked down at the table, her shoulders hunched in defeat. Tonight had turned out to be a bust and she wasn't in the mood to sit and be grilled. Her pride had been wounded and now she had to sit across from a woman she earlier thought she wanted to get to know. Now, it was a cop/victim relationship and she knew better than to cross that line. The look of impropriety was enough for her.

"Well that's good to know. I'm not sure I would've had your restraint, Tyler. She pushed my buttons, just sitting there listening to her. I can only imagine how you felt."

Tyler looked up at Ashley, surprised by the admission. Even in the dark, Tyler could see sparkling green eyes that conveyed understanding.

"So, she was pretty explicit in what she said," Ashley continued, her hand resting on Tyler's. "She said, and I quote, 'who wouldn't want a hot chick crawlin' all over 'em?' Unquote."

Tyler smiled at the remark from Cassie. *She definitely thinks highly of herself,* Tyler thought. Ashley cleared her throat, obviously waiting for an answer from Tyler. But for once, Tyler didn't have anything to say or want to say for that matter. Turning her head, she looked over to where her motorcycle jacket lay.

"Is that a bite mark on your neck?" Tyler felt Ashley pull back the collar of her t-shirt, exposing the mark. "Tyler?"

"What?"

"Really?"

"What?"

"Look, that's battery. She could have some kind of disease—something serious like Hepatitis or HIV. You need to get that looked at now. I don't have to tell you, Ms. Hot Paramedic, that these types of things can be serious. There are so many germs in the mouth ..." Ashley stopped mid-sentence and looked at Tyler who had a cocky smile on her face. "What?"

"Did you just call me Ms. Hot Paramedic?"

Tyler watched as a blush crawled up Ashley's neck and warmed her face. A slow smile from Ashley captured Tyler's attention and she smiled back.

"What?" Ashley said, looking back down at her pad and writing something.

Tyler grabbed her jacket and slipped it on. She

needed to get out of Ashley's space or she would say or do something stupid. Her nerves had gotten the best of her all week and the final act with Cassie was the coup de grâce. Edgy, Tyler pressed the ice pack to her face and shifted from foot to foot waiting for Ashley to finish. She could smell Ashley's perfume as she leaned closer to see what Ashley was writing. The fresh smell reminded her of the lake for some reason and wildflowers. Tyler loved camping; the smells, the freedom, and the outdoors nourished her soul, revived and replenished her. *So why haven't I gone lately?* The thought hung out there, but lacked an answer.

"Where are you going?"

Tyler was sucked back into reality by the question. "Me? I'm going home. I've had a crappy week and an even crappier night. So if you don't mind, we're done here." It was a statement more than a question. "If you need more information, call me," Tyler said taking out her wallet and passing Ashley her card.

"I'm going to need more information, Tyler," Ashley said following Tyler out of the bar.

Just as they both exited the bar, Cassie was being put into a police cruiser. Seeing Tyler, she began to yell.

"Tyler, damn it, you need to fix this. I didn't do anything wrong. Tell 'em you like it rough. Come on, Baby. Don't do this to me." Kelly slammed the door shut, but Cassie continued her rant.

"Geez, that's some bruise, Tyler," Kelly said walking over to the two women. "So what happened in there, Stud?" Kelly smiled and bumped Tyler's shoulder with hers.

Tyler looked down at Kelly and wondered what was going through her friend's mind. A banging made all three women look at Cassie as she pounded her head against the window. Kelly walked over to the car and opened the door slightly.

"Look, if you don't stop, I'm going to hog-tie you and that won't be pretty with you in a skirt and all."

"Tyler, fix this. Tell them I didn't do anything wrong," Cassie screamed.

"It isn't Tyler's choice. We witnessed the slap. So you're going downtown to booking and that's the end of it. Everything will be explained when you get downtown."

"Bitch."

Cassie tried to spit on Kelly as she shut the door for the second time. Pulling out her pad she added another charge to the list of charges the woman would be facing.

"Disgusting," Kelly said, rejoining the group. "You look like hell, Tyler. You need to go get that looked at, now."

"She's got a bite on her shoulder, too. I suspect from the lovely woman in the car," Ashley added, pulling down Tyler's collar.

"Geez, Tyler. Did you ask for that?" Kelly grimaced looking at the bite.

Tyler's look said it all. She was a lot of things, but she wasn't into painful foreplay like that. Pulling her neck away, she tugged the t-shirt back into place and zipped her jacket.

"Wow, when did you get the haircut?" Kelly reached up and scuffed up the short hair. "You look like George."

George was Tyler's younger brother, the other playboy in the family. Tyler pulled her head back and smiled at Kelly's joke. She should get used to the comments, because they were a regular way of life at the station these days. So why should her friends be any different.

"Can I go now? I've had a rough week and tonight was just the icing on the cake." Tyler sighed, wishing she hadn't gotten out of bed that morning.

"You okay?" Concern showed on Kelly's face.

"Yeah. I've just had a tough week and now all I want to do is go home and try to forget all this," Tyler said giving a weak smile to her friend. "Look, I don't want to press charges against Cassie. She just had a little too much to drink and wouldn't take no for an answer."

A camera flash caught both women unaware as Ashley clicked off a few pictures of Tyler's face. Puzzled. Tyler looked at Ashley and frowned.

"Evidence," Ashley said, giving Tyler a half smile. "Sorry."

"Can I go now?" Tyler turned not waiting for an answer. Her week sucked, her life sucked and she couldn't wait to go home, pull the covers over her head and try to forget everything. *When am I ever going to learn?* Tyler slammed her car door. *When am I ever gonna learn?*

Chapter Fourteen

Wow, Tyler looks totally different," Kelly said, finishing her report before she passed off Cassie to booking.

Ashley smiled. Tyler did look different. In fact, she looked smokin' hot with her new haircut. If Ashley had a type, the new Tyler was definitely it. But there was something else different about Tyler and Ashley couldn't quite put her finger on it. During the brief interview, if one could call it that, Tyler seemed reserved, almost embarrassed about what had happened with Cassie. She didn't know Tyler well, but she knew when a victim was hiding something and Tyler Jackson was hiding something.

"Did Tyler seem different to you tonight, Kell?" Ashley questioned.

"Different how?"

"I don't know. I just got a sense that she was hiding something or something wasn't quite right. Maybe it was just me she was avoiding. It wasn't like the last time we saw each other was a good thing."

"You think she's still smarting about the ticket you gave her?" Kelly asked, as she poured something that passed for coffee into a paper cup and sat on her desk. "She doesn't usually hold a grudge, but I didn't get a chance to talk to her tonight."

"Hmm."

"What did she say when you questioned her about

Cassie?" Kelly's interest was piqued now. Tyler and she had been friends for a long time, but the hair cut, the silent treatment, and the events of the night were definitely different behavior for Tyler.

"That's just it. She didn't want to talk about it. I told her she needed medical treatment for the bite and the swelling, but she blew me off." Ashley took the offered cup of coffee and continued, "In fact, she didn't want to press charges at all."

"Yeah, that last part sounds like Tyler. She loves 'em in all their forms, and she wouldn't want to see any woman get in trouble, not because of her."

"I don't understand?" Ashley felt like she had stepped into a movie that was half over.

"Tyler hates violence in any form. She'd rather walk out of a restaurant and leave her date sitting there than deal with an outburst or a verbal confrontation. Jill used to tell me that was one of the things that pissed her off about Tyler. She never liked to argue, about anything. Period."

"Really? Wow. I wouldn't have guessed that. All that bravado and ego packed into that butch package. Hmm." Ashley was starting to like this Tyler she didn't know.

"Look, don't get me wrong. If you mess with someone she loves, she's a pit bull. But, when it comes to herself, she hates confrontation. Just look at how she acted with you and the ticket incident. She didn't fight it, did she?"

Ashley remembered the ticket and Tyler's passive attitude when it came to the whole incident. Tyler never asked for a professional courtesy, she didn't argue with the speed Ashley had put down, and she didn't engage Ashley in anyway. Except when Ashley called her sir.

Smiling, Ashley remembered Tyler's face when she looked up from her ticket book. The mistake had been an honest one and she had tried to apologize, hadn't she? Suddenly, Ashley felt like she needed to call Tyler and apologize for her mistake, but that was weeks ago and probably forgotten. At least she hoped it was forgotten.

"Something doesn't make sense. Knowing Tyler like I do, why would she turn Cassie down?" Kelly asked, looking at Ashley.

"Huh?"

"Cassie said she was the one that took it personal. That 'who'd be stupid enough to turn down a hottie like her.'"

"Well, that's not exactly what she said," Ashley corrected Kelly.

"You know what I mean. I've never seen Tyler turn down any woman who was willing and at least halfway cute. So why tonight?"

"Interesting."

"I'll give her a call later and see what's up. Better yet, I think I'll go by on my way home and talk to her. Besides, I wanna give her crap about the new cut." Kelly smirked before taking a sip of her sludge, then grimaced. "Shit, this stuff must have been made a month ago. Hey! Who makes this shit?" Kelly yelled across the squad room, which evoked more than a few wise cracks from the officers on night shift.

"Aw, don't give her a bad time about the hair cut. I think it makes her look sexy." Ashley signed off the last of her report on the evening's events. "Did I just say that out loud? Forget I said anything. Just professional observation."

"Really?" Kelly smiled at her partner, who was blushing all the way to the tips of her ears.

###

Tyler stepped into the hot spray of the shower hoping it would wash away the remnants of the night. Bracing her hands on either side of the shower head, she let the pulsating spray hammer her body, which was begging for a release from the evening's tensions. Cassie had started something Tyler would normally finish, but tonight she just wasn't interested. Squeezing shampoo into her hands she ran her fingers through her short hair. Chuckling, she realized she had once again poured too much and the suds ran down her face and neck. Next time she would remember not to squirt so much, but she told herself that every time she showered lately.

Tyler winced as she ran the washrag over her left breast, still tender from Cassie's torture. Tyler cursed the woman under her breath. The burning on her neck didn't help matters as she let the hot water clear the stinging soap from the bite mark. She could feel her foul mood returning as she turned away to avoid the intense heat on her bruised face and ego. So much for relaxing in a hot shower. Pulling the showerhead out of its holder, Tyler sprayed the shampoo and soap off her back and legs. Trailing the spray up her thigh, she accidentally hit her sensitive clit and her body jerked in response. Soaping herself again, she directed the warm spray again at her clit and enjoyed the tingle it sent through her body. She hadn't been intimate with anyone for a couple of weeks and her body was letting her know it didn't appreciate the lack of attention.

Closing her eyes, she leaned against the warm, moist tiles of the shower and indulged in the pulsating tempo the showerhead thrummed on her clit. She could almost imagine a woman touching her, sliding her fingers over her hardened clit, the warm body pressed up against hers. She felt a slow stroke down her thighs, and then the push of a wet pussy against her ass. *I think I saw this in a porno somewhere,* Tyler thought as she kept massaging her clit. *I bet those women aren't even lesbians in those things. What's the saying: gay for pay?* Shit! She murmured as the pulsating jets hit the right spot. Her body arched from the intense contact and goose bumps sprouted all over her body. Time had been her enemy lately. That and self-pity, but who's asking. Besides, anything that would help her escape tonight was fine by her. Tyler let out a deep sigh. The hot water was turning her skin beet red, but she didn't care. She was just about to do what every woman with a pulsating showerhead did at least once in her life, orgasm from the damn thing. It started off as a slow roll through her body, but the more she tightened her muscles, the quicker the orgasm came. She felt the tremor start in her vagina and finger its way throughout her body. Quickly, Tyler slid two fingers inside and worked the orgasm. Pumping faster she felt her cunt clench down on her fingers and stop her progress. At the tips of her fingers was her G spot, so she began rubbing it and felt her body spasm again at the rhythmic pressure. Another quick jerk and she relaxed against the warm tiles, sliding down to the floor.

Tyler buried her face in her crossed arms and began to cry. The turmoil of the week had seeped its way into her soul and she cried for release. She hadn't realized how hard it was to put Jill in a box the first time and now she had done it for a second time this week. Leaving that part of her life in the past where she knew it needed to be was agonizing, but she was resolute in moving on. The incident at the bar though, had thrown her for a loop. Letting Cassie treat her like she always had was her first mistake. Not stopping the situation from escalating was her second. Trying to change how she lived her life was going to take time, but she didn't have a choice. Not in her mind, not now.

The doorbell caught her by surprise. "Who the fuck comes by at this late hour?" Tyler complained, turning the water off and grabbing a towel. The persistent ringing announced that whoever was at the door wasn't leaving. "I'm coming, I'm coming."

Looking through the peephole, Tyler sighed and reluctantly opened the door.

"What?" Tyler said, swinging the door wide. She knew it was useless to deny her persistent visitor, so she walked to the couch resigned to the fact that she was in for an ass chewing. "Come on in and make yourself at home."

"God, Tyler. Nice to see you, too," Kelly said closing the door behind her with a smack.

"Sorry, you caught me at a bad time."

"Oh, do you mean …" Kelly nodded her head in the direction of the bedroom, "you have company? If that's the case I just go and we can touch base another time." Kelly rose to leave, but Tyler stopped her.

"No, I mean I was just getting out of the shower. Isn't it kind of late for house calls, Officer?" Tyler's voice oozed with condescension.

She knew Kelly would notice the absence of Jill's pictures and wonder what was happening, so she braced herself for the pending questions. She just hoped she was ready for her own response.

"So, you wanna talk about tonight? What happened, Tyler?" Kelly looked first at the bite mark, then the bruised face. "This isn't like you. I mean the bite mark, the slap. I get the 'not wanting to press charges', but I've never seen you let someone do this to you. I'm worried. What's going on?" Kelly studied Tyler's face, waiting for answers.

"Nothing," Tyler said nonchalantly. "Nothing."

"I haven't seen you for weeks."

"I've been busy."

"I can see that," Kelly said looking around the barren room. With the exception of two pictures, the room looked like a cell rather than a home. "You need some plants in here, Tyler."

"Can I get you something to drink, since I know this is going take a while?" Tyler asked, walking to her bedroom and putting on a robe.

"Tyler, don't be that way. I'm worried about you, that's all."

"Yeah, well you don't need to be. I've been taking care of myself just fine without you, Kelly. I'm a big girl now."

"Tyler don't be—"

"Don't be what, Kell? Don't be a player? Don't ride my motorcycle to fast? Don't be mad Jill's gone? Don't what?" Frustration flowed with her words and she knew Kelly wouldn't take them personal. Her bruise throbbed as she felt her blood pressure increase.

Tyler tossed a beer at Kelly, hoping she saw it before it smacked her in the stomach. Twisting hers open she took a long pull and then gently placed the cool bottle against her face as she sat down across from Kelly. Her stomach ached from the stress and she doubted talking to Kelly would make it feel any better. The tension she had succeeded in reducing earlier was returning with a vengeance and now her head was starting to throb.

Pushing Kelly away wouldn't solve anything. Besides, Kelly was like a dog with a bone, she wouldn't be put off.

"What's going on, Tyler? The haircut, the pictures, or lack thereof, and the hibernation?" Kelly quizzed Tyler, then took a swig of her beer.

"Hibernation? Is that what you call it?" Tyler smiled.

"Well, what would you call it? You do it when you start thinking about Jill. You bury yourself deep and don't come up for air except to work. So what would you call it?"

"Hibernation works," Tyler said not wanting to argue with Kelly.

"What happened tonight with Cassie?"

"Is this a professional question or a personal one, Kelly?" Tyler was starting to get edgy now.

"I'm here as your friend, Tyler. As someone who cares about your well-being. Is that okay? Are you still allowing yourself to have friends, Tyler?"

Tyler didn't miss the condescension, or was it concern, in Kelly's voice. Their long history was what allowed Kelly to still be sitting in her house, but Tyler hoped she didn't push it too far tonight. She wasn't in the mood for motherly advice or the hand of the law.

"I changed the rules and Cassie didn't like it. There, now you know." Tyler took another swallow of her beer and put her feet up on the coffee table.

"Now I know what, Tyler? Cassie practically said all that, but what I want to know is why?"

"Why what?"

"Okay, let's play twenty questions."

Tyler sat avoiding Kelly's stare. She knew it would just be a matter of minutes before Kelly came unglued, so she waited. The ticking of the cat clock, its eyes moving back and forth with every tick, counted off the time. Another swig and Tyler waited. She looked straight ahead while she adjusted her robe. A long sigh followed by another swig and this time Tyler smirked knowing if she looked at Kelly smoke might start shooting out her ears. She could practically feel the steam rolling off Kelly as she took another swig and sighed again. This time she started to mentally count, *one, two, three, four—*.

"Tyler, what the fuck is going on with you? God damn it! Have you finally lost your fucking mind? Don't you know that we're here for you? All you have to do is ask and we'll be here in a heartbeat."

Raising an eyebrow, Tyler finally looked over at Kelly. "Are you done?"

"I haven't even started, sister." Kelly tilted her bottle and drained it, then slammed it on the coffee table.

"Hey, careful there. You break it you buy it," Tyler said, smiling at her frustrated friend.

"Very funny, Tyler. Very fucking funny."

"Do you kiss my godson with that mouth? I hope you wash it out first. I would hate to think he would pick up your bad habits just through contact." Tyler smirked again.

"I'm not leaving until you tell me what is going on. So get me another beer and let's talk."

"Oh, girl talk? I love girl talk. What do you want to talk about? That dreamy boy in gym? He is so cute, but don't tell him I said so. He'll get a big head."

Smiling, Tyler walked into the kitchen and retrieved two more beers. She was certain smoke was billowing out Kelly's ears right about now, but she didn't care. If Kelly was going to push her, she was going to earn her paycheck on this one.

"So what do you think about that boy in gym? Isn't he dreamy," Tyler settled her chin in her palm and batted her eyes at Kelly.

"Okay, enough. I get that you don't want to talk to me," Kelly surrendered, throwing her hands up.

"Finally."

"But you have to talk to someone, Tyler, and right now I'm the only someone you have."

"Not true. I have the guys at the station. They listen to me all the time." Tyler was starting to sound like an impetuous child and she knew it, but she hated being bested by Kelly.

"Right. They like hearing about all the women that you—"

"Hey now," Tyler said, putting her finger up. "You kiss my godson with that mouth. Remember, exposure to toxic fumes kills."

"Ha ha. I bet you think you're funny?"

"I've been told on occasion that I have a good sense of humor, yes."

"Look, I know you miss Jill, but ..." Kelly hoped the change in tactics would make Tyler open up.

"Stop right there. For once this isn't about Jill, Kell." Tyler looked down at the label she was picking at. "It's about me."

"What do you mean?"

"Look around you. Don't you see anything?" Tyler swung her arm wide motioning around the room.

"Yeah, but I didn't want to say anything."

"Now you don't want to say anything. Before I couldn't shut you up, now you don't want to say anything?" Tyler continued picking at the label, anything to keep from looking at Kelly. "I boxed her pictures up, sent some of her things to the charity store, and gave her family some things I thought they might like. The pictures are in a box in the closet. I couldn't …" Tyler felt a lump in her throat as she tried to finish. "I sat here for a week and looked at that box. Believe me, there were times I just wanted to unpack those pictures and put them back, but I knew if I wanted to move on I needed to make a few changes. So there you have it, Kell." Tyler wiped a tear from the corner of her eye and swallowed hard. She hadn't given voice to her mission. She had only done it in the dark of night, away from her friends and without their love and support to help her through it. It was better that way, reasoned Tyler. Besides, she didn't want anyone to see her at her lowest, at her weakest. No, she wanted to shoulder the pain by herself, without the help of friends and family.

"Oh, Tyler. I'm so sorry," Kelly moved to sit down next to Tyler.

As Kelly wrapped her arms around Tyler, Tyler laid her head on Kelly's shoulder and started weeping, softly at first. Then sobs wracked her body as she finally let go of Jill.

"Why did you do this by yourself, Tyler? Why?" Kelly questioned as she hugged Tyler tighter.

"I had to, Kell. I needed to put Jill to rest once and for all. I needed to let her go and I needed to do it alone." Tyler cried harder as she realized what she had done. "I loved her so much that it's killing me." Tyler wiped at her eyes and continued, "I had to make a change. I had to do it by myself to prove to myself that I could do it." The floodgates had been released and Tyler felt her soul finally mourning Jill's death. Tears streamed down Tyler's face. Looking up she saw Kelly crying, too.

"I know it's hard, Honey." Kelly dabbed at Tyler's tears trying to stem the flow.

Tyler felt Kelly's fingers run through her hair as she continued to sob. She had finally told someone and it was done. She cried hard when she thought about not being able to go to her mom and cry on her shoulder. She missed her mother's strength and wisdom and now she cried even harder. Her mom, her rock, the person who had held her hand during Jill's funeral. The person who held her when she tried to sleep, rocking her like she did when Tyler was a child. She had grieved for her mom when she died. She didn't have a choice. It was a family affair. Her father and brothers all came together and stood strong, but they cried, they shared, and they loved their mother. They shared stories and held each other when they cried. They had a process that helped everyone get through it, but her grieving for Jill was cut short, denied a full process when her mom died two weeks later. And Tyler had paid the price for it. Shutting herself off and carrying around all that grief had changed Tyler and now she had to make another change—finally accept Jill's death and move on.

"Is that the reason for the haircut?" Kelly asked, still stroking Tyler's head.

"Yeah, I needed to make a few changes personally, so I cut it off. Do you like it?" Tyler questioned. She knew Kelly would be blunt and honest.

"Ashley likes it." Kelly slapped her hands over her mouth. "You didn't just hear that from me. Shit."

Raising an eyebrow at Kelly, Tyler smirked through the tears. "Really?"

"I like it, too. It makes you look younger."

"Yeah, well, I get called 'Sir' all the time, so I look like a guy, too, I guess."

"Well they're just not looking then, 'cause with those," Kelly said pointing to Tyler's generous breast, "you do not look like a 'Sir', trust me."

"Jealous, huh?" Tyler kidded her friend.

Laying her head back on Kelly's shoulder, she let out a big sigh and relaxed. She thought about Jill and her mom and said a silent prayer for them. Tyler knew they would never be far from her thoughts and she was grateful she had the time she did with them. More time with Jill would have been nice, though. Tears rolled down her cheek, but this time she just let them come, silently. Kelly's strong arms wrapped around Tyler and pulled her close. Kelly was a great friend and she would never be able to repay that friendship, no matter what Tyler did. Kelly had stood by as Tyler tried to self-destruct and she always picked up the pieces. A gentle reprimand always followed, but she let Tyler work out her grief in her own way. And for that, Tyler was thankful.

"So what happened with Cassie, Tyler?"

"I told you, I changed the rules on her and she wasn't happy." Tyler pulled back to look at Kelly and explained further. "I told her I wasn't interested in a quickie and she got pissed. She tried to convince me that I really wanted it." She pulled her robe open and pointed to the bite mark. "When I said I didn't play like that anymore, she slapped me and walked off. End of story." Tyler threw her hands up and shrugged.

"Well, you know that's battery, at a minimum."

"I'm not pressing charges, Kell."

"Fortunately, you don't have to; we saw and heard the whole thing."

"I know, but can't you just let it go? Cassie's not a bad gal; she just knows what she wants and goes after it."

"It's out of my hands."

"Kelly."

"I'll see what I can do. If she doesn't have any priors, the Judge will probably go easy on her. But I can't promise anything, okay?"

"Okay. So, tell me what else Ashley said about my haircut." Tyler smiled at Kelly, hoping she would be forthcoming.

Chapter Fifteen

Ashley pulled her pants on and tucked her t-shirt in. She knew she wasn't the slim, waif-like female some people preferred for a girlfriend, but she could hold her own in a fist fight if she had to and that counted for something in her world. She liked her curvy figure and while her uniform hung with razor sharp creases, the bulk of the vest just wasn't appealing. She hated it because it made her look like a linebacker and it took time to get used to the bulkiness of the vest.

"Well, it isn't a fashion show out there and I'm no fashion model," she whispered to her reflection. Pulling her red hair back into a bun she pinned the few strays that had made their way loose.

"I wonder what kind of woman Tyler's attracted to?" Ashley let out a sigh as she realized for about the umpteenth time that morning her thoughts had wandered back to Tyler. Last night was somewhat of an eye opener for Ashley as she watched how Tyler had handled the conflict with Cassie. A big strapping butch like Tyler, whose ego seemed to outshine everything else about her, had a hidden soft spot. Then, listening to Kelly talk about how Tyler hated confrontation.

Reaching for her shirt she slipped the short sleeve, navy blue uniform on and buttoned it. The color made her look more paler than she really was. Even if she were promoted to an upper rank, the color of the uniform wouldn't change until she was much, much higher.

Ashley looked at her reflection in the mirror, admiring her uniform.

"Detective is starting to sound more and more appealing, if just for the change in wardrobe," she said chuckling. She had finished her four hundred hours of rookie duty. Two years and she was suddenly ready to give up the glamorous life of patrol for the opportunity to wear civilian clothes. Well, maybe not yet. She knew she had to pay her dues, but knew that professional exams were just around the corner. She was hopeful she would do well enough to put another stripe on her uniform.

Her green eyes sparkled as she pinned on her silver badge. She remembered the day she graduated from the academy. While her mom didn't agree with her decision to become a police officer, she never stopped Ashley from pursuing her dreams. Their conversation about the police force had been strained at best.

"Explain to me why you need to be a police officer, Honey," Ashley's mom asked quietly.

"I don't need to become a police officer. I want to become a police officer, Mom," Ashley said resolutely.

"I don't understand, Honey. You're college educated and your grandfather has left you a sizable inheritance. You don't have to work, so why are you?"

Ashley remembered her mom's gentle voice, pushing ever so slightly for her to reconsider her decision.

"Mom, I'm not a trust fund baby. I refuse to act like some dilettante, who has nothing better to do than spend her daddy's money." Ashley had said the last part with a sickening sweet accent. "Besides, I like working. It keeps my mind active, and you know what they say about wasting it?"

"No Dear. What do they say?"

"Use it or lose it. I don't feel like losing mine yet."

The vibration of her cell phone pulled Ashley from the memory, but not before Ashley laughed from the recall. She still remembered the perplexed look her mother gave her before she dismissed Ashley. Looking down at the number on the phone, Ashley flinched.

"How the fuck did she get my number?" Ashley wondered, tossing the phone on the counter. A minute later the phone vibrated again alerting Ashley that she had a message. Panicking, she quickly went to voice mail and deleted the message without even listening to it. She didn't know how Leslie had gotten her new number, but she sure as hell wasn't going to confirm it by answering the phone. Once again Ashley's phone went off, this time alerting her that someone left a text message. Ashley's hands shook as she reached for her phone. Her heart raced as she closed her eyes and wished that it was anyone other than Leslie. She hadn't heard from Leslie in months, so why now? Looking down, Ashley's throat tightened as she read the message:

Hey Babe. I knew you wouldn't pick up the phone. Let's get together and talk. Love ya Leslie.

A chill ran down Ashley's body. Nothing good ever came from contact with Leslie and she wasn't about to respond to this message either.

"Fuck," Ashley said, walking into her bedroom.

Ashley's body started to shake and she threw the phone at the wall breaking it into tiny pieces. She could feel cold sweat start to take over her body, her chest tighten and her knees start to buckle. Sitting on the bed, she put her head between her knees and took slow, deep breaths. She tried to calm herself down and think about something else. A pair of smiling brown eyes popped into her head, making her jerk. Tyler. Of all the things and all the people she could think about, Tyler was what popped into her head?

Suddenly, her house phone rang. Panicked, she slowly walked over but was too afraid to look at the caller ID, so she let it go to voice mail.

"Hey Ash, it's Kelly. Gosh I was hoping I could catch you before—"

"Hey, Kell. Sorry. I was getting ready for work and I didn't hear the phone. What's up?" Ashley felt a rush of relief wash through her. At least Leslie didn't have her home phone number.

"Hey, is everything okay? You sound like you just ran a marathon, Girl."

"Yeah, yeah everything's fine. I just ran across the house to get the phone. What's going on?"

"I just wanted to give you a heads up that you're going to be riding on your own today. Robbie's home sick and it's my turn to stay home with him. I called Sergeant Owens and told him. He said you were probably good to ride by yourself. Besides it's a Tuesday and nothing happens during the day on Tuesdays." Ashley could hear Kelly saying something to someone in the background. "Oh, wait Honey; put your hand over your mouth. Hey Ash, I gotta go. Robbie's getting sick again. Call me later." The line went dead.

"Sure, no problem, Kell," Ashley said into the dead receiver.

It was going to be one of those days, so she needed to focus and be ready. Unfocused led to mistakes, and in her line of work mistakes could mean disaster. Closing her eyes, she tried to clear her mind and think about her job, the people who needed her, and those who didn't know they needed her, yet. Leslie was a nuisance but she could handle a nuisance easily enough. If she didn't engage Leslie, she wouldn't be an issue, period.

Ashley put her Batman belt, as some called it, on the bed and went through the dual magazine pouches to make sure the clips were loaded and ready. She checked her two sets of handcuffs and made sure all the other equipment was checked and ready. Strapping her utility belt on, she went to the cabinet that she kept her gun box in, unlocked it, and loaded a clip into her gun. Taking another deep breath, she slid the automatic into her holster and snapped the hook closed. Looking at her reflection again in the mirror, she saw a determined stare looking back at her. She wasn't about to let Leslie get to her, ever again. Making her way to her vehicle, she waved at her neighbor, a petite older woman who had told her how much she appreciated having a 'cop' in the neighborhood.

"Morning, Mrs. Reilly," Ashley said, waving again.

"Morning, Ashley. Stay safe out there, okay?"

"You got it. Have a good one."

"You, too."

With that she was off to work and another day sitting behind the wheel on patrol.

###

Just as Kelly had said, Ashley's Sergeant had informed her she would be on patrol by herself. She knew it would eventually happen. Lots of the officers did patrol by themselves during the day. But with a city the size of hers, it wasn't standard protocol. With more gangs moving into new neighborhoods, it was becoming dicier to have a single officer on their own when they patrolled. Part of Ashley's patrol was the neighborhood she grew up in. With its affluence, she was sure the Chief got more than one call if someone didn't see a police officer at least twice a day. Driving through the old neighborhood gave her a feeling of melancholy. Her childhood was fun, carefree, and anxiety ridden. The fun, carefree part included all the things kids do when growing up. The anxiety came when she realized she had a crush on her best friend, Mary.

She carried that crush around as she watched Mary have boyfriend after boyfriend. Ashley never had the guts to tell her how she felt. How was she supposed to do that? Lesbian wasn't even a word in her vocabulary at the time and she didn't know girls could feel like that. Mary didn't know it, but she would set the model by which all other women would be compared. Mary's dark hair, brown eyes, and tan skin would be the ideal by which Ashley would be attracted to other women. Smiling, Ashley wondered what had happened to Mary. They had stopped being friends in high school, not because they had a falling out, but because their lives had taken different paths. Mary was probably married to a successful financial advisor, with two point five kids, a membership at the country club, and driving a kid hauler to soccer, dance class, and whatever parents do with younglings.

"Patrol Six?" Ashley's radio pulled her back to reality.

"Patrol Six," Ashley said into the mic on her left shoulder.

"Can you check out a report of a suspicious person at 1132 South Laurel?"

"Do you have a description?

"Negative. RP was on a cell phone and hung up before I could get one." RP was the reporting party. "They did say they would meet the officer on the street.

The RP was female if that helps."

"Okay, I'm in route."

Ashley turned her cruiser around. A suspicious person was unusual and most times it ended up being a homeless person sleeping in the comfort of the bushes or sitting in front of someone's business. Business owners had businesses to run and a vagrant sitting in front usually ran off customers who didn't want to deal with them. Pulling into a space in front of the four-story building, Ashley looked around for the RP, but didn't see anything. In fact, she didn't see anything out of the ordinary at all.

"Dispatch, show me at the location. I don't see anyone suspicious so I'm going to go try and find the RP. Location is Bank of Meridian," Ashley said into the mic. Opening the door, she looked around and still couldn't see anyone. Raising her hand to shield the sun out of her eyes, she heard what she thought was a firecracker go off and then a searing pain shot through her right arm pit. Twisting to her right, she heard another shot and her mic exploded on her shoulder. Ashley felt herself take another shot to her chest which sent her backwards with such force her head hit the pavement and knocked her out.

Chapter Sixteen

Tyler stood next to the crew cab of the fire truck adjusting her turnout bottoms. The call had come from dispatch as an officer down with a possible medical situation and hostages. Every police officer in the city was on scene.

"What do we have, Captain?" Tyler asked, tossing her ball cap on the seat and putting her helmet on.

"We got an officer down, hostages and injuries, but we can't get to the injured officer because of the shooter or shooters."

"Do we know how many are injured?" Tyler walked with Captain Russo closer to the scene. Ducking down, they both peered over the sedan and looked over at a police cruiser riddled with bullet holes.

Captain Russo tossed his head in the direction of the cruiser and said, "See that cruiser? On the other side is an officer lying on the ground. We don't know how badly injured they are. They haven't seen movement for a few minutes now. So they're not sure if she's dead or if she's playing dead to avoid being shot again."

"She? Who she?" Tyler bent down and looked under their cruiser to see if she could make out who the officer was. It didn't matter. There were only a few females on the force and Tyler knew two of them, Kelly and Ashley. She felt herself get lightheaded and start to sway as she sat back down on her heels. Tyler broke out in a cold sweat and felt her heart start to race. She had been here before and it had ended badly. The memories started flooding her mind as she took a deep breath.

"Hey, you alright? Maybe you need to go back to the rig and wait this one out, Tyler." Captain Russo eyed Tyler cautiously. "I don't need to worry about you, too."

"I'm good." But Tyler didn't sound good. Her voice quivered with despair as she tried looking under the cruiser again. The body hadn't moved and Tyler couldn't see any blood. "Why hasn't someone gone over there and helped her?"

Fear was starting to grip Tyler's heart as she continued to watch the still body. Whoever was over there was alone, scared, and might be dying, while someone decided what to do. At least she had been able to hold Jill while she lay dying. Her stomach started to revolt and she felt bile rise up, starting to gag her. Swallowing hard, she tried to maintain her composure while she waited for an answer.

"Every time they make a move towards her, someone starts shooting. So we wait until SWAT gets here."

"She doesn't have time for us to wait, Captain. She could be dying right now while we wait for a plan."

"We wait, Tyler." Captain Russo's words were a silent command to stand down until they had other options.

"Fuck. Well, have they at least tried to radio her?"

"Yeah, but they don't get any response. They have two other officers in the building somewhere and no one is communicating. They think the shooters have scanners, so everyone's on radio silence until they can come up with a plan."

The incident had only been going on for ten minutes but it felt like a lifetime to Tyler.

"So, you never said. Do they know who's down over there?"

Captain Russo shook his head. "They have an idea, but they aren't willing to speculate yet."

Tyler looked at the cruiser again and noticed it was Kelly's car and she was partnered with Ashley. So that meant it was one of them, but which one? Looking up again, she noticed the door was open; whoever was down had probably taken cover behind the door. The way the cruiser was positioned gave the shooters access to the fallen officer. Extracting her from her current position was impossible without someone getting hurt. Looking around the closed off street, Tyler noticed it was littered with police cars and a few civilian vehicles. The sun was directly over them so that would offer no help. Hiding in the few shadows wouldn't offer any cover and she was almost certain that the officer would be dead by the time it did.

Getting up, Tyler walked over to the paramedic that had gone out with them on the motorcycles earlier in the week.

"Mike, we can't let that officer die out there. We just can't." The fear in Tyler's voice made the paramedic take notice.

"Tyler, we can't do anything until they give us the all clear sign." He didn't look up from rearranging the supplies in his kit.

"Mike, I think I can get in and out quick, but I need your help to do it."

The paramedic now looked up at Tyler and shook his head. "Tyler, we can't."

"I can't sit back and watch another officer die, Mike. You can help me or you can walk away and let me do what needs to be done. But I refuse to see another officer die on my watch." Tyler pleaded, waiting for Mike's answer. She wouldn't be surprised if he walked away. Her plan had risks, but hadn't the downed officer put her life at risk going into a no win situation? "She's out there on the other side of that car and I'm not going to let her die like Jill did. So you can help or get the hell out of the way."

Tyler took off her turnout coat and tossed it into the ambulance. It would weigh her down if she did what she wanted. Looking at the paramedic, she waited for his answer.

"You're going to probably get us fired, you know." Mike closed the kit and pushed it into the ambulance. "Tell me what your plan is first and then I'll decide."

Tyler and Mike huddled as they went over all the possibilities of Tyler's plan. It was definitely a risk, but the way Tyler explained it she would be taking the bulk of the risk. If it went off as planned, it would get the officer out of harm's way and open up an opportunity for the police to end the situation. Tyler was used to putting herself in difficult situations, but the paramedic was just that, a paramedic. He had been hired on as a paramedic and wasn't one of those who had been taken from the firefighter ranks and trained as a paramedic. His fear was palpable and Tyler could feel it.

"Look, just trust me on this. It will work. But if anything goes wrong, you just get the officer and the bus out of there. I can handle myself."

Tyler had taken fire before so the idea of being shot at didn't scare her. She felt the adrenaline surge through her body as the plan started taking shape.

"Maybe we should tell Captain Russo what we're going to do, just in case anything happens."

"Nope, he'll just tell us to wait. I'm not waiting,

not this time." Tyler jumped into the ambulance and asked over her shoulder, "You coming? Or am I doing this myself?"

"I'm coming. You can't do this yourself." Mike strapped everything down and closed the back doors on the ambulance behind them.

Chapter Seventeen

Tyler backed the ambulance out of the protected perimeter and started down a side street that paralleled the one the crime scene was on. If she was right, she would barely have enough time to get to the corner and do what she needed to do. She hoped surprise would be on their side. Reaching the corner, she turned the ambulance around and started backwards toward the scene. Maneuvering the ambulance was easy at first. No traffic and no cars gave her the advantage she hoped would save Kelly's life. Spotting the open door of the cruiser she pushed the gas pedal down. Avoiding two officers who were waving her down, she moved fast hoping they would get out of the way. No one was going to stop her, including the police. Hopefully, they would see what she was doing and put a diversion together so she wouldn't get shot at.

Then it happened. The first shot at the ambulance missed Mike by inches, causing him to hit the floor.

"Fuck, Tyler, they're shooting at us."

"Just stay down, Mike. I got this." Tyler continued on her path towards the open door of the cruiser. A few more yards and they would be close enough to save Kelly's life, hopefully. Another shot came through the cab and broke Tyler's side window, glass showering all over her. Unperturbed, Tyler continued her methodical path towards the police car, dodging another cruiser and the officers who had taken refuge behind it.

"Tyler, is that you Tyler? What the fuck are you doing?" Captain Russo squawked on the radio. "Get your ass out of there or I'm gonna fire you."

Tyler didn't lose her focus on her target. She was about fifty yards away when another bullet hit the ambulance, coming through the roof and lodging in her seat. Clearly, the shooters were aiming for the driver, trying to stop her progress.

"Tyler, you're going to get yourself and Mike killed. Get the hell out of there now, before they shoot you," Captain Russo radioed again.

Tyler could hear someone in the background questioning what was going on and who had given the order to rescue the fallen officer. At worst, she would be fired. At a minimum, she would face a reprimand with a letter in her personnel file. But she didn't care. Kelly's husband and son were not going to go through what she had when Jill died.

"Hold on, Mike. We're almost there. Remember, stay back until you hear me call you." Tyler kept her eye on the cruiser as the ambulance neared its target. As she inched closer, the radio squawked again. Before she heard the voice on the other end she turned it off, choosing to risk losing her job rather than losing much needed concentration. The corner of the ambulance was diagonal to the cruiser's bumper, so she had about five feet until she reached the downed officer. If she got any closer, she wouldn't be able to open the barn doors of the ambulance, so she was as close as she was going to get. Grabbing her helmet, she put it on and hoped it would offer her head some protection. Snapping it closed, she walked between the seats and looked over at Mike who was obviously shaken by the gunshots.

"Mike, once I open those doors they're going to

be shooting at me. So timing is critical. Once I get her over to the bus, I need you to floor it. Once we're out of harm's way we'll trade places and you can work on her." Tyler peeked out the back window but still couldn't see who was down. The officer's hat hid her face and she still wasn't moving. From where Tyler was, she still couldn't see any blood, but that didn't mean anything. She might have internal wounds and be dying right before her eyes. "Ready?"

Mike gave her thumbs up and stood up.

"Stay down and against this panel," Tyler said pointing to her left. "I don't think a bullet can reach you here. The angle's all wrong." Taking a deep breath, Tyler put her hands on the handle and said a little prayer.

"Be careful out there, Tyler."

"Always." With that, Tyler pushed the doors and ran as fast as she could to the cruiser, diving for the tight space just under the car.

Luckily, she had her turnout pants on, so her legs were protected but her palms and elbows took the brunt of the asphalt rash.

"Fuck," she said, wishing she had put on her gloves.

"Tyler?"

"Ashley? Shit." Tyler suddenly felt lightheaded realizing that it was Ashley and not Kelly next to her. "How badly are you hurt? Can you move? What are you doing in Kelly's cruiser? How did—"

"Tyler, I don't know how much longer I can stay awake. Help me." Ashley's voice was barely a whisper now.

Scooting closer to Ashley, Tyler ran her hands over the fallen officer's chest looking for something, anything that would tell her how badly Ashley was injured. A bullet hole in the center of her vest at breast level, one on her right side and one more dead center of her abdomen was all she could feel. Her mic clip on her left shoulder was all that was left of her mic. A few shattered pieces had embedded in her neck and jaw.

"Hey, you lookin' for a cheap thrill?" Ashley coughed and then turned her head slightly towards Tyler. "Under my arm pit. The bullet went in above my vest right there. I'm having a hard time breathing."

"Shh, try and relax. I'm gonna get you out of here, but you have to do exactly what I say. Okay?" Tyler crawled closer to Ashley and looked up at the building across from the cruiser. So far, the shooters hadn't started shooting again, but it was only a matter of time. Looking back at the ambulance, she could see Mike peeking out from around the cabinet watching her. Nodding in his direction, she watched him give another thumbs up.

"My vest, Tyler. Take my vest off and put it on. The ambulance is too far."

"No, I got this. Don't worry. Besides, your vest might be compressing your injuries just enough to keep you alive." Tyler grabbed Ashley's wrist and checked her pulse. She could barely feel it. "This is probably going to hurt, but I'm gonna pick you up and carry you to the bus. Sorry."

"Don't worry about me. Please promise me you'll be careful."

"Okay, if you promise me you'll stay alive long enough to go out on a date with me."

"Really? You're asking me out on a date at a time like this?" Ashley could barely open her eyes as she responded to the request.

"Really. Okay, be ready. On three," Tyler said,

squatting next to the fading officer. "One." Tyler slid her arms under Ashley and pulled her gently against her legs. "Two." Tyler started to stand, the limpness of Ashley's body sent a frightening chill through her. "Three." Standing, Tyler pulled the light body tight against her chest and started for the ambulance.

Ping. The glass window in the ambulance door shattered. Without missing a step, Tyler pushed her body hard to stay upright. The weight pitching her forward almost made her lose her balance. Ping. Tyler felt a stinging on her neck. Finally getting her stride under her, she ran towards the ambulance and the waiting paramedic, his arms outstretched.

"Get back, Mike."

Ping. Tyler felt herself stumble as she listed to the right. A sharp stinging pain almost caused her to drop Ashley, but she kept going. Ping. Another shot buried itself as it hit the pavement where her right foot had just been. Pushing harder, she barely reached the ambulance when she heard another shot hit the back of the ambulance.

"Grab her Mike," Tyler said, barely able to push Ashley into Mike's waiting arms.

Tyler jumped, twisted, and landed on her back against the diamond plate floor. She watched as Mike picked Ashley up and laid her on the gurney, starting oxygen immediately. Tyler turned to her right and tried to push herself upright, but found herself face down on the deck of the ambulance.

"Fuck," Tyler said, her head spinning as she rolled on her back.

"Tyler."

Tyler looked up to see Mike swimming above her head. She vaguely saw a gauze pad pressed to her neck with instructions to keep applying pressure.

"Just take care of Ashley, Mike. I got this," Tyler said, rolling to her left side and pulling her legs into the ambulance. Suddenly, Tyler's world went dark.

###

Ashley faded in and out of consciousness. Each time, she tried to focus on the words swirling around in her head.

"She's lost a lot of blood."

"Let's get her into surgery."

"Her mom's here. What do we tell her?"

Ashley tried to talk when she heard the last statement. She felt her lips move, at least she thought her lips moved, but nothing came out. She tried to swallow, but her throat rubbed against something. A tube. She was intubated. Darkness started to slowly creep back in and her mind started to fog again. It took all her strength to push out a moan.

"She's awake, Doctor."

Opening her eyes, she found herself staring into a set of caring blue eyes. "Officer Henderson, you've been shot. Can you understand me?"

Ashley barely nodded her head as she continued to stare at the man.

"I'm Doctor Wainwright. You have a tube in your throat so you aren't able to speak. We're going to take you into surgery. You have a collapsed lung with internal bleeding and we need to get that bullet out." Nodding in another direction he spoke to someone else, "Nurse, let's get her to surgery." Looking down at Ashley, he continued, "Officer Henderson, I'll see you when you get out of surgery."

Ashley felt a gentle pat on her shoulder just before her world faded to black.

###

"Tyler?" A soft whisper caressed Tyler's ear.

Turning her head towards the whisper she smiled as she recognized the voice.

"Baby."

"Tyler, what are you doing, Honey?"

"What? Nothing. I'm just laying here thinking about you, Jill. Come here and let me hold you." Tyler held out her arms waiting for Jill's soft body to fill her grasp. Warmth filled Tyler as she relaxed in the embrace. Jill's touch was always healing and today was no different. "How was your day today, baby?"

Tyler laid back on the bed reveling in her wife's touch. Jill had a way that made Tyler crave her touch. The soft way Jill caressed Tyler's face and body sent a charge right through her body. A soft fragrance filled Tyler's senses as she inhaled deeply. The sharp motion caused a stabbing pain in her thigh. Grabbing the bandage, Tyler winced remember the day before.

"Are you okay?" Jill's soft melodic voice reverberated through her ears.

Tyler's journey between the two worlds was starting to confuse her. The edge of the sharp pain dissipated, helping her start to center herself in the here and now. Her mind was clearing, but her heart lost in the memories of her love for Jill kept her firmly anchored in both worlds, for now.

"Tyler, you need to stop this destructive behavior." Fingers feathered through Tyler's short hair.

Leaning into the stroke, Tyler whispered, "Jill, I

want to be with you. Either here or there. Clearly, I'm there right now or I wouldn't be able to touch you." Looking up into big, brown eyes told Tyler she was right. She stood somewhere between Jill and life. It felt good to be so close to Jill, to touch her and feel Jill finally touch her. But the pain in Jill's eyes tore at Tyler's heart. "What is it baby?" Tyler grabbed Jill's hand entwining their fingers, and then pulled them to her chest. She knew what was coming, but she wasn't ready for that yet, not just yet.

"Baby. You need to live. You need to go on without me. There is so much still waiting for you out there. Someone waiting for you out there. Don't you understand, baby?

"I don't care. I want to be with you." Tyler smiled into Jill's brown eyes. "I'm done here, Jill. There isn't anything else for me here. Besides, you and my mom are where I want to be."

"Your mom is pissed Tyler. She sees everything and is so worried about you."

"Where is she? I want to see her."

"You can't. It isn't time yet, Honey." Jill's warmth infused Tyler's body. "Honey, it just isn't your time. You have things that still need to be done. Trust me on this. You've got a full life ahead of you and all I can say is that you're going to meet someone special, Tyler. Be open to it."

"But—"

"Honey, you've already started the transition to your new life. You don't need me anymore. Besides, as long as you're holding on I can't transition either." A tear rolled down Jill's face and Tyler wiped it away as her own tears fell. "She's a wonderful woman, Tyler. You just have to be open to it. Promise me you'll give love another chance."

"Jill, please!" Tyler pleaded with her wife, holding her tight. She didn't know why, but she knew she didn't have much longer with Jill.

"I'll be waiting for you when it's your time, Baby. But trust me, this isn't it."

Tyler watched as Jill stood. A light popped behind her and started to envelope Jill. Shading her eyes, she gripped Jill's hand tighter but felt her grip loosening. Soft lips touched hers and a whisper in her ear told her something that made Tyler smile. Shaking her head, she felt a peace come over her that she hadn't had in a year.

"I'll always love you, Baby." Tyler started to cry.

"I'll always love you, too. Remember, I'm always with you and you know it."

"I know, I know," Tyler whispered as Jill disappeared into the light, which dimmed suddenly and was gone.

Tyler laid her head back and closed her eyes. Tears streamed down her face as she thought about what Jill whispered in her ear. Tyler knew that she wouldn't see Jill again. In her dreams, in her mind, she would have *that* Jill. Tyler had finally released Jill's spirit to go be with her mom. She was on her own, but then again, she had probably always been on her own and just didn't know it.

Chapter Eighteen

Her eyes still closed, Ashley took a shuddered breath, and at least breathing was easier. The smell of flowers mixed with coffee permeated her brain as she tried to focus on something, anything but the pain radiating through her body. The beeping of the monitors told her everything she needed to know about her condition, she was still alive. A warm touch ran up her arm and then back down grabbing her fingers and giving them a squeeze.

"Hey, Mom," Ashley whispered, her eyes still closed.

Her throat was killing her and every time she tried to swallow it felt like sandpaper was rubbing against sandpaper. Coughing, she winced at the shooting pain through her chest. She lifted her hand to grab her chest and realized she was tethered to two I.V.'s. Reading her mind, her mother lifted a spoon with ice chips to her lips. Greedily, she took the offer and slipped back to her pillow.

"How do you feel?"

"Like someone punched me in the chest. How bad do I look?" Ashley looked at her mom through slits. The light hurt her eyes and she couldn't stand it. "Can you close those blinds, Mom? I've got a splitting headache."

"The doctor said you have a concussion from hitting your head on the pavement."

"No shit."

Ashley tried to assess everything that hurt. Her chest felt like a mule had kicked her, not that she knew what that felt like, but she had a pretty good guess. Her head and neck were killing her, so moving fast wasn't an option anytime soon. Every deep breath hurt like a son of a gun. Smiling at the joke, she turned to look at her mom who was studying her closely.

"How long have I been here?"

"Two days. The doctor said you would wake up when you were ready."

"Not sure I'm ready, but I'm awake." Ashley felt something being pushed into her hand.

"The doctor said this was for pain. You just push it and it'll give you a dose of pain medication. He said you can push it as often as you want, but it'll only give you one dose. It's timed so you can't get too much."

Ashley could tell her mom was nervous because when she was nervous she talked too much. Putting her hand on her mom's she tried to reassure her with a smile.

"It's fine, Mom. Could you get the nurse? I want this damn catheter out."

"Oh, sure. Let me get him."

"Ah, no. Get a female. No offense, but I would feel more comfortable with a woman."

"I'll go to the nurse's station and see what I can do. Relax, Honey. I'll take care of this."

Ashley watched her mom go into mother mode. She felt sorry for anyone who didn't agree with her wishes. Trying to move, Ashley felt her body fatigue with just the little movements she had made. It looked like it was going to be a long recovery if she tired this easily.

"Ah, our patient is awake. How do you feel this morning, Officer Henderson?" the short stocky woman asked as she took Ashley's pulse and looked at a monitor over Ashley's shoulder.

"Good."

"Really? With your injuries I would've thought you'd be feeling like a punching bag right about now," the nurse said as she went about her routine. "So, I hear you want the catheter out. Well the only way it comes out is if you can get up to use the bathroom. We're pushing a lot of liquids through your system right now and that means what goes in must come out." She smiled at Ashley, raising her eyebrows and pursing her lips.

The nursed flicked on the irritating fluorescent light over Ashley's bed making her wince in pain. Closing her eyes, Ashley covered her head with her arm and groaned. "Okay. I can do that."

"Okay." Gloving up, the nursed moved down to Ashley's waist and looked at her mom. "You might want to go outside, just for a minute. Can you close the door? We wouldn't want anyone to see your daughter in her delicate position. Thanks," she said going back to her work.

Ashley rolled her eyes and waited. She hadn't had a catheter before. Heck, she'd never had surgery, so this was all new to her. A slight pressure and it was done. The bag, the tubing and the nurse were all whisked away so fast she couldn't ask her the question that was on the tip of her tongue.

"You know, you've had visitors in and out of this place since you got here," Ashley's mom informed her as she pushed the privacy curtain back. "You're a pretty popular woman, Honey."

"Mom, can you get the light?" Ashley pointed to the fluorescent above her.

"Sure, Honey. Do you remember what happened

to you?"

She remembered getting up that morning, dressing, checking her firearm, and then getting a call about a suspicious person. She remembered getting out of her car and then a searing pain shot through her chest. Reaching up, she touched the bandages on her face and remembered the mic exploding on her shoulder. Then Tyler was by her side lifting her and running. After that she didn't remember anything.

"I remember everything up until a firefighter starting carrying me to the ambulance. After that, nothing." Ashley winced again in pain. Pushing the button on the pain machine she hoped it didn't take long to work.

"Knock, knock. Anyone awake?" Kelly's voice was barely a whisper as she peeked around the privacy curtain. "Hey, you're awake. How are you, kid?"

Kelly leaned down and kissed Ashley on the head, then turned and smiled at Ashley's mom and patted her shoulder.

"Hi, Kelly. Well, I guess I'll go home now that my replacement is here." Leaning down, Ashley's mom kissed her on the forehead. "I'll be back in a little while, Honey."

"Bye, Mrs. Henderson," Kelly said taking her place next to Ashley.

"Mom? Mom, you don't need to come back today. I'm awake, but I'll probably sleep all day, so stay home and just call me tonight. If I need you I'll call you, okay? Please, Mom?"

"Okay, Ashley. Call me if you need me. It was nice to see you again, Kelly."

"Bye, Mrs. Henderson." Kelly waved and looked at Ashley.

"She's pissed," Ashley whispered. "She wants to feel needed and I just told her to stay home. Being a daughter can be so hard. Can you hand me that cup of ice?"

"Here, I'll do it," Kelly said, slipping a few chips in Ashley's mouth.

"So how bad is it?" Ashley steeled herself for what was about to come. She could feel her eyelids start to droop, which meant the pain meds were starting to work. She focused on Kelly's lips that were moving but she couldn't really hear anything, except one word.

"Leslie."

Chapter Nineteen

S he should be waking up soon. She's been in and out of consciousness for the past two days," a male voice said as Tyler tried to focus on it. "She's got a long road ahead of her. She's going to need to rehab as soon as she's able to get out of bed. We want to try and get her up as soon as possible, so when she's able we need to get her on her feet."

"She's not going to like that," another voice said.

"She'll be fine. She's a fighter, Doctor." Tyler recognized that voice. It was her dad's.

Trying to open her eyes again, she realized she was freezing. *Geez, don't they heat this place,* Tyler asked. At least she thought she asked it, but she didn't get a response to her question. Trying to clear her foggy mind, she licked her lips and tried to talk, but nothing came out. *Shit, now what?* She could still hear the conversation going on around her as if she wasn't even there. Finally, she moaned in frustration.

"Hey, Kiddo. How are you feeling?" Tyler's dad came into her field of vision giving her something to focus on.

Tyler made a writing motion with her hand and looked desperately at her father.

"Sure, Ty," her father said, pulling out a pad of paper from his front pocket and a pen from his jacket. "Here you go, Kid."

Tyler tried to sit up, but her body rejected the idea.

It seemed to take forever for her to scrawl her request, but she finally finished the word. Handing the pad to her father she laid her head back on the pillow and sighed. Never had something taken so much out of her, but a single word was all she could muster. Looking up at the paper she frowned at the childlike scratching and started to cry.

"Honey, don't cry. It'll be okay." Picking up the pad, her dad started to chuckle. "She wants water."

"Sips, small sips. Her throat is probably dry and scratched from the breathing tube," the doctor said moving into her field of vision. "Hi Tyler, I'm Dr. Smyth. I'll be treating you while you're in the hospital."

Tyler smiled at the simple name. Had she been able to talk, she probably would've given the good doctor a bad time over the name, but now she just wanted a drink of water. Looking back up, she saw Doctor Smyth pull out his penlight to check her eyes. Instructing her to look in different directions while he checked her pupils, it was clear Doctor Smyth was going to check her out first. The things she had to do to get a drink of water. Tyler grunted again and raised her eyebrows, dramatically making a swallowing motion.

"Okay, Okay. Chief Jackson, she can have a drink, but small sips. She hasn't had anything in her stomach and I would hate to see her get sick." Looking back at Tyler he continued, "Tyler, you have two injuries. One was to the neck, which needed surgery. You were lucky the bullet just missed your carotid artery, but we had to go in and make sure that the jugular wasn't compromised in anyway. We did find a few fiberglass fragments from your helmet when we irrigated the wound so we cleaned the wound out and sewed you back together. We did an MRI and didn't find any bullet fragments so that's good.

Your hip, on the other hand, is another story. It looks as if the bullet ricocheted off the pavement and entered under your right buttock, nicking the femur about 3 inches below the trochanter, which is the outer part of your femur, and to the ..." Looking down at his own legs he tried to visualize which side Tyler was shot. "right of the head of your femur. We noticed on the MRI that there were bullet fragments there so we wanted to make sure that the joint wasn't impacted. So we had to go in and do surgery to check everything out. We also needed to get the fragments out so you didn't develop lead toxicity. The nick should heal without any additional surgery, but we did put in drains because I'm worried about the formation of a fistula, which is a pocket of blood or pus. The surgical drains will allow those fluids to discharge and we can check the content and treat you accordingly. Okay? Well that's a lot of information for you to take in. It's going to be difficult to walk around with the I.V.'s and drains in, but we've got everything taped down. You're going to have a little trouble talking because your throat is bruised, but don't worry. It will go down. Sips of water, maybe some lukewarm broth, and we'll see what we can get dietary to send up that will be soft and palatable. Questions?"

Tyler's head was spinning with all the information. She had two gunshot wounds, wasn't dying and would be able to walk. Nope everything sounded good on her end.

"Peeing?"

"Aw, you want to get up and walk around. Slowly. You'll need help so don't walk alone. I'll get a walker sent up and that should help. You'll find lying on your left side is much more comfortable. Also be careful sitting.

Lean more to the left when you do sit and then lay on your side."

"Pee?"

"Oh, right. Yes, you can get up to pee. In fact that will help with the healing process. So yes, by all means pee, but with help. Okay Tyler, I'll see you later tonight when I do rounds. If you need something, let the nurses know. I've given you something for the pain, but if you need more we can set you up on a pain management system. Don't wait though to ask and don't think you can tough it out. You've been seriously injured and we want to make sure pain doesn't stop the healing process. You know what? I'm going to order it when I get out to the nurses' station. That way we don't have to worry." Turning to Tyler's father, he extended his hand and they shook. "I'll see you both later."

Finally, Tyler thought. *Now I can get that damn water.* Moaning again she motioned to her throat.

"Oh, sorry, Sweetie." Tyler's father came to her side and quickly moved her bed to an upright position. He put a pillow behind her back so she would roll over, placed a small paper cup with a straw in her hand and helped her take a sip of water. "You scared the shit out of me. I thought I was going to lose you, too."

Tyler looked at her father and saw a tear start to roll down his check. Reaching up, she wiped his face, then cupped his check. Taking another sip of water, she smiled at him and squeezed his hand hoping it would lend some reassurance. Tyler's dad had been a pillar of strength when her mom died, but he had his moments when she found him by himself crying. One day, she found him sitting in his office with a picture of her mother in his lap. He had fallen asleep, but it was evident he had been crying. It broke Tyler's heart to see her father worried about her.

Tyler reached up and touched the gauze on her neck and tried to twist her neck slightly, but pain shot through her forcing her to stop. Tapping her father's arm, she reached for the pad again. This time she was able to write somewhat better. The shaking in her hand was gone and she felt a little clearer as she scrawled one word on the paper again. Handing it to her dad she waited for his response.

"Ashley? Oh, Officer Henderson. She's doing better. Kelly was in here checking on you and said that she was finally starting to come around." Tyler's dad smiled at her.

Giving him a thumbs up, she took another sip of water and laid her head back on her pillow. Trying to move in the bed she felt another shooting pain at her hip. Pulling the covers back, she pulled her gown to the side and saw a long gauze with two drains coming out of the skin. Looking panicked at her father, she pointed to her hip and grunted out, "Oh shit!"

"You don't remember much from the incident do you?" Tyler shook her head and motioned for her father to continue. "Well you got shot-up pretty bad, Tyler. In fact, we didn't think you were going to live. You took one in the neck there," he said pointing to the pain in her neck, "and you took one right there in your hip. Mike said he was surprised you made it to the ambulance. Tyler, I don't know if I can save you from yourself, but this has to stop. I'm going to put you on administrative leave until I can figure out what to do."

Shocked, Tyler looked at her dad and shook her head. She had known there would be some repercussions from her decision, but right now she didn't care. She had saved Ashley and that's all that mattered. At least

Ashley wouldn't end up like Jill, hanging on the Wall of the Fallen at the police station. Tyler felt her dad's warm hand rub her shoulder, trying to smooth over what he had just told her.

"Mike … wasn't his fault," Tyler whispered in her raspy voice. "I made him do it. I threatened him, Dad. Not his fault."

"I had a long talk with Mike. He explained that he wasn't going to let you go out there alone, so I put him on admin leave for a week. I just can't have my firefighters breaking the rules or worse, putting themselves and others in danger, just 'cause you think you know better. Can I Tyler?"

Tyler slumped her shoulders and head and slowly shook it in agreement. She felt like she did when she as a kid and had disappointed him. She almost wanted to cry, but not in front of her dad and her chief. Now, Mike had to pay for her stupidity. Her reputation as a cowboy was firmly intact, she was sure of it. Pulling the pad to her again she wrote something down and showed it to her dad.

Smiling and shaking his head, he ran his fingers through her hair and grasped her head and kissed it. "I know, Honey. I know."

Writing something else down, she showed it to her father and waited.

"Well, I can help you with the first thing, but I'm not sure you're ready to get out of bed. The pajamas and robe, I'll bring in later. Okay?"

Another thumbs up from Tyler and then she was trying to lower the bed as far down as it would go. She wasn't going to be stuck in that bed any more than she had to be, so it was now or never. Motioning to her father, he helped her swing her feet to the floor. Tyler noticed the pink booties on her feet and groaned. It wasn't that she didn't like pink. It just wasn't a color she wore unless it was a polo shirt or a button down.

"Wait, Honey. Let me page the nurse."

Tyler waited while everyone assembled for her grand adventure to the bathroom. Tyler hoped her ass wasn't hanging out for her dad to see. She was sure the last time he'd seen it was when she was a baby, if he even changed her diapers. Slowly rising to her feet, she felt the room start to spin.

"Down," she grunted, motioning with her hands to sit again. Turning to her left side, she felt the pull on her right thigh and butt. Oh this is going to suck, she thought as she broke out in a cold sweat. Taking a long deep breath, she focused on her mission. It was a simple one but urgent, pee. Putting her hands on the side of the bed, she started to push herself up and felt a set of hands on each side of her helping. This time the dizziness wasn't as bad. Putting one foot in front of the other, she slowly made her way to the open bathroom door. Turning slightly, she looked at her dad, raised an eyebrow and shook her head. Mouthing the word no, she walked into the bathroom with the nurse and closed the door. A minute later Tyler let out a deep moan, which she was sure the nurse could hear.

"Good Girl," said the nurse with such enthusiasm that it embarrassed Tyler.

She wasn't a six year old and didn't need the accolades that went to someone so young when they made their first poopoo after surgery. Tyler washed her hands and made her way back out of the tiny box they called a bathroom. *Someone could get claustrophobia in a little place like that,* she reasoned. Tyler's dad walked over and wrapped his arms around her, squeezing ever so slightly, but the intent was felt. Tyler was safe in her dad's arms and she laid her head on his shoulder as she heard him sniffle, a sure sign he was crying.

"Come on. Let's get you back into bed. That little jaunt to the little girls' room is gonna tire you out. Trust me."

Tyler reached for the pad again, wrote "blanket", and handed it to her dad. She was sure her nipples were hard enough to cut glass and it didn't do Tyler's ego any good to know her dad had probably noticed.

"Yeah, I figured you were cold," he said walking Tyler to the bed. The look she sent him could have withered a weaker man, but he withstood the glare. "Sorry, Honey. Guess that was better left unsaid, huh?"

Tyler's face said it all. She had suffered the humiliation of having her dad see her bare ass, now he had seen her high beams on full. What else could happen?

"Hey kids, is our sleepy head up yet?" Kelly asked whispering as she came into the room.

Tyler rolled her eyes. *I just had to ask didn't I? Now Kelly could see me in all my bare-ass, high beam glory. Why hadn't I just gotten into bed and not hugged my dad? Shit!*

Chapter Twenty

The smell of coffee assaulted Ashley's senses again, this time her stomach rumbling from the enticement. She knew her mother would be sitting across from her so she relaxed, trying to sleep a bit longer until the pressure in her bladder made it almost uncomfortable to sleep. Cracking an eyelid open, she found the room in almost complete darkness. *Thank heavens*, she thought as she opened both eyes. Looking over at her mom, who was asleep, she wished her mom had taken her advice and stayed home until Ashley had called her. Ashley didn't get her stubbornness by accident and that genetic marker was sitting across from her, snoring.

The pressure on her bladder was painful and she needed to get up soon or the nurse would be scolding her for wet bed sheets and the lack of the catheter.

"Mom," Ashley whispered, hoping not to startle her mother. "Mom," she said a tad more forceful. "I have to pee."

Ashley's mom adjusted her position slightly and kept sleeping. Looking around for something to toss in her mother's lap, she spied the nurses call button. She hated to do it but she really needed to pee. Pushing the button, she heard a loud cranky voice come over the intercom.

"Do you need something two thirteen?"

Ashley's mom jumped at the question and then

responded, "Oh shit, I must have accidentally hit the button." Looking around for it, she found it dangling from Ashley's hand twisting ever so slightly.

"Oh, did you need something, Honey?"

"As a matter of fact, Mother, I need to use the bathroom. That's why I buzzed the nurses' station, since I couldn't wake you up. What are you doing here anyway? I thought I told you to go home and rest."

"I did rest, Dear. But I kept thinking about you and your being shot, and the pain you're in and … well I couldn't sleep. So I came down here and sat with my only daughter. Is that a crime, Officer?"

Ashley knew when she was being bested at her own game. So it was time to play the subordinate daughter and concede defeat.

"No, Mom. I'd do the same thing if I were in your shoes. I'm sorry." Ashley patted her mother's hand and then laid a soft kiss on it. "Can I pee now? Please?"

Just as Ashley finished, the privacy curtain was moved back and a nurse walked in.

"You forgot to take your finger off the button. We heard everything at the nurses' station." Scrunching her nose at Ashley and her mom she continued, "You two are so sweet. I think we all got a cavity just now. Okay, so this is how we move Ashley so she can go to the bathroom …"

The nurse demonstrated the correct procedure to move Ashley from the bed to the bathroom. Since her ribs had been severely bruised under her arm pit, she would have to be extra careful of the sling and brace she had on her right side. The IV stand went everywhere Ashley did and eventually Ashley could use it to lean on, but only a little. With her mom's help, she made the trip in ten minutes. *Who knew ten feet would take so long?* Trying to unravel all of the IV tubing, power cords and pain unit was an exercise in futility. Then came the parting of the gown. Never had Ashley felt so exposed in her life. One minute she was covered head to knee, the next minute everything was flopping out for all eyes to see. Forget tying the damn thing. That had been her mother's first mistake after Ashley used the bathroom the first time. The second time, Ashley had to buzz the nurse from the bathroom for assistance as her gown and IV's got tangled and the IV stand almost went into the toilet. *All of this just to pee. How had my life become such a tangled mess?*

"Mom, PJs. I need my flannel PJs. At least when I go to the bathroom I can just pull one thing down and only have my ass exposed. With these hospital gowns, I'm in a peep show."

"Fine, I'll bring your flannels."

"Mom?"

"Yes."

"Could I have a sip of your coffee? It smells so good."

"I don't know. You know what the doctor said."

"Mom. If you don't want to see your daughter have a full on temper tantrum —"

"Fine, fine. Let me go warm this up or maybe I'll get a fresh one for my little girl," Ashley's mom said, rubbing it in.

The walk back from the bathroom had been a little more than Ashley could handle so she pressed the pain button. Gently lying back on the upright bed, she pulled her legs onto the bed and sighed. *If this is what recovery is going to be like, someone shoot me now 'cause I don't think I'm gonna make it.* The medicine seemed to be working faster lately, as her eyelids became heavy again. *Damn it, stay awake. I want that coffee.* Ashley heard her mom come back into the room humming. She liked it when her mom hummed. She had such a pretty voice. It reminded her of a scratchy record. *What?* No it was beautiful like a bird pooping on her patrol car. *What? Oh man.* The medicine was really starting to have an effect on Ashley's thought process. Maybe the coffee would help counteract it.

"Here you go, Honey. What were you saying about bird poop?"

Ashley raised her eyebrows and rolled her eyes.

"Well you don't have to be so dramatic, Honey. It was just a question." Ashley's mom laughed at the face Ashley made. "I think someone needs to go to sleep. Here, let me take that coffee before you spill it and then you'll have scalding burns to go with that gunshot. Won't that be nice?"

"No, no. I want a sip. Sit, mother. Maybe it will help me stay awake and we can talk."

"Okay, Dear. What would you like to talk about?"

Ashley thought this must be some kind of trick question, because every time her mom said she wanted to talk about something, it was usually something bad. Wait, she was the one who wanted to talk. Wasn't she?

"Tyler. Have I told you about Tyler Jackson? She's the one who risked her life to save me."

"Yes, I know, Dear. She was very brave to do that. If it wasn't for her…well, I don't know what I would've done without you."

Ashley heard her mom sniffle and then wipe her nose with the hankie she kept either up her sleeve or in her bra. *Yuck! Shit like that grosses me out. Why do women do that? Keep stuff like that around, isn't that what tissue was made for? Geez.* She knew her mother was frugal. It came from a time when she had nothing as a child and an embroidered hankie was a gift to be treasured, her mom told her once. *Yeah, but still, it's gross,* she reasoned.

"So you were saying about Tyler?"

Raising the cup to her lips, Ashley tried to snake her tongue out and test the coffee, but instead burned the tip of it.

"Ouch."

"Here, let me hold it for you."

Swatting her mother's hand away, Ashley informed her she could handle a cup of coffee quite easily. Resting it on her chest, she continued her thoughts of Tyler. Seeing through the fog of medication wasn't easy, but she willed her mind to focus on Tyler's face. Ashley smiled when she thought about the "new" Tyler. The short hair was very becoming on Tyler. Had she told Tyler that? She couldn't remember.

"She's beautiful Mom. I mean, you know, in that roguish, butchy sorta way." Ashley slurred her words and let her head roll back, her grasp still firm on the coffee cup resting on her chest. "She has this way about her that just makes you want to scoop her up and hug her like a puppy. You know what I mean?" Ashley's eyes still closed, she smiled again as she thought about kissing Tyler's lips. Jerking her head up in a moment of lucid thought, she realized where her mind was going and how easily her body was following.

"Hmm," was all she heard from her mother, her mind once again inching its way through the impending fog. Squinting her eyes as if to see better, she tried focusing on the hand washing instructions on the mirror over the sink in her room. Reading the instructions over and over again to help focus wasn't helping. Then another thought crept into her head. *Coffee, coffee,* she thought over and over again. Taking a sip, she let the warm liquid soothe its way down, a slight burn trailing behind it. The burn was nothing compared to what her body was feeling as she thought about Tyler again.

"Did I mention she saved my life? Hey," she said in her medication-induced stupor. "How is she? No one's told me how she is or what happened to her. I need to thank her. Can you get her for me, mom?" was the last thing Ashley remembered before passing out.

Chapter Twenty-one

Lying on her side, Tyler faded in and out of consciousness. Tyler was grouchy way beyond her normal cynical attitude. Her ass hurt, the pain in her neck kept her from finding a comfortable position, and her headache pounded with each beat of her heart. Sleep was impossible to find with all the nurses coming in on the hour to chart her medications, heart rate, and blood pressure. Every time she fell asleep, someone, usually a nurse or nurse's aide, flung the curtain, flipped a light on or asked her a question. She needed to get out of the hospital if she wanted to recuperate, so that would be her first question when she saw the doctor again.

As Tyler closed her eyes again she felt warmth cover her hand and stroke her hair.

"Jill?" she said without thinking.

"No champ. Just me," a familiar voice whispered in her ear.

Without opening her eyes, Tyler responded, "Kell."

"Hey, kiddo. I hear you got a real pain in the ass."

"Don't you mean 'I am' a real pain in the ass." Tyler grasped Kelly's hand and kissed the back of it. "Thanks for coming by when I'm awake. I hear you've been here a couple of times."

"Well, you need your beauty sleep, so I didn't want to wake you. Besides, you're not the only person I have to see in the hospital, you know."

"Aw gee and I thought I was your favorite?" Tyler smiled and opened her eyes, finding Kelly squatting next to her bed. The compassion in her eyes told Tyler volumes. "How is Ashley? No one's said anything and I've been too doped up to really think straight." Squinting her eyes and smiling, she pointed at Kelly, "No straight jokes."

"She's okay. She's got a few bruised ribs, a collapsed lung and a concussion, but she'll be okay. If you hadn't gone in there and saved her, we probably would've lost her, Tyler."

Kelly's voice was serious and Tyler could probably guess what she was thinking. Tyler had a ton of questions, but she wasn't sure which ones to ask first. She had been thinking of Ashley every time she was awake. The other question of why this happened ate at her. She could barely remember the incident, except the urgency of getting to Ashley and getting her out of there. After that, everything was a blur, thankfully.

"Did you catch the guy who did this?"

The question hung there and Tyler could see Kelly struggling with the answer. Kelly seemed to pale as Tyler waited. Something was wrong, and she knew it. Tyler was close enough to see a thin bead of sweat break out on Kelly's lip. Tyler took a deep breath trying to mentally steady herself for Kelly's answer. "Did someone else get shot? Tell me you caught this guy?" Tyler could feel her blood pressure rising at the thought that someone else had been shot. The monitor behind Tyler started beeping faster as both women looked up at it.

"Calm down, Tyler. We got the shooter, but I'm not sure how much I can tell you. I mean, it's complicated."

"Complicated, what's so complicated about someone deliberately shooting me?"

Tyler tried to sit up but the pain coursing through her body was making it impossible to act impulsively. Taking a deep breath, Tyler tried to relax to alleviate the pain shooting through her. The room was stifling and, suddenly, Tyler felt as if she couldn't take a deep enough breath. Anxiety started its evil journey through her head, her body acting in concert with the racing thoughts. *A slow deep breath in, hold it and exhale slowly,* Tyler told herself. There was nothing Tyler could do about the situation now, but she definitely felt she had a right to know the details of her shooting.

"It's just that…"

Kelly fidgeted with the band around Tyler's wrist, twisting it one way and then back the other. Tyler grabbed Kelly's hand and squeezed it gently.

"What?"

"It was a woman."

"What? You've got to be kidding me? Who?"

Tyler watched Kelly's face as she bit her lower lip. Tyler knew this Kelly. This was the Kelly that had bad news and didn't know how to deliver it. Tyler closed her eyes and slowly pushed herself up from a lying position to leaning on one hip.

"Help me stand, please."

"Tyler. Are you sure you should be standing. I mean, do you want me to call the nurse to help you?" Kelly panicked, reaching for the call button on the bed.

Tyler stopped Kelly's hand before she could grab the button. She didn't need the nurse's help. She needed Kelly to tell her what had happened and having a nurse in the room wouldn't help.

"No, I don't need the nurse. Just give me a hand," Tyler said reaching for Kelly's arm.

Slowly, Tyler let her left foot touch the floor,

placing her weight on it. She grabbed Kelly's arms for support and pulled herself to her feet. A bit wobbly, but none the less for wear, Tyler smiled and looked at Kelly.

"See, I'm good. I've been up to the bathroom a few times already. So stop worrying and tell me who shot me or I'm going to find Ashley and ask her."

"NO, you can't," Kelly said, stopping Tyler from moving.

"What the hell is going on, Kelly?" Tyler said, flinching at Kelly's response.

"You probably should be sitting down for this." Kelly led Tyler to the chair by the window.

"I just got up, I'm not sitting down. Bring me that walker and let's take me for some exercise. I'm sick of this room. Besides, you…will…tell me what's happening, Kelly," Tyler said sternly, grabbing the walker.

The pace was slow, but it gave Tyler the chance to stretch her tired muscles and get a much needed change of scenery. She also knew Kelly was stalling. Whatever Kelly was mulling over in her mind, Tyler could almost see the steam coming out of her ears. Kelly's fidgeting continued as she pushed Tyler's IV stand, playing with the rubber tubing winding its way around and down the moving unit. Tyler cleared her throat and raised her eyebrows while looking at Kelly. Surely, it was enough to prompt Kelly, but she still stayed silent, following Tyler's slow pace.

Stopping at a door that led to a room with a greenhouse, Tyler waited for Kelly to push the button for the automatic door. The lushness of the room was in stark contrast to the squeaky clean interior of the hospital. Tyler could feel the humidity as soon as she entered. The vast diversity of the vegetation was impressive and gave the room a cool, damp feeling.

Leaning against a wall, Tyler looked at a flowering plant, admiring the beautiful blooms that cascaded over the retaining wall.

"Okay, Kelly, spill." Tyler turned and gave Kelly her best I-mean-business stare.

"Look Ty, we haven't had a chance to tell Ashley everything. So whatever is said here is between us. Understand?" Kelly's discomfort was palpable.

"How bad could it be, Kelly? I mean getting shot is pretty bad, but you got the guy and he's in jail, so why all the cloak and dagger?"

"The 'woman,'" Kelly said, making air quotes for emphasis then continuing, "was Ashley's ex-girlfriend, Leslie."

Stunned, Tyler tried to wrap her mind around what Kelly had just said. Ashley's girlfriend had just tried to kill them? *The shooting wasn't an accidental shooting, it was attempted murder.* Tyler couldn't imagine someone hating so much that they would rather kill their girlfriend than let her go. Suddenly, Tyler felt sick to her stomach. Feeling flushed, Tyler reached for an available chair and gently sat on the edge of the seat.

"Are you okay?" Kelly pushed the IV stand closer and bent down to touch Tyler's face. "You don't look so good. Maybe I should call the nurse."

Tyler stopped her. "No, I'm fine. I'm just shocked. Poor Ashley," she whispered, catching her breath. "Is she dead?"

"Who, Ashley?"

"No, Einstein. Leslie."

"No, but we had a heck of a time getting to her. She had the whole place booby-trapped. It was a mess. I have to be honest here, Tyler." Kelly sat on the floor next to Tyler and ran her fingers through her hair. Clearly, Kelly was having a hard time with the details of the incident. "For once, I'm glad you decided to be reckless. Leslie was entrenched on that third floor and it took us hours to get her out of there. If we had waited until Leslie was immobilized, Ashley could've died out there."

It was Tyler's turn to comfort her friend. Reaching down she stroked Kelly's hair and then laid a kiss on her head. Tyler didn't know Ashley well, but she was almost certain Ashley was in for a long, drawn out ordeal. Through the investigation, Ashley's personal life would be exposed and everyone would know about her lifestyle, if they didn't already know. The trial, the testimony, and the questions would be intrusive and her choices in partners would be questioned, too.

"You know I couldn't let her sit out there. It was too much like Jill. I just … I just couldn't sit by and watch." A tear rolled down Tyler's face, remembering once again how Jill died. Would she ever be able to remember Jill and not cry? She doubted it, but this wasn't about her and Jill, this was about Ashley. "So, when are you going to tell her?"

"Well, the captain wants to talk to her as soon as possible. I asked him if I could be the one to break the news to her."

"What happened to Leslie?"

"She had a superficial gunshot wound, but she's already lawyered up. So she isn't talking."

"Did you meet Leslie? What's she like?" The hair on Tyler's neck stood up as she wondered again what kind of person would want to kill someone they professed to love.

"No. In fact, I just learned about her the night of your battery."

"That wasn't a battery. Come on," Tyler said

defensively.

"You know what I meant."

"Anyway, what did she say about her?"

"It wasn't so much what she said, but her reaction," Kelly said, gazing off as she thought about that night again. "I've never seen Ashley so upset." Shrugging her shoulders, Kelly continued, "She was nervous, maybe even scared. She said something about burning Leslie's stuff and their relationship being abusive and that's it. Gosh, Tyler. I wish I'd paid more attention, but she just shrugged it off and said it was over. She doesn't talk about her personal life at work. They're two separate things and she likes to keep it that way."

Kelly's body caved as she finished and Tyler reached over, again rubbing her friend's shoulders. Tyler was sure Kelly was beating herself up inside for not being a better friend to Ashley, but Tyler knew it wasn't Kelly's fault. Tyler had lived with someone who kept work at work and her personal life at home. Those two things were paths that never merged for Jill and Tyler had come to understand the need to keep them separate. While they socialized with Kelly and her husband and other officers, Jill never talked shop, period.

"When are you going to tell her?" Tyler asked standing and stretching her back. Sitting or standing, it didn't seem to matter. Tyler couldn't do either for very long without pain shooting down her hip and leg. She had held off as long as she could, but the stress of Ashley's situation was probably to blame for her lack of pain management. Grabbing the pain pump, she pressed the button and wished it worked faster. She was trying to work through the pain, but right now she just wanted relief.

"Hey, let's get you back to the room. I don't want

to have to throw you over my shoulder and carry you back when that stuff takes effect."

"Quit avoiding my questions, Kelly," Tyler said, the pain clearly making her irritable.

"Today, after I walk you back to your room, I'm going down to see her."

"Do you want me to come? You know, for moral support." Tyler smiled, her pain had eased slightly.

"I don't think that's such a great idea. Once she has time to think about who did this, I think guilt is going to eat her up when she sees you. Besides, I have to ask her some questions and I can't do that if you're there. Sorry buddy, it's business this time."

Slowly, they started the long walk back to Tyler's room, each woman lost in her own thoughts about the shooting.

Chapter Twenty-two

Beeping machines, the warmth of the room, and another pump of her pain meds had finally allowed Ashley to sleep for a few hours. The medication also buried her so deep that whatever dreams she might have had weren't remembered. For the first time in a long time, Ashley was able to avoid the nightmares that plagued her on a regular basis. Turning onto her right side, Ashley jerked awake when her ribs protested the new position.

"Shit."

Rolling onto her back, she slowly opened her eyes and sighed. Her days and nights were a jumbled mess. She tried to maintain some type of schedule, but the medication made it nearly impossible, so she gave up trying. The empty room was a welcome sight. Her mother had finally left late last night after much cajoling and a promise that Ashley would call her if she needed anything. While she appreciated her mom, she was tired of the idol banter she had to engage in as she tried to avoid talking about the shooting. Her mom had been relentless with her questions, but Ashley had a hard time remembering much after Tyler saved her. She hadn't seen who shot her and the few officers that had stopped by to see her didn't say much when she questioned them. In fact, her last visit with Kelly had been embarrassing. She fell asleep just as Kelly was getting ready to tell her who had shot her. When she woke up, Kelly was gone and her mom was sitting in her usual place, drinking coffee.

Ashley knew the peace and tranquility, if that was what you could call it, would end when the nurses did their rounds so she enjoyed the brief respite. Running her hand down her right arm, the stiff hospital gown had been replaced with the soft flannel pajamas her mother had brought. But putting on her pajamas had been an exercise in torture and her shoulder and ribs still ached. Trying to move her shoulder around, she groaned in pain. The nurse had warned her that a frozen shoulder would bring more pain than she was experiencing moving it now. So she had been a good patient and started to make more of an attempt at stretching the painful appendage. A protesting bladder let Ashley know she would see the nurse sooner than she would like.

Lowering the bed as low as it would go, Ashley swung her feet off the bed and inched her way to the floor. Determined to go to the bathroom without an audience, Ashley began the slow process of getting off the bed. Smiling, she looked at the pink footies she still wore since she had been admitted. While she didn't think she was exerting herself, her body said otherwise. She had tensed her shoulder and kept her arm tightly wrapped around her body as she placed more weight on her feet. At least her legs still worked. She couldn't imagine what she would have done had she been shot in her lower body. She had broken her leg skiing one winter and the hassle of walking with crutches had been almost more than she could bear until she got her walking cast.

A slow shuffle to the bathroom and she had successfully made it when she heard someone come in the room.

"Ashley?"

Startled, Ashley replied, "In here, but don't go away. I'll be out in a minute."

Feeling lightheaded, she sat for a minute longer and composed herself. *Why did company always come at the most inopportune times?* Finishing her routine, she dried her hands and peaked around the doorframe. Kelly. Finally she would get some answers, as long as she didn't press her pain button.

"Hey. Are you supposed to be up by yourself?" Kelly asked walking towards Ashley. "Here, let me help you," she said grabbing the IV stand. "I'm getting good with one of these." Kelly grabbed Ashley's elbow and helped her to the bed.

"Thanks. So what brings you to this neck of the woods?" Ashley leaned her butt against the bed looking at Kelly. She'd rather poke a stick in her eye rather than crawl into that bed, so she stayed standing, at least as long as her body would let her. "You don't happen to have a café latte hiding somewhere on you, do you?"

Kelly smiled and shook her head. Ashley had a coffee addiction in a bad way and loved the icy drink. Often times, it was one of their first stops when on patrol.

"No, sorry. I can go down to the coffee shop in the lobby and get one if you want?"

"No, I'm fine. It'll just make me pee anyway and I hate that walk to the bathroom." Ashley smiled at the weak joke and motioned for Kelly to sit. "So, what are you doing here? How's Robbie?"

"He's good. I just came from seeing Tyler and thought I would drop by and see how my favorite partner is doing."

Ashley cocked her head and squinted her eyes at Kelly. Something wasn't right. Maybe the drugs were doing a number on her system, but she could have sworn Kelly made it seem that Tyler was here in the hospital.

"You came all the way from the fire station to see me. Why?"

"Tyler's not at the station, she's here in the hospital. Didn't you know? Tyler was shot while saving you."

Ashley felt herself become lightheaded and grabbed the bed for support. *Why hadn't anyone told me that Tyler had been shot? How serious was it?* Suddenly she felt sick to her stomach and started to gag. Motioning for the trashcan by the nightstand she held her mouth until she was over it. What little was in her stomach was emptied into the plastic bag in the can. Kelly's cool hand covered her forehead as she handed Ashley a paper cup with water.

"Here, take a sip of this and try to relax. She's okay. She was only shot twice." Kelly guided Ashley back on to the bed and instructed her to sit. "I think you need to lie down. We need to talk, Ash." Kelly helped Ashley swing her legs onto the bed and pulled the sheet over her.

A cold sweet broke out over Ashley's face and she could feel her heart racing. Tyler had been shot because of her, because she had been careless on a call. Guilt replaced the sick feeling and Ashley had a sudden urge to see Tyler, to make sure for herself that Tyler was all right. Looking at Kelly, Ashley tried to say something, but words wouldn't come. Her ribs and shoulder began throbbing, each heartbeat a reminder of what had happened.

"How bad is she hurt?"

"How bad?"

Ashley nodded her head and waited. Looking at

Kelly she had a pretty good idea she didn't want to know, but she needed to know.

"Define bad," Kelly said, sadness flashing across her face.

"Oh god. Please tell me she isn't paralyzed. Please tell me she'll be okay, normal, anything but—"

"Relax," Kelly said putting a hand on Ashley's arm. "She was shot in the neck and in the upper thigh. The bullet nicked her thigh bone, and the one in her neck just missed her jugular."

"Oh god," Ashley moaned.

"She's up and moving, sorta. They have her on pain meds and she's finally awake." Kelly gave Ashley a reassuring smile and then patted her arm again.

Ashley's tears started to fall as she looked at the ceiling. She was responsible for getting another human being hurt. She swallowed and ran a barely wet tongue over her lips, licking at the tears that ran across them. How could this have happened? Who could have done such a horrible thing? Thinking about the shooting it was clear that whoever did this was deliberately trying to hurt them. Tyler had been hit twice and she had been hit once, but not for a lack of trying on the shooter's part. Remembering her mic exploding on her shoulder, she reached up and touched the bandage on her face. *If I had moved just a few inches, I would be dead right now. But who would do this and why?* She wondered.

"Ash?"

"Hmm?" Ashley turned and looked at Kelly.

"There's more."

"More?" Ashley felt dazed, almost like she was dreaming. Only it wasn't a dream, it was a nightmare. Wiping her eyes, she bit her lip and tried stopping the tears that continued to fall. She needed to see Tyler. To tell her how sorry she was and explain everything. But what was she going to explain? She didn't know what to say, actually.

"Ashley," Kelly began as she sat on the side of the bed and took Ashley's hand in hers, "we caught the person who did this to you."

Looking into Kelly's eyes, she saw something she'd never seen before. Pain or shame, she wasn't quite sure, but she had seen it when her mother had bad news.

"What?"

"It was Leslie Freeman."

"Leslie? Leslie did this? Leslie tried to kill me?" Ashley couldn't believe what she was hearing. Leslie, her Leslie, had tried to kill her. Shocked, Ashley felt sick to her stomach again, but this time there wasn't anything to throw-up. Ashley felt a cold sweat break out all over her body again. *Is this nightmare ever going to end?* "Are you sure? I mean I just heard from her and she said she was going to see me …."

A sudden realization hit Ashley. The text message. Remembering back to the day of the shooting, Ashley remembered the text message Leslie had sent, but she hadn't thought anything about it at the time. It was just Leslie being Leslie, or so she thought. A groan escaped Ashley's lips as she grabbed her head. The room was spinning now and she felt as if she would faint if she had been standing.

"Ash, are you okay? Would you like me to call the nurse?"

"Oh my god! Leslie sent me a text that morning, but I didn't think anything of it. She had called and I didn't answer the phone, so she texted me and told me she would see me later. Oh god, Kelly, I didn't know. I didn't know." Ashley started to cry again.

Her life, her career was spiraling out of control. There would be an investigation and everyone would know about the abuse, about her relationship with Leslie. They would know everything. *How could this be happening?* She wondered.

"Ashley, calm down, Honey. It'll be all right. I promise." Kelly cradled Ashley in her arms and gently rocked her.

Minutes passed before Ashley stopped crying. Her life was in shambles. But more importantly, she had only herself to blame for Tyler being shot. If she had reported the abuse she had suffered from Leslie, none of this would've happened. Her shame and guilt would be ten-fold now. How would she apologize to Tyler for what Leslie had done? What would she say? What could she say?

"I hate to say this, but please tell me she's dead." Ashley knew the only way she wouldn't have to face the fallout from what Leslie had done was if Leslie had died.

"I'm afraid not."

"Oh god."

"Ashley, I have to ask you some questions. Do you think you're up to it?"

Ashley nodded. She knew she didn't really have a choice in the matter. Besides, she would rather have Kelly be the one asking than one of the male detectives. Eventually, they would question her too, but this way Kelly would write everything up and pass it on to the investigating officers.

With each question Ashley felt her body weaken a little more. The more Kelly asked the more Ashley was sure she was being judged. She knew Kelly couldn't help it, it came with the job. They were trained to look for answers, to figure out the who, what and why things happened. Her life was now an open book and Ashley wished she could tear out the chapters that contained Leslie and burn them. Slowly and methodically, Kelly wrote down Ashley's answers. Each question seemed to have a follow-up until Kelly's pen finally stopped. Ashley watched as her friend closed her narrow pad, tucked it in her back pocket then looked up at her. Her eyes asked the question before her mouth did.

"Why, Ashley? Why didn't you report this? We could've done something," Kelly said moving to sit on Ashley's bed again. "Why did you think you had to go through this by yourself?"

Ashley dropped her head back on her pillow in shame. Squeezing her eyes tight, tears seeped out and down her face. How could she tell her friend that she was ashamed by what had happened? How could she explain it to Kelly when she couldn't even explain it to herself?

Chapter Twenty-three

Ashley sat watching Tyler sleep. After Kelly left, she had tried to sleep, but she couldn't get rid of the guilt that plagued her. The noise of the machines beeping throughout the hospital and the pitter-patter of the nurses making rounds was no match for the noise in her head. Staring at the ceiling, all she could think about was Tyler lying wounded somewhere in the hospital because of her. Once she had found out what room Tyler was in, Ashley decided to check in on Tyler herself to make sure she was all right.

There was just enough light in the room to see Tyler's face. It took everything she had not to start crying when she saw the huge bandage on Tyler's neck. Clearly, Kelly had downplayed the seriousness of Tyler's injuries. The fact that she was still on a pain machine was proof enough to Ashley that Tyler was still in serious condition. Bending closer, she studied Tyler's face. With the exception of a crease between her eyebrows, Tyler looked like she was sleeping peacefully. Ashley finally had time to look at Tyler, really look at Tyler, without all the bravado and cocky attitude she was so famous for. Ashley resisted the urge to move several locks of hair that hid part of Tyler's face and run her fingers through the short hair. Tyler moved slightly, her hand coming to rest hanging slightly off the bed. Moving closer, Ashley looked at the strong hand and long fingers that tapered to well-kept nails. A scar ran parallel to the side of her hand, the stitches barely visible. Ashley wondered how Tyler had gotten the now fading mark.

Moving her gaze back up, she looked at Tyler's mouth and noticed how her lips seemed to be in the start of a smile, a dimple marking one cheek. She always thought Tyler had a brooding feel about her, yet looking at her tonight she thought she looked handsome, not in a male sort of way, but more like a… Ashley couldn't quite put her finger on it. Perhaps it was her new haircut that gave her that boyish quality Ashley found attractive in women.

Ashley froze as Tyler moved again, this time letting out a groan as she tried to lie on her back. Returning to her original position, Tyler moaned, then licked her lips and sighed. Clearly Tyler was in pain. Pain Ashley was responsible for. She wanted to reach out and comfort Tyler, to take her pain away, but how would she explain what had happened. Seeing Tyler had eased Ashley's guilt, but only a little. She wanted to talk to Tyler, to explain what had happened and to tell her how sorry she was for getting her involved. Resting her head in her hand she briefly closed her eyes. Her body was rebelling from sitting so long, but she couldn't bring herself to leave quite yet. Running her fingers through her hair, she felt a tear slide down her face. She wiped it away before it dropped.

"Hey, don't cry. It'll be alright," she heard Tyler say softly.

Startled, she grabbed Tyler's hand and pressed the palm to her face. More tears started to flow at the gentle words.

"I'm sorry, Tyler. I am so sorry this happened to you. It's all my fault—"

Tyler's thumb gently pressed against Ashley's lips,

stopping her from continuing.

"It's not your fault."

Ashley felt the softness of Tyler's thumb over her lips. The touch sent a charge through Ashley. If she had been anywhere else, she might have kissed the thumb or even playfully bit it. But she was in a hospital with the person who had been shot by her ex-girlfriend. How was she going to explain to Tyler who had shot them both? It was one thing for her to be shot, it came with the job and the crazy ex, but Tyler was just doing her job. Leslie had purposefully made a decision to try and kill Tyler, too. Would her life ever get better or would there constantly be a dark cloud hanging overhead? Only time would tell.

"Tyler, I need to tell you something," Ashley said, reaching for the hand that still stroked her lips. "I don't know how to say this, but the reason you were shot is because—"

"Officer Henderson, I was just doing my job. We all take risks and I knew what I was doing when I backed the bus up to get to you." Tyler's smile was faint, but Ashley felt the sincerity in her words. "Besides, you can't control what other people do. You know that, right?"

Ashley had an urge to kiss the palm of the hand she was holding, but thought better of it as she looked into Tyler's eyes. Tyler's eyes held her firmly in place as she tried to think of a way to explain Leslie. Not that she could really explain Leslie, but it was going to come up eventually. She had a choice, take on the subject head on or wait until later. Tyler's smile reached her eyes and started Ashley's body throbbing. The room suddenly felt stifling as Ashley returned the smile with a weak one of her own. Guilt was the great emotion that made people do strange things.

"Well, I should let you get some sleep. But remember, I promised you coffee. So when you're ready, I could go for a latte. In fact, I would kill for one, but don't tell anyone," Ashley said winking at Tyler.

Standing, Ashley became lightheaded. She had stood too quickly, surprising herself, especially in her condition. Now, she felt as if she would topple over. Grabbing the rail on the bed she steadied herself.

"Hey, are you okay?" Tyler's hands covered her own, trying to help steady her.

"I'm fine. I think I just stood too fast." Pulling her hands from Tyler's grasp she smiled again and turned to leave.

"Why don't you sit for a minute? I would hate to think you passed out because you visited me."

Watching Tyler pat the bed next to her, Ashley raised an eyebrow and bit her lip again. *I have to work on those nervous habits,* she thought looking at the space Tyler had made for her on the bed. As the bed was lowered, Ashley considered her options, making the long trek back to her room or gathering her strength and sitting next to a handsome woman. Oh, it sucked to have options and what a hardship it would be sitting next to Tyler. Ashley shook her head looking at the bed.

"I can always call the nurse and have a wheelchair sent down. Would that make you feel more comfortable?" Tyler quirked her eyebrow at the suggestion.

"Okay, here, twist my arm. That way I can at least say you twisted it to get me to stay."

"Oh, come on. I don't bite, regardless of what you've heard," Tyler said smiling. "Unless, of course, you want me to."

Ashley blushed at the innuendo and slowly sat down with her back to Tyler. She wouldn't give Tyler the satisfaction of seeing her blush. It was bad enough that Tyler's touch made her ache for more, now she had to admit that the "new" Tyler was having an effect on her. She was sure once Tyler learned who shot her, Ashley wouldn't have to worry about the few tingles she was getting from Tyler. No, Ashley was positive Tyler would distance herself from her. Suddenly, Ashley felt her body flinch from the warm path Tyler's hand took down her back.

"It'll be okay, trust me." Tyler smiled.

Why did she have to do that? Why did Tyler have to been so understanding, so warm, so sympathetic? Taking a deep breath, Ashley knew she needed to come clean or it would tear at her until she did.

"Tyler, I need a favor," Ashley said as she wrung her hands.

"Okay."

"I need you to listen to what I have to say and not interrupt me. Otherwise, I'll lose my nerve and I really need to tell you something."

"Okay?"

"Once upon a time." Ashley looked at Tyler when she heard her clear her throat. The smirk on Tyler's face made her grin. "Okay, I had a crazy ex-girlfriend not too long ago and—"

"Haven't we all?"

Ashley flashed Tyler a puzzled look.

"A crazy ex. I mean haven't we all had at least one?"

"Not like this. Believe me, not like this." Ashley continued her explanation. "Her name's Leslie and... Kelly told me she's the one who shot us." Turning towards Tyler, Ashley covered Tyler's hand and caressed the back of it with her thumb. "I had no idea she would do something like this, I swear, Tyler. I'm so sorry. You just can't imagine how bad I feel. I'm so, so sorry."

A tension descended between the two women. Ashley's internal voice was screaming run, but her heart was telling her to stay and take her punishment. She deserved Tyler's wrath, but instead, Ashley felt Tyler softly caress her face. How could Tyler be so understanding, so sympathetic, after being shot twice? Ashley realized she really didn't know Tyler at all. All the stories, all the bravado and all the ego were a smoke screen Tyler lived behind. Something to throw everyone off of the sensitive person she really was, at least that's the person Ashley saw in front of her right then.

"How bad was it?" Tyler asked, still stroking Ashley's face.

"What?"

"The abuse."

Ashley's dirty little secret was being revealed and she didn't know whether to confide or deny. But eventually it would all come out, so there was no sense in denying it, not now. Turning into Tyler, Ashley slid her leg up on the bed, pulled her IV stand closer and leaned back on her good arm. This was going to be a long conversation and Ashley might as well settle in for it. The pain on her right side was starting to get the better of her so she hit her own pain button and waited. Biting the inside of her mouth, she relived the pain Leslie had created in her life as the medication took the edge off.

"Bad."

Remembering Leslie's anger made Ashley cringe and withdraw from Tyler's touch. Her mind wandered back to an incident early on in their relationship. A pivotal night, because Ashley chose to go with her heart and not her head.

"Leslie lit up a room when she walked in, kind of like you do. She was bigger than life sometimes and I just happened to meet her one of those times." Ashley faded into the memory and continued, "She had just closed a big deal for her firm and was celebrating at the same restaurant I and a few friends were having drinks and dinner." Picking at the tape on her arm she wandered through the dream, selecting what she would and wouldn't tell Tyler. She didn't know Tyler all that well and didn't want her to get the wrong idea.

That day she met Leslie had been hell, but work was particularly tough that week and she was ready for some down time. She had finished her second gin and tonic and was ready for a nice dinner when Leslie walked in with her coworkers. The room practically exploded when Leslie walked in. It was hard to miss her, but Ashley didn't give her a second look. But, she had come up on Leslie's radar the minute Leslie walked into the restaurant.

Dinner was filled with talking, laughing, and relaxing as Ashley was finally able to let go of the dreadful week. A bottle of wine was delivered to the table, *compliments of the woman at the bar,* she was informed. Looking up, Ashley noticed a striking woman smiling and raising her glass in a toast to their table. Ashley would have sent the bottle back but her friends were already pouring wine into their glasses, each one raising their glasses acknowledging Leslie's generous offer. That's how it had started, innocently enough, Ashley explained to Tyler.

"We started seeing each other, infrequently at first, but then she wanted more. So we dated, exclusively I thought. I found a slip of paper with a woman's name and number on it when I had her jacket on one night. I questioned her about it, but she told me it was nothing. The more I pressed the more she denied it until she slapped me. 'Snapping me back to reality' she said. I should have left, but I didn't. She apologized profusely and said it was a knee jerk reaction to my being out of control." Ashley rubbed her face as if the slap had just happened. "I wasn't out of control."

"Ashley."

Ashley felt Tyler touch her face, but she couldn't look at Tyler. She was sure her shame was written all over it and if she looked at Tyler what would she see? She wasn't ready to be judged, not by someone she barely knew. She took a deep breath and tried to control the tears she knew would come if she continued.

"Ashley, it isn't your fault. Leslie obviously has issues and no one deserves to be hit, no one."

Nodding her head, Ashley felt herself cave in emotionally. She had carried her secret around inside for months and now it had hurt an innocent person. How would she live with herself now? What would she say to the detectives she knew would come and ask her questions? What would she say to her mother? Oh god, her mother. Her secrets would spill out and there was no way she would be able to stop them from spilling, not now. Her pain had been replaced with grief and guilt. Now if she could only take another shot of pain medicine to make it all go away.

Putting her hand on Tyler's arm for support, she knew she needed to get back to her room. Her head felt as if it were swirling down a drain, her secrets finally free to follow. The purging had been too much and she needed to rest both her mind and her body.

"Come here. Lay down," Tyler said patting the bed next to her. The look on Ashley's face must have told the whole story because Tyler smiled. "I might be a cad, but taking advantage of you in this condition is low, even for me," she said patting the bed.

"I'll be okay."

"I know you will, but humor me."

Ashley gently lay beside Tyler and stroked the arm that engulfed her waist. Her head stopped spinning but her mind worked at the loose ends of her memories of Leslie.

"Two months," Ashley whispered.

"Huh?"

"Two months. We were only together two months, but in that short amount of time she turned my life upside down. Amazing isn't it?" Ashley continued to whisper, as if whispering kept it hidden.

Slowly she drifted into a dream, a quiet, calm place that she hadn't been to in a long, long time.

Tyler's heart ached for Ashley, for the torment she had to endure at the hands of someone who loved her. She didn't know how Ashley felt. She'd never had to go through something so traumatic and wondered how Ashley had kept it so well hidden from everyone.

Ashley had fallen asleep on Tyler's shoulder, snuggling close as she drifted off. Tyler tried to move backwards on her bed, giving room between her and Ashley, but each time, Ashley moved herself closer to Tyler. Now, she was practically leaning on Tyler's body, her red hair cascading down Tyler's chest. Reaching up, she fingered the soft locks of hair, bringing one up to her face and brushing her check with it. Luckily for Tyler, Ashley had pajamas on. Otherwise the open back of the hospital gown would put Ashley's shapely rear in her groin. Still, the contact was intimate and was starting to have an effect on Tyler. She had thought Ashley was beautiful the first time she saw her at the bar, now here she was practically laying right on top of her. She was being tested, she knew it.

It was clear guilt had placed itself firmly in Ashley's grasp and now she had to carry around the extra baggage of the shooting. Lucky for Tyler, Kelly had given her a heads up on the ex-girlfriend being the shooter. It had given Tyler time to process the shooting and the connection between Leslie and Ashley. Otherwise, she wasn't sure what her reaction would have been when Ashley told her about Leslie. Oh, she was sure she wouldn't hold it against Ashley, but the thought that it could have been prevented would have nagged at Tyler. Kelly had made it clear that she thought something was wrong with their relationship, but Tyler was sure she didn't know the half of it. Kelly would have to find out from Ashley herself. She wasn't about to repeat what had clearly been a difficult situation for Ashley.

Without a doubt, Leslie had issues, but Tyler couldn't connect the dots that it took to hurt another person. Life was valuable and yet it was so easily taken away. If being in a war zone hadn't taught her that, losing Jill had. The more she thought about what Leslie had done, the madder she got. Holding Ashley a little tighter, she let herself enjoy the feel of Ashley's body against her own.

Chapter Twenty-four

Tyler woke up to find herself alone in her bed. Sometime during the night Ashley had gotten up and left, leaving Tyler with an emptiness she couldn't explain. It had been a long time since she had spent the night with a woman. Even if it was in a hospital room, Tyler liked the feel of Ashley lying against her. She blushed at the memory of Ashley's ass planted firmly in her groin. She had resisted running her hand down Ashley's arm or responding when Ashley moaned in her sleep. At one point in the night, Tyler was so stimulated by the contact she thought she might combust, leaving only a wet spot behind.

"Hey, where's Sparky," a young man's voice boomed through her room. "There you are." J.J. and Mike came into the room in their typical loud and obnoxious way.

"Shh, you're in a hospital for God's sake," Tyler said, shushing the guys.

"Oh, right. Sorry," Mike said, sitting on the corner of Tyler's bed. Mike looked none the worse for wear from his experiences at the scene of the shooting. In fact, he couldn't have looked better to Tyler. She worried he would get caught in the line of fire, but seeing him now gave Tyler some peace.

"Hey, how are you doing Mike? No nicks, no scrapes, no burns?' Tyler asked jokingly.

"Naw, it's all good, Sparky. You're the one that took all the shrapnel. How's the neck and the leg?"

Mike inquired, nodding his head in the direction of her ass. "Heard you took one in the ass. Man that's gotta be painful. Oh wait, you're already a pain in the ass, so you know what that feels like," Mike said, high-fiving J.J. "Awe, you know I'm kidding, right?"

Tyler smiled at the young gun. His time was coming and he knew that as soon as she went back on shift he was fresh meat. Time was her friend, and he would have forgotten his little dig at her by the time she got back, but she wouldn't.

"It's fine. You know the saying, 'you can't keep a good woman down,'" Tyler said, wiggling her eyebrows at the guys. "So how's work?"

"Awe, you know, same ol', same ol'. I think the captain's still pissed at the stunt you pulled. But other than that, nothing new."

"You guys miss me, don't ya?" Tyler knew she would be the talk of the department. Her practical jokes and escapades were legendary, according to J.J. But now they had the shooting to talk about.

"Seriously, Tyler, you okay?" J.J. grabbed her shoulder and squeezed.

They both came on the department at the same time and had been tight friends ever since. Tyler smiled up at her friend and patted his hand, nodding. His concern for her touched her and she couldn't give voice to her thoughts without the possibility of crying, just a little.

"So, did you hear the news about the cop that got shot? Her girlfriend's the one that shot you guys, I mean gals." Mike quickly corrected his mistake. "So, I guess this means she bats for your team. Damn, why are all the cute ones lesbians?" He asked rhetorically.

"Really? Well aren't you glad I didn't take you up

on that stupid bet at the restaurant?" Tyler smiled. How lucky could she be to have a cute one batting for her team?

"So, Sparky, when are you getting out of this palace?" Mike raised his hands and turned looking around. "I mean, you get all the breaks. Hot nurses waiting on you hand and foot, your meals being catered, and to top it all off you get to sleep all day. What more could a firefighter ask for?"

"Well, the pain in my ass keeps me from sleeping on my back and you see that walker over there. I need that just to walk the ten feet to the bathroom. Oh, and I have all these lines and that contraption to pull along with me when I take a pee." Tyler smirked at her buddies. "But the scenery is nice. I got to admit that."

As if on cue, a cute, young nurse pulled the privacy curtain back and smiled. "Morning, Ms. Jackson," she said, making Tyler feel old. "I need to take your vitals." Looking at the men in attendance, "If you gentlemen don't mind?"

"No, please don't let us stop you from doing your job, Nurse…"

"Wakefield." She smiled, clearly not influenced by the firefighter's uniforms.

"Nurse Wakefield, please don't let us stop you from doing what you need to." Mike smiled at Tyler then bit his knuckle.

Tyler raised an eyebrow at the antics and then gave them both a dirty look. She hated when the guys acted like overgrown adolescents and right now they were worse. As the nurse went about her duties, the guys kept checking the nurse out. Their gaze worked from the top of her cute little brunette head all the way down to the sensible shoes. *Why didn't nurses have to wear dresses anymore,* thought Tyler, as she extend her arm for the blood pressure cuff. The scrubs were cute with little thermometers and nurse's hats on them, but it left little to the imagination. *There was something to be said for a white dress and stocking and those cute little high heels they wore. Oh wait, that was the nurse's outfit from a recent Halloween party,* Tyler remembered. *Oh well, one can dream.*

"So Ms. Wakefield, are you single?" Mike asked, puffing his chest out and trying to look buff.

"No," she said, peering at his name tag.

"Oh, you can call me Mike."

"No, Mike, I'm not, but thanks for asking." Turning to leave she looked at Tyler and continued, "I'll be back, Tyler, to take that IV out and those leads off." Winking, she smiled and left.

Tyler smiled back, then looked at her buddies and smirked. "Guess she bats for my team, too."

"Fuck, no way," Mike said, shaking his head.

Tyler shrugged her shoulders and smiled again at the frustrated paramedic.

"So I guess that means you'll be getting out of here soon, Stud." J.J. clapped her back. "And back to the grindstone, huh?"

"Yeah, I guess it'll be desk duty for me until they clear me to come back."

Desk duty was the kiss of death to an active firefighter. There was nothing more boring than answering phones and doing the mountains of paperwork that got left behind. Whoever was on desk duty did all the school tours, cleaned around the station and often times did the lunch detail. Unfortunately, cooking wasn't her forte so she hoped it was the one thing she could skip. Every time the alarm sounded her blood pounded, adrenaline pulsed through her and she amped up. How would she cope with that when she sat behind the desk? Oh life was going to be miserable while she was on desk duty.

"Well," J.J. cupped his hand and lowered his head to her ear. "I heard the captain say he thought they might put you on suspension for what happened."

"What?" Tyler looked at J.J. surprised. "The chief didn't say anything to me when he visited."

Shrugging his shoulders J.J. said, "All I know is he's pissed you went against orders."

"What orders? He never gave me any orders! That's bullshit." Tyler's face flamed when she got angry.

How could the little weasel do this to me? She had never gotten along well with her captain, but she was a damn good firefighter and he had no right to request she be put on suspension. She would get to the bottom of this when she talked to her dad later. She would quit before she got suspended, that was all there was to it. Piss on that little rat bastard, she hated him anyway. Maybe she would ask to rotate to a different station instead. There was no way she was going to let him win, no way.

"Well, we gotta go, Sparky. I'll come by later and we can chit chat about that officer of yours."

"She's not my officer, J.J., so don't be starting any rumors."

"Too late," Mike said, slapping her back as he walked by. "That's the talk back at the station. Well, that and the fact that her lover shot you both. Man, you just can't make this stuff up. Can you?"

"No gossiping, you guys. Jeez you're as bad as some women I know. God!"

Tyler waved at the men as they left with a promise to kick their butts if they talked about the shooting at the station. She heard them laughing all the way down the hall, then nothing. Laying her head back on her bed, she wondered what else everyone was saying at the station. Then she remembered what J.J. told her, she was facing suspension if the captain had his way. Well that wasn't going to happen if she had anything to say about it. Picking up the phone, she pressed the button for an outside line and dialed the phone.

"Hey, Dad, got a minute?"

Chapter Twenty-five

There you go, all done," Nurse Wakefield said, pulling off her gloves and disposing them and the bandages into the trash. "I've gotten as much of that adhesive off as I could, Tyler. There are just a few spots left. But if I rub the areas any more, you'll be raw there. So maybe when you take your shower you can see if soap and the washrag will do a better job."

Tyler looked down at the red spots on her chest and arms. Not pretty, but better than the alternative. Pulling her top closed, she smiled at the pretty nurse. She was going to miss the extra attention she got from the nursing staff when she left, so she enjoyed it while it lasted.

"Oh, I brought you a cane. The doctor thought, since you've been up and around, the cane might make walking easier now that you don't have to pull the IV stand around."

"Did he say when I was being released by any chance?"

"Well …" Nurse Wakefield fidgeted with a piece of tape on her scrubs. "He said he wanted to wait to see how you do without the drains, so a day or two. But let's wait and see what he says, okay?" She smiled at Tyler, grabbing the rest of her supplies and turning to leave. "I'll be back to check on you. Do you need help with your shower?" she asked, smiling again.

"No, I think I got this, but thanks," Tyler said,

smiling back. *I am a lucky woman.*

"Just buzz me if you need me."

A shower sounded good. Now with no leads, IV or a bulky stand to pull behind her, she felt like a prisoner who had just been released. The bulky dressings on her neck and leg had been exchanged for non-stick three by four bandages. Stretching, she flinched when she felt the tug on her leg and butt. Pulling herself up, she slid down to the floor, her feet jerking at the cold tiles. She had tossed the pink booties the hospital had given her because they made her feet sweat. Now, she looked around the room for them, sure she was going to need them after her shower.

"Screw it. I'm tough," Tyler said, grabbing the cane Nurse Wakefield had brought in. Putting her weight on her good foot, she tested out the cane as she moved forward. She realized that there was no way she could put all her weight on her right leg as she felt the stabbing pain arc through her upper thigh. *Just how much digging did they have to do in there to get the bullet fragments?* She wondered. A slow walk around the room and Tyler had tackled the cane successfully. Dragging the walker around had been more of a pain than the pain in her ass and her aching shoulders were the testament. Walking to the closet, she noticed her street clothes folded next to her clean pajamas. *What I wouldn't give to be putting those on right now and getting the heck out of Dodge.* Grabbing her robe and clean pajamas, she let the thought linger for a moment more before she headed to the shower.

The steam billowed from the shower head as she sat on the bench naked. She wondered why her father hadn't said anything about the possible suspension. Surely, he would have told her something if he was considering it. Taking a deep breath, she let the moisture coat her lungs and relax her. She had asked the nurse to put a plastic cover over her neck bandage to protect the wound, but she was still tentative as she ducked under the shower head. The warm spray felt good, no great, as it pelted her body. She'd only had sponge baths the whole time she was in the hospital so the shower was a welcome change. Not that the nurses giving her the sponge baths weren't nice, but she liked to see to her own personal hygiene. Looking down at the cane, she wondered if the darn thing would rust since she hadn't thought anything about bringing it in the shower with her. No matter, she wouldn't be using it long enough anyway. She would talk to the doctor about physical therapy, so maybe she wouldn't need it. It was only a muscle tear and a chipped bone. Those wouldn't need much she was sure.

A knock at the door startled Tyler as she rinsed the shampoo from her hair.

"Are you okay in there, Tyler?" Nurse Wakefield inquired through the door.

"Yes, I'm fine thanks," Tyler said, smiling. She was almost certain she heard a soft giggle on the other side.

"Well, you've been in there a long time so we thought something might have happened."

"No, I'm fine. I'm just enjoying my first shower in days, that's all." Tyler smiled.

"Okay, well you let me know if you need anything. There's a button on the wall in there if you need immediate help."

"Thank you, Nurse Wakefield."

Had she been daydreaming that long? Time had slipped right through her fingers as she thought about the suspension and work and she hadn't even thought about Ashley yet. She let the water cascade down her body for a few more minutes before she turned the shower off.

Her dad was coming that afternoon and she wanted to be ready for his answer when she questioned him about the suspension. Was quitting an option if she didn't like his answer? Surely, he would understand why she had to rescue Ashley. What would he have done? That's what she would have to ask him. Put him in the situation of rescuer and see what he would do.

###

"Good Morning, Officer Henderson," a voice said breaking into Ashley's drowsy mind.

Swallowing, Ashley licked her lips and tried to smile, but she had a rough night and just wanted to rest. It wasn't that she couldn't sleep last night, it was the fact that she was laying on Tyler's warm body. Ashley's own body vibrated from just remembering how inviting Tyler felt. She nearly came undone when Tyler wrapped her arm around her waist and buried her nose in Ashley's hair. Tyler's arm under her head had exposed her breasts to Ashley's back. She thought she could feel Tyler's nipples when she adjusted her position. Embarrassed, Ashley tried not to move again.

If there is a God, she is torturing me, Ashley thought trying not to move. Her shoulder ached and her ribs were killing her. *When would the pain ease?* Moving was a bitch, still, and she was almost a week post op. Eventually, she knew she would lose the pain pump, but hopefully not before she could deal with the pain on her own terms. Making an effort to ease up on the medications had left her cranky, but it was doable. While hospitality had hospital as its base, this was not a place where people enjoyed the surroundings and could relax. She yearned for her own bed, her own house, and she missed her dog. Oh shit! She hadn't thought about Mongrel since she arrived. Her mom had a key, but had she thought to go by and check on her dog? It wasn't like her mom was a dog person but, hopefully, she remembered that Ashley had one and he needed attention. Her panic was almost palpable as she tried to think about who she needed to call. Grabbing her cell phone from the bedside table, she flipped it open.

"Oops, I'm sorry, you're not allowed to use that in here," said a voice from across the room.

Ashley had forgotten about the nurse who woke her earlier. The nurse had been busy taking notes on her chart and Ashley hadn't even noticed her until now.

"On the arm of your bed is a landline. Just hit nine for a line out and then dial the number."

"Thanks."

Ashley bit her lip. For the life of her she couldn't remember her mom's phone number. She hadn't actually dialed it from memory in…years, maybe. *Think, think, think, Ashley,* she said to herself holding the handset in her hand. In fact, she couldn't remember anyone's number, not Kelly's, not work's, not anyone's. Now she started to really panic. What was she going to do? How would she make sure Mongrel was taken care of? She needed to get out of the hospital now, or she was going home to a desperate dog at best. At worst, she didn't want to think about the worst case scenario. Ashley groaned at the effort it was taking to right herself on the bed.

"Here, let me help you, Officer Henderson."

Ashley reached out and grabbed the nurse's arm, hoisting herself upright. Once again her head spun. She needed to spend more time sitting up or get used to the ride her head took every time she stood. Steadying herself, she walked to the closet and grabbed her clothes.

"What're you doing, Officer?"

"I need to get home. My dog is home alone and I don't think anyone has been home to check on him."

"Officer Henderson, I can't let you just walk out of the hospital. Why don't you call your mother and see if she can check on your puppy?"

"I would but," Ashley blushed with embarrassment, "I can't remember her phone number and my phone is probably dead so I can't turn it on to get the number. So as you see, I need to get home and check on him."

"Officer Henderson, you're a police officer. Think. I'm sure you can call a fellow officer and have them check on your pet. Do you have an emergency card in your wallet or do you have an emergency number on file somewhere. Surely you have your mother as your emergency contact."

Ashley tried thinking, *did I have an emergency contact number listed somewhere? Oh God, what am I going to do?* She couldn't think straight, the pain was really clouding her head.

"Yes, yes you're right. My wallet, in my wallet I have my mother's business card."

Why her mother had a business card was beyond her. She didn't work and she didn't own a business, but she had insisted on having them made because she was tired of going to events and being asked for her personal information. This way, her mother explained, she could just hand out the plain, clear, plastic cards with her phone number on it. The fact it didn't have her mother's name on it was perfect she told Ashley. If they didn't remember who gave it to them, then they didn't actually need her information. Shaking her head she muttered, "Mother."

Dialing her mother's number, Ashley finally

relaxed. "Answer, answer, answer it, Mother."

Waiting, she was just starting to think her mother wasn't home when she heard her voice on the other end.

"Mom!"

"Honey, are you alright?"

"Yes, I'm fine. I need a huge favor. Mongrel, I completely forgot about him, Mom. I need you to go over and take care of him."

"Honey," Ashley's mom said dragging out the endearment. "I took care of everything already."

"Oh God, thank you, Mom. I just realized I forgot about him." Relief flooded Ashley's body.

"No problem, Honey. Do you need me to come down there right now?"

"No, Mom. I'm good. I appreciate you taking care of Mongrel."

"Okay, Sweetie. I'll be down there later then. I love you."

"I love you too, Mom. See you this afternoon."

Ashley smiled as relief surged through her. Mongrel was fine and being spoiled, if she knew her mom. It was one less thing she had to worry about. Now, if she could just find her appetite. Pushing the food around on her tray hoping it would make it more appetizing, Ashley put the cover back on and sighed. She had graduated from broths and gelatin to more solid foods, but it wasn't quite bacon and eggs. More like goop and the worst coffee she had tasted. Biting off an edge of her toast, she slowly chewed the dry wheat. *The least they could have done was not burn it,* thought Ashley, trying to swallow the clump in her mouth.

"Hello?" a soft knock on her door and a whisper broke the silence.

"Come in?" Ashley wondered who would be

visiting. Kelly was on shift and she just talked to her mom, so who could it be?

"I'm looking for Officer Henderson. I have a special delivery for her?" The voice behind the curtain said gruffly.

"I'm Officer Henderson. Please come in." Ashley waited, trying to connect the voice to a person, but she couldn't.

"I heard that you like café lattes and I just happened to be in the neighborhood and thought I would drop this off."

A hand appeared with a drink holder, a café latte on one side and diagonal from it a large hot cup of tea. Ashley clapped her hands, almost bouncing in her bed. Her mouth started to water just looking at the cold drink. Her prayers had been answered. A café latte was all hers and hers alone.

"Get in here so I can kiss you." Ashley didn't know who she just offered to kiss, but she didn't care. She wanted that latte and she wanted it now. "Don't make me get out of this bed and chase you. I'll do it, trust me. I'm a desperate woman."

Peeking around the curtain, Tyler raised her eyebrows as a cute smile crossed her face.

"How bad do you want this?" Tyler asked, moving the tray back and forth.

Ashley squinted her eyes at the beautiful woman and pursed her lips. Waiting, Tyler stood moving the drink holder back and forth, just out of Ashley's reach. Clearly, the evil stare wasn't working on Tyler, so Ashley had to take a different tactic.

"Okay, come get your reward, handsome." Ashley held her hands out waiting for Tyler to enter her embrace. "Come on ya big lug. I pay my debts and I owe you a kiss." Ashley closed her eyes and puckered her lips. When Ashley didn't hear any movement, she opened her eyes to find Tyler staring at her. Following her gaze, Ashley looked down to find her shirt part way open, exposing part of a breast. Blushing, she yanked her shirt closed and gave Tyler a dirty look. All she wanted was the latte and she would be fine, now if she could just get her hands on it.

"Are you going to come in or not?" Ashley was cranky now, her latte mere inches away, but Tyler was playing games with her. Any other time she would play along, but today she needed her coffee fix. Ashley's fingers drummed a cadence on the bed rail. Waiting, Ashley looked up at the T.V. on over Tyler's head. Two could play this game.

"Okay, okay. Here's your coffee," Tyler said handing Ashley the cold latte and smiling. "You need your coffee in the morning, don't you?"

"We all have our vices, don't we?" Ashley returned a smirk as she took a long draw on the straw. The cool liquid coated her tongue, making her taste buds dance. Goosebumps popped up on her arms as the cold drink took its effect on her. Leaning her head back on her pillow, she let out a long sigh.

"Heaven. Finally," she said smiling.

Ashley looked over at Tyler who was smiling at the display of sheer joy found in a café latte. Tyler's hair was wet and messy, as if she had taken a shower but forgot to comb her hair. *So this is what she looks like when she gets out of bed,* thought Ashley looking Tyler up and down. Her robe pulled tight around a narrow waist, and flannel pajamas peeking out below her robe, gave her that little kid look. The only thing missing was a teddy bear hanging from her grasp. Ashley really liked the new Tyler. She just couldn't help herself as she let her gaze roam again over the lanky woman. A warmth shot through her body at the assessment, causing her to take another long pull on the straw to her café latte.

Letting the cold liquid rest on her tongue again, Ashley closed her eyes and enjoyed the melting sensation. The sweet coffee slid down her throat and she nearly choked as she watched Tyler open her robe. It wasn't like she could see anything, but the teddy bear pajamas almost made Ashley choke again as she admired them. Who knew Tyler was such a kid at heart?

"What?" Tyler said, smiling at Ashley.

Oh how she could get lost in that smile if she let herself. A kiss, she owed Tyler a kiss for the café latte, but how would she work that into the conversation and not have it seem like she was begging. Ashley smiled again as she watched Tyler cock an eyebrow and watch her tongue as it darted out and licked whip cream from her lips. Tyler licked her own lips then dropped her gaze to the hot tea in her hands.

"So, what's your vice, Tyler?" Ashley said stirring her latte.

"Huh?"

"Your vice. Mine's a good café latte. What's yours?"

"A beautiful woman," Tyler said matter-of-factly.

Ashley felt her face and neck heat as she blushed at the statement. Coffee, alcohol, or even food, Ashley expected. But Tyler's confession of a beautiful woman made her ache with desire. Focusing on the cold drink, she cleared her throat and took another drink. She had put her foot in it now and she wasn't sure how to redirect the conversation.

"I'm sorry. Did I embarrass you?" Tyler smiled.

"No, of course not."

"Of course not."

"I mean, your taste for women is legendary." Ashley instantly regretted the statement as soon as she said it. Why did she always have to say things she knew would destroy a conversation, especially with someone who had risked her own life to save Ashley's?

"Yes, well, you shouldn't believe everything you hear," Tyler said icily.

The once warm room took on a chill and there wasn't anything Ashley could do about it now. What was it they said, regret is a dish best savored cold, or was that revenge? It didn't matter. Tyler's stiff body language and expression showed Ashley the arrow she had accidentally launched had firmly landed on its intended target.

"Tyler, I'm so sorry. You didn't deserve that. I have a tendency to lob grenades and I have no idea why. Please forgive me." Ashley tried to get up but her broken ribs protested.

Tyler's hands reached under Ashley's shoulders and then a pillow slipped behind her back helping her sit upright. Ashley flinched and took a deep breath, the smell of soap wafted around her. Turning toward Tyler, she was close enough to kiss her neck. The temptation lasted less than a moment, but long enough that Ashley considered it. Ashley grabbed Tyler's arm before she could sit back down and pulled her closer.

"I owe you a kiss for the latte," Ashley whispered, kissing Tyler's cheek before she could reconsider the impulsive action.

Tyler turned towards Ashley and studied her lips and then looked into her eyes. Seconds passed between them, their eyes locked only inches apart.

Chapter Twenty-six

Tyler's heart was hammering in her chest. *God, one kiss on the cheek and I'm a goner. Great.* Tyler thought staring at Ashley. Looking back down at Ashley's lips was her undoing. Closing the distance between them, she kissed Ashley and let her lips linger on the sweet taste under them. Tyler could taste coffee as she let her tongue glide over Ashley's parted lips. Venturing further, she felt Ashley's mouth open welcoming her tongue inside. A moan echoed in the warm room, spurring Tyler further in her advances. Reaching a hand up, she ran her fingers through the soft, red locks and then held Ashley's head while she continued her exploration. Pulling away slightly, she ran her lips along the soft skin of Ashley's jaw, her tongue leaving a wet path as it traveled down her neck. Kissing the base of Ashley's neck, Tyler felt her breasts tighten and her nipples harden as she continued to explore. It felt as if the room had jumped twenty degrees, sweat broke out on her neck, a sure sign she was excited. Ashley's fingers slipped through Tyler's hair, a gentle pull keeping her firmly against Ashley's neck.

"Tyler." Tyler heard her name barely spoken as she tasted the saltiness of Ashley's skin. A primal need was beginning to take over and she felt herself getting wetter. Women didn't usually have this kind of effect on Tyler and she was enjoying her body's reaction. Ashley released the grip in her hair, moving to her breast, palming the hard nipple and sending a jolt through Tyler's body. She was ready to explode. Just the right touch and she would come undone right in front of Ashley. Remembering where she was Tyler tried to center herself. Pulling away from Ashley was the hardest thing to do when she wanted her, but this wasn't the time for her to put Ashley in a compromising position.

Clearing her throat she spoke softly, "I'm sorry, I don't know what came over me," she said without looking at Ashley. Pulling her robe tight around herself and tying it, she sat back down almost missing her chair as she gripped the arms for support and lowered herself down. "I shouldn't have done that. I'm really sorry."

Tyler could feel her body shake inside, raw emotion taking its toll. She hadn't had that kind of reaction with a woman lately and it was unsettling. Jill had been the last woman to make her lose control and now Ashley stirred that reaction in her. Was it the environment, the shooting, the guilt? She wasn't sure, but this wasn't an average situation and she wasn't about to take advantage of it in that way.

"Don't be sorry. I wanted that as much as you did. Besides, I'm the one who should be sorry. If it wasn't for me you wouldn't be here. You would be at the station, hanging with the guys and saving lives." Ashley looked down at her hands resting in her lap.

Tyler felt sorry for Ashley, for the guilt she clearly carried and for the psycho girlfriend that nearly ended her life. Reaching over she patted Ashley's hands then covered them with her own. Ashley had a long road ahead of her, Tyler knew that much. She suspected guilt was like loss, until you accept it you have no control over the situation. It will always be a constant companion. Looking down at their entwined fingers Tyler smiled.

She liked the way Ashley made her feel, the energy, the warmth, and the protectiveness all made her feel needed. She knew she was projecting onto Ashley, but she couldn't help it. Ever since that day at the shooting she had worried about Ashley.

"I'm fine, Ashley. You're not responsible for the actions of Leslie. The sooner you accept that the easier it will be to move on. Trust me. I definitely know what I'm talking about here." Smiling, she hoped her words would give Ashley some comfort, but she doubted it. "Besides, you still owe me a coffee date."

"Oh, it's a date now?" Ashley smiled back at Tyler.

"Well, it's not a date date, but you did promise to go for coffee with me. Unless you and I in our pj's are date material. But I'll have you know, I don't wear pjs on a date or to bed." Tyler wiggled her eyebrows at the implication. She watched Ashley blush and smirked. "You are so easy."

The shocked look on Ashley's face made Tyler laugh. It was too easy to bait Ashley and yet Tyler couldn't resist. Patting her hand Tyler sat back in her chair and steepled her fingers resting her chin on the tips.

"So, you wanna talk?"

"About?"

"Anything."

Tyler watched as Ashley went somewhere far away. Studying Ashley's face she noticed the dark circles under her eyes and the shallow cheeks. Ashley looked like a fragile porcelain doll that needed protection and Tyler felt the need to protect her right now. It was obvious the shooting was taking its toll on her, physically, but what was going on in Ashley's head? Tyler could only guess at the trauma she had gone through at the hands of the abusive girlfriend, but she wasn't a mind reader and she wouldn't know unless she asked. But should she? Nothing ventured, nothing gained as they said. Taking another sip of her lukewarm tea, Tyler worried she might be intruding if she tried to get Ashley to talk, but she knew from experience that talking was the only way to give voice to the pain she carried. It was the only way to release it, to purge it from her soul.

"Tell me more about Leslie."

Ashley looked at Tyler puzzled. Of course she wanted to know about the woman who almost killed them, but was Ashley ready to tell Tyler everything? Was she ready to let someone in that deep?

"It's okay, you don't have to talk about it if you don't want to. I just thought perhaps talking about it might help." Tyler still couldn't shake the turmoil from her own body and she needed to divert her attention. The more she looked at Ashley's lips, the more she felt the need to kiss them again, to hold her, and protect her from the pain she felt rolling off the fragile woman. A weak smile creased Ashley's face as she laid her head back against the pillow. Moving the head of the bed down a little she took a deep breath and held it, then released it.

"I told you how we met and the first few weeks we were together. It all started with that slap when I confronted her about a woman's number. I should have stopped seeing her then, but I didn't. Things were pretty good. I mean, she yelled, but that was Leslie. She said it was all part of her heritage, how she was raised. We decided to move in together and take our relationship to the next level, as she called it. Things were good and then, one day, we got into another argument about another woman. Guess she'd been cheating on me the whole time. Leslie reared back like she was going to slap me and I stood my ground. I told her if she touched me there would be hell to pay. Guess she didn't care and slapped me anyway. I fell against the coffee table and broke my collar bone."

Tyler looked at Ashley and knew she was there, living that moment all over again. Moving to the bed, she cradled Ashley's wounded body in her arms and rocked her. Ashley's body went rigid at the contact and Tyler relaxed her hold. She heard Ashley start to cry as she buried her head into Tyler's shoulder.

"It's okay, she can't hurt you anymore."

"I didn't think she could anymore, but I was wrong." Ashley looked up at Tyler and whispered, "She hurt you, too."

"Hey, I'm okay. It's just a pain in the ass, that's all." Tyler laughed at her own joke, hoping to lighten the mood.

"You are so gallant Tyler, but it's more than a pain in the ass. You could've been killed that day."

"Naw, I'm hard to get rid of. You'll see." Tyler cupped Ashley's face and made her look at her. "It's going to be okay. Nothing a little time and therapy can't fix." Tyler hoped minimizing the incident would ease Ashley's guilt, but she knew she wasn't succeeding.

"Do you know how much counseling I went through after the break-up? Tons," Ashley said, sniffling.

"I think everyone should get their head shrunk at least once in a while. I went a lot after Jill died. I'm not sure it helped, but it gave me something to do, I guess," Tyler said once again downplaying her own pain and anger at losing Jill.

Really, Tyler had gone to counseling because of the suicide attempt, but once there she knew she needed to deal with the anger of losing Jill. She just wasn't sure she had been successful implementing the counselor's suggestions. She still rode her bike too fast, screwed too many women, and took too many chances at work. So she guessed the answer was no, the counseling hadn't helped, maybe only to lessen the anger, but it definitely didn't diminish the pain, not until recently.

Everyone gets to their own place of healing at their own time, Tyler thought. She knew she couldn't push Ashley to hers. It was a journey for one, and two on the path only made it a crowded journey. She wasn't sure time healed either, living did. Living life, making a new path, and taking on a new purpose might help Ashley. Surely it had helped her. Hadn't it?

"I know this might sound weird, but would you like a shower or maybe a hot bath? That always helps me think and relax when I've had a tough time." Tyler smiled down at red, swollen eyes. Ashley looked so helpless that Tyler's heart ached for her.

"Is that a come on, Tyler?" Ashley questioned, and then smiled.

"Of course. You know what a cad I am. Besides, I had my first shower today and I thought I had died and gone to heaven." Tyler winked at Ashley. Reaching over her shoulder she buzzed the nurses' station.

"Yes?" came a voice over the speaker.

"Officer Henderson would like to take a shower or a bath. Is that possible?"

"Of course. I'll be right there."

"Thank you."

"Thanks, Tyler. I've only been able to brush my teeth and get a sponge bath. Maybe I'll start to feel a little more like myself."

"Well, I can't vouch for its healing powers, but a hot shower always seems to help me." Tyler leaned her head against Ashley's. "Don't let her win, Ashley. Don't give her that power over you. Okay?"

Nodding, Ashley closed her eyes, tears squeezing out and running down her face. Tyler turned Ashley's face up and kissed the trail of tears on each side of her face and then placed a soft kiss on the tight lips.

"It will get better. I promise."

"Okay, who wants a bath?" The nurse said flinging back the privacy curtain.

Chapter Twenty-seven

Tyler lay back on her hospital bed, the doctor's voice droning on. Her thoughts were of Ashley. Her soft lips and beautiful smile were all she could think about. The kiss had nearly sent her into an orgasm. She had plenty of women who fulfilled her needs for sex, but this was different. Ashley was different. She had a strength about her, whether Ashley knew it or not, that turned Tyler on, that she found sexy. But she also had a softness, a…how would Tyler describe it, a need to be protected that Tyler loved, too. In Ashley's capacity as a cop, Tyler was sure Ashley didn't think she needed protecting, but Tyler did. Tyler wanted to wrap her arms around the petite red head and protect her from the world. To hold her, to comfort her. Ah who was she kidding? Circumstances had thrown them together and she was just experiencing some type of rescuer's syndrome. The doctor's voice continued to grate on her nerves. Blah, blah, blah was all she heard until she heard the words 'doing good enough to be released' and then she sat up.

"I'm sorry. Did you just say I can go home?"

"Well that sure perked you up."

Tyler was more than ready to get the heck out of the hospital, she was bored beyond belief. The only bright spot was Ashley a few floors above her. Suddenly realizing she wouldn't be close to Ashley, she questioned the doctor again.

"Are you sure I'm ready to go? I mean I wouldn't

want to push anything, I mean, you know, do something that would put me right back in." Tyler questioned the doctor.

"No, don't worry. I'll give you some light pain medication and as long as you take it easy, you should be fine," he said scribbling on her chart.

"When can I go back to work?"

"As a firefighter, not for a while. I still want you to be on bed rest. Then, after a follow-up in two weeks, we'll reassess your ability for light duty and then when you can go back to work full-time." The doctor kept writing on Tyler's chart while she fidgeted with the belt of her robe.

"What about riding my motorcycle?"

"Are you trying to be funny? No motorcycle, period. Not for now anyway."

"Do you know when they are going to release Officer Henderson?"

Tyler didn't know if her doctor treated Ashley as well, but it was worth a try.

Shaking his head he handed her a prescription slip. "Nope, I'm not her attending. She's the one who came in with you, right? Bruised ribs, bullet wound, and collapsed lung?"

"Yeah."

"A few days. Probably no more than that as long as there weren't complications."

"I see."

"Okay, Tyler. I told your father that you would be released this afternoon. So, he should be here to take you home. Any other questions?"

Shaking her head she extended her hand, "Nope, I think I'm good. Thanks Doc."

"Be careful out there. Okay?"

"Always," Tyler said smiling. "Always."

###

"So are you ready for some lunch, Officer Henderson?" the nurse asked while helping Ashley back from her shower.

Smiling, Ashley had to admit she was hungry, "Yeah, I think I am, actually. But not that broth or gelatin. How about something more substantial?"

"I'm sure we can arrange something like that. I can't vouch for the taste, though."

Shaking her head, Ashley couldn't wait to get out of the hospital and back to her own home, dog, and serenity. A hospital wasn't a place where one got better, it was the way station on the way to getting better. Home was her sanctuary and she wanted the peace and quiet it afforded her. Running her fingers through her wet hair, Ashley wished someone had brought her a comb. Without conditioner it would take forever to detangle the wet mess. Tyler had been right. The shower did improve her mood and outlook. The days ahead were going to get better. They had to. No more looking over her shoulder, no more wondering where Leslie was, and no more worrying when the phone rang.

Setting her things on her bed she rifled through the overnight bag her mother had brought. Ah, a comb. It was the small things that made Ashley happy right now. Surprisingly, combing her hair was one of those small obsessions Ashley needed to fulfill to be happy. Being right handed had presented a problem with many of her routines and this one was no exception. Struggling, she scratched her scalp as she dragged the comb through the tangled mess with her left hand. What started off as a triumph was proving to be a disaster as she yanked more hair out of her head than ran the comb through. Grunting, she tried once again to gently glide the comb through, starting at the bottom and working her way to the top as her mother had shown her when she was little. Ashley thought about all the things her mother had taught her in that subtle motherly way she had. How to cook a three-minute egg might not mean anything to some, but in her family the three-minute egg was routine every Saturday. Ruin it and it spoke volumes for how the day would progress, make it right and it wasn't even an issue on the radar. Her dad, when he was around, had shown her how to take a car engine apart.

"It should be mandatory for every girl your age," he said as she looked at the engine of her Dodge Dart laying in pieces on the garage floor. It was a gift for her sixteenth birthday, *but who got a Dodge Dart for their first car?* She wondered. It was a gift she would have gladly given back if she could. But after spending a week reassembling it with little help from her father, who only grunted when she selected the wrong tool or car part, she felt the satisfaction of success when the car's engine turned over and started for the first time. Her heart felt heavy as she thought about her dad and how he had turned his back on her mother and her. Oh well, water under the bridge as her mother would say. Looking down at the comb in her hand she remembered what she was supposed to be doing. It was a 'shiny object moment' as her mother referred to them, the times when Ashley got sidetracked from what she was doing.

Ashley jerked and let out another grunt as she wrestled with another tangle.

"Hey, need a hand?" Kelly asked, reaching for the comb now stuck in Ashley's hair. "Let me do that."

Ashley flinched in surprise at Kelly's voice. She hadn't heard Kelly come in, too focused on her task to pay attention. Turning towards Kelly she presented her back to her partner and slumped when Kelly pushed her head down. Clearly Kelly had done this before. She had all the tell-tale signs of someone who knew how to comb out long hair.

"Thanks. Trying to do this left-handed was frustrating enough. Then to pull out chunks of my own hair, I thought I would be bald by the time I finished," Ashley said, relaxing at the gentle strokes through her hair.

"My sisters and I loved combing each other's hair. We would sit for hours and do it. Why do you think that is?"

"Bonding I suppose. Kind of like when monkeys groom each other and eat the bugs from the other monkey's fur."

"Gross," Kelly said, slapping Ashley with the side of the comb. "All done."

"What're you doing here?" Ashley faced Kelly noticing she had her uniform on. "Ah, you're working and I'm on your to do list, aren't I?"

"Sorry, duty calls."

"More questions?"

"Yep, more questions."

"Hmm." Was all Ashley could say. She knew the last time Kelly was here she had taken it easy on her, but as the days went on Ashley would have to answer more questions. "Fire away."

Kelly pulled out the pad she kept on her and flipped it open just as she had done before.

"I'm sorry, Ash, but I'm going to have to ask some very intimate questions about your relationship with Leslie.

She's said some things and I need to either verify them or put them to rest. Her lawyer is determined to get the charges reduced." Kelly wrote a few things down and then looked up at Ashley, who could see how uncomfortable Kelly was getting. Ashley's stomach tightened and she suddenly felt nauseous, fearing what Leslie might have said.

"Let's get this over with so I can puke and you can get back to work," Ashley said snidely. Kelly didn't deserve the attitude, she was only doing her job, Ashley realized and apologized. "Sorry, it's just…I just want this over, the sooner the better."

Kelly put a comforting hand on Ashley's shoulder and smiled. "I know it's tough, but this is only the report side of things. Wait until the DA gets a hold of you. The upside is I hear she's quite a looker, if you like tall, authoritative, sexy brunettes."

Kelly closed the door to Ashley's room and pulled the privacy curtain. Sitting down, Ashley could see the *all business* Kelly, her posture straight and her face guarded, had taken the place of her *friend* Kelly.

"Ready?"

"Yep."

Chapter Twenty-eight

Tying the waistband of her sweat pants, Tyler grabbed her cane and looked at her father. "Ready?"

"Yep."

"Good, let's get out of here."

Tyler reached for her bag, but her dad slapped her hand away. "I got it."

"Thanks, Dad."

"No problem, Sparky."

"Cute."

"I know. That's what your mother says all the time." Tyler's dad stopped and looked at Tyler's shocked face. "Sorry, sometimes I forget she's gone."

Tyler grabbed her dad's shoulder and squeezed it. If she had a hard time with things, what could she say to a man who had been married to the same woman for thirty-five years? Nothing, so she just hugged him wishing she could help him as much as he had helped her. Tyler knew what he was feeling so no words were needed between father and daughter. His weak smile said it all.

"Excuse me," a male voice said. Both turned to see a man pushing an empty wheelchair towards them. "Hospital rules, you need to go to the door in a wheelchair."

"I might have come in on a gurney, but I'll be damned if I'm going out in one of those," Tyler said pointing her cane at the wheelchair. "Besides, it's bad enough I have this," she said shaking the cane at the poor fellow who was only doing his job. "Now, unless you want me to put this—"

"Tyler."

Tyler looked at her father who had grabbed her forearm and was shaking his head. She didn't want to say anything that might embarrass her father so she toned down her statement.

"I can't sit on anything right now so unless you fill that with about five feather pillows, I'm going out on this," she said holding up the cane again. "So call the doctor if you need to. We'll wait right here for his answer."

Tyler turned and started for the door, her father following close behind, smiling. Jacksons weren't a family that took easily to orders and Tyler's behavior was proof of that. But they did have a selfless need to serve, either publicly or in the military, and Tyler's dad was proud of his children and their successes. Right now though, Tyler was sure her father had wished he was anywhere but next to her when she dressed down the nurse, who was only doing his job.

"I hope you have some pillows in that car, Dad, or I'm going to be screwed. My ass is killing me." Tyler chuckled realizing she had a self-fulfilling prophecy of pain ahead of her.

"I got it taken care of, Honey," he said patting her back.

Warm sun greeted Tyler as she felt it for the first time in days. Taking a deep breath, she reveled in the sweet smell of the flowers that bloomed all around the hospital. A peace descended over Tyler as she finally realized she was putting this part of her life behind her. The shooting, the pain, and the constantly being woken up to have her vitals taken lay behind her. Life was good. The chief walked over to his car sitting in the fire zone.

"Really, Dad?" Tyler blushed at the liberty her father had taken.

"What? It's the chief's car and I'm the chief, right? Besides, you don't have to walk very far this way."

"It's the fire lane, Dad."

"Well thanks, Einstein. I see you got your mother's brains and my good looks," he said holding the door open with a smirk.

Tyler looked in the sedan, ready to sit down when she spotted the eight-inch pad filling the seat. Looking back at her father, who only shrugged, she gently lowered herself to the thick foam. *Hmmm, not bad,* Tyler thought swinging her long legs into the car.

"But I get to play with the lights and siren, right Daddy?"

"Cute, Honey, Cute," he said closing the door just a little too hard.

The trip home would be a long one and Tyler's stomach made its presence known.

"Hungry?"

"Yeah. I guess I forgot to eat in all the excitement of going home." Tyler slapped her head. "Oh shit. We have to go back, Dad."

"What? Why?"

"I forgot to tell Ashley I was being discharged. Shit."

"She's a big girl, Honey. She doesn't need you checking in with her. Besides, I saw Kelly this morning on my way into the hospital, so she's probably with her as we speak."

Tyler looked out the window, the buildings ticking off like roadside markers. Distracted by the thought of

Kelly being there, Tyler didn't notice the drive-through or the question her father had asked.

"What?"

"Tyler, what would you like?"

"The usual, Dad. You know me, I like my routine."

"Two dogs, the works and a soda, and I'll have a burger with extra onion, fries, and a diet root beer."

Tyler's dad parked the car under a tree as Tyler handed him the burger. She had wanted to talk to him about what J.J. had told her earlier in the week, but time had gotten away from her, so now was as good a time as any.

"Dad?"

"Huh?"

"Are you suspending me?" Tyler said before shoving the overloaded hotdog in her mouth and taking a bite.

"What?"

"I heard that the captain wants me suspended. So, I'm asking you not as your daughter, but as a firefighter, are you suspending me?"

"Captain Russo wants a lot of things and usually gets them, but this isn't one of them. Besides, the police chief called me personally and told me to thank you for saving Officer Henderson's life," he said popping the last bite of his burger in his mouth.

"Oh, he did, did he?"

Nodding his head, he looked at Tyler and smiled. "Tyler, you need to stop taking risks, though. Luckily you've never put anyone's life in danger. When that happens though, you're out of the department."

Tyler appreciated her dad's honesty. They had always had a great relationship and he had always supported her, no matter what. That was as close to a dressing down as she was going to get, but she knew he was right. Looking back, she had been lucky the few times she had taken a risk and saved lives, but it wouldn't last.

"Maybe a transfer's in order then. I'm not sure it's good for either of us to work together considering I know he wants me out. I mean, Captain Russo wants what he wants and I would be a constant reminder that his judgment was questioned, or worse he would think favoritism was at play because I'm your daughter."

"Tyler, you're a solid firefighter and if he has a problem with my decision he can take it up with me. As for a transfer, no need. Since you're on light duty you'll be at the main station so you're good there. Anything else you want to talk about?"

"As a matter of fact, I have this girl problem I wanted to talk to you about," Tyler said, smiling at her dad.

Chapter Twenty-nine

The check-out process had been a breeze once the doctor gave Ashley the okay to be discharged. There wasn't anything the hospital could do for her that she couldn't do at home, with the help of a home-health care nurse her mother promised the doctor she would get. She felt bad that she hadn't told Tyler she was being discharged, but she promised herself she would call once she got settled. It had been difficult convincing her mother she was fine, but the idea of staying at her mom's house was overwhelming, to say the least. Ashley looked around the big empty house. She had conceded that bringing Mongrel home wasn't a good idea. Ashley's body ached from the ride home. The bandages pulled tight around her chest made it hard to take a deep breath and her shoulder would catch when she tried to rotate it to keep it loose. Still in her pajamas, she slowly walked around her house, making sure every door was locked and all the windows were closed and locked tight. Even though she knew Leslie was in jail, the nightly ritual would be a hard one to give up.

Mongrel was still at her mother's, because she didn't think she could handle him jumping all over her. The doctor had been specific about her after care routine and it didn't include taking care of her mixed breed, jumping machine. She really did need to take him to some discipline classes, but where was the fun in a well-behaved, composed pet? Mongrel needed to be walked daily and if the truth were told she wasn't ready for that kind of commitment yet. She missed him and she knew he missed her, especially when her mother informed her that he wasn't eating. Her mom blamed it on the food she had purchased, but Ashley knew he got like that when she wasn't around.

"Well, at least someone misses me," she said to the empty room.

Ashley looked at the pile of stuff her mom had dumped on the floor of her living room, but on the couch were her uniform pants, hat, badge and utility belt. It had been there when she walked in the door. *Kelly must have brought it over,* she thought looking at the pile. Her uniform top had been cut off and kept as evidence. Thankfully they thought to keep her pants and other items, giving them to Kelly. Her pants contained her identification, her note pad and other things Ashley would need when she returned to work. Picking up the pants, the smell of blood rushed her senses, taking her back to the day of the shooting. Her heart sped up, and she felt herself flush and get lightheaded. Remembering the sickening ping of the bullet as it bounced off her car and into her body made her flinch. Her stomach felt as if it would revolt right then and there, as the painful memories assaulted her senses. Tossing the clothes towards the laundry room, Ashley straightened up and took a deep cleansing breath.

Ashley jumped at the sound of a car backfiring down the street. She grabbed her tightening chest as a pain shot through it. Was this what she had to look forward to every time she thought she heard a shot? Ashley felt as if she was on sensory overload and she had only been home forty-five minutes. The blood, the torn clothing, and the car backfiring made her feel as if she was speeding over a cliff, and all she could do was hang on for dear life. *How did soldiers survive when they came home from a war zone?* she wondered. *How did they cope with being shot at or worse, injured? How will I cope with my own injuries and trauma?* She needed to get a grip. She needed to take back control and remember Leslie was in jail and couldn't hurt her ever again. At least for now.

Looking through the pile she pulled out her utility belt and noticed her weapon was gone. Fuck, who would have taken it? She needed to call Kelly and give her a heads up on the missing side arm. Everything else was there though. Cuffs, flex cuffs, and collapsible baton. Even her reserve magazines for her weapon were there. Another sickening feeling overcame Ashley. *What if I lost my gun at the scene and someone picked it up and used it to commit a crime? Stop,* she told herself. She was letting her imagination get the better of her and she knew it. Sitting on the couch she tried to reason with her over active mind. No one had her gun. She had pulled it when she lay on the ground, ready to shoot anyone who came near her. Resting it on her chest she waited for the perp to come calling, to finish what he had started. She corrected herself, what she had started. She still couldn't believe that Leslie hated her enough to kill her. The hitting, the pushing, even the slapping were all part of Leslie's abusive behavior, but it had never escalated beyond that, not even when she threatened Ashley. Ashley was so mad her hands began to shake. Adrenaline pulsed through her body fueling her anger as she thought about the shooting again.

"That fucking bitch," she said through clinched teeth. "It's a good thing she's in jail already. God only knows what I would do if she were out." Ashley made the hollow threat knowing in the back of her mind she would never do something so brutal. At least giving voice to her thoughts helped her calm down and see reason again. Leslie deserved everything the court system was about to do to her, and Ashley realized it was everything she hadn't done that put her and Tyler in this position. She was on a roller coaster ride of emotions, hatred one minute, guilt and self-loathing the next.

But her gun, what had become of it? *Think, think, think.* Someone had taken it in the ambulance, Mike. After that she had no clue as to its whereabouts. Opening her closet she put her utility belt and vest inside next to her gun box. Pulling the gun box to her she grabbed the handle and set it on the floor. Punching in her code she pulled the handle when the green light went on. Inside laid her weapon, with the trigger lock in place. Relief surged through her body. At least she didn't have to worry that the gun would fall into the wrong hands.

Ashley rubbed her temples. Frustration another car on the rollercoaster she was on. How had everything turned so upside down? One minute her life was finally going exactly where she had planned, the next minute she was fighting for her life. To make matters worse, Tyler had accidentally come along for the ride.

"Tyler!"

Ashley had wanted to stop by Tyler's room and check in with her before leaving, but in her haste to get out of the hospital she had completely forgotten about Tyler. What was Tyler's room number at the hospital? Oh it didn't matter. She could call the switchboard and they would connect her. At Ashley's request, her mom had been nice enough to replace Ashley's phone while she was in the hospital. The last one still lay in pieces against the wall behind her. Flipping the phone open, she waited for it to boot up. In less than a minute, the phone vibrated letting her know she had messages. Looking at the screen, forty-five messages and texts waited for a response. Most were probably co-workers wishing her well, and the others were probably reporters wanting a scoop on a story. How they got her number she would never know, it seems they had an insider at the police department who didn't have a problem passing on information to the news reporters. Ashley decided to listen to the voice mails first, since it would be her first step at clearing her messages. Pressing one on her phone she waited for the messages to start.

"You have thirty-seven messages. Press seven to listen to the first message," the automated voice instructed.

Pressing seven Ashley hit speaker on the phone and set it on the bar. At first she couldn't hear anything. Then suddenly, she could hear heavy breathing and someone running. Recognition rocked her when the voice finally spoke, Leslie.

"Hey Sweetie, I'm just getting everything set up to meet you. It is fucking amazing up here. The view is killer." A maniacal laugh punctuated her sentences. "Oh, God, Ash, I wish you were up here to see this. I've got some really great stuff up here. Oops, there you are now. Gotta run babe."

Ashley hated it when Leslie called her babe. Her stomach started revolting just as she started to hit delete. Hesitating over the delete button she wished she could delete the bitch's voice, but the cop side told her she needed to save it. Pressing nine she saved it and moved on to the next message, dreading it.

"Hey babe. Ouch, that looked like it hurt. Oh, I guess you won't be joining me for dinner tonight will you?" Another bout of laughter and then silence.

Ashley pushed the save button and pressed on. The detectives would ask her what was on the messages, so she might as well listen to them. Her stomach started cramping as she pressed seven again for the next message.

"Hey, baby, you doin' okay down there? I know you won't answer your phone, but come on…" This time there wasn't any laughing, no jokes just silence before the line went dead.

Ashley repeated the process of saving the message, but this time she sat back and stared at the phone. She couldn't bring herself to play another message if her life depended on it. She twisted her neck, trying to release the stress that had collected there. A steady pain had taken up residence in her head and now her ribs were throbbing. She could barely focus on anything around her except the phone that sat on the bar. Tunnel vision closed in around Ashley, and the only thing she could see was that damn phone. Closing her eyes, she took a deep breath and, with all the resolve she could muster, she picked it up and dialed Kelly. She couldn't do this alone and she knew she would have to listen to the damn messages to verify that it was in fact Leslie who had left them. The detectives would tell her that there were probably important details of the shooting in the messages and hopefully incriminating evidence. But thinking back to the three she had heard, Leslie was smart, but not smart enough. Ashley had Leslie incriminating herself on her phone.

"Hey partner, how're you doing?" Kelly's bubbly response calmed Ashley, but just barely.

"Not so good I'm afraid. Can you come over tonight?" Ashley's voice quivered at the request.

"What's wrong, Ash? What happened? I'm close to the hospital, I'll be right there."

Ashley knew Kelly would pick up on the fear in her voice. How could she explain she was afraid to listen to messages left by someone who was behind bars? Someone who couldn't hurt her now or probably ever.

"No, wait, I'm home now." Ashley informed her.

"You got out today? Why didn't you call me?" The silence on Ashley's end was her answer. "Oh, right, you are calling me, duh. Okay, give me about ten minutes to get there. Do you need anything? Have you eaten?"

"I'm good, just hurry, please."

Popping open the pain meds, Ashley looked around for something to wash them down with. A slow trek to the frig reminded her of what a lousy shopper she was. Nothing, absolutely nothing was in the frig, except a science experiment masquerading as leftovers. She would have to settle for a glass of tap water or the half bottle of white wine in the frig door. Mixing medication and alcohol was a no-no, so she filled a tumbler with water. If she had been a throw-caution-to-the-wild kind of gal, she could tempt fate right about now and chase her pain meds with the wine.

The knocking at the door stopped her from further contemplating her options between the wine or the water. Choking down the pain medication she thumped her glass on the counter and made her way to the door, wishing she hadn't been so thorough when she secured her house.

"Coming, I'll be right there."

Ashley finally made it to the door and looked through the peephole. A smirking Kelly stood on the other side with her hands up in the air. Ashley flung the door open and spread her arms wide, welcoming Kelly.

"Oh, Ash. You look scared. What's up?"

Pointing to the phone on the bar, Ashley's hand began to shake. "She's on the phone."

"What? She can't call your phone unless you accept the charges from jail. You know the rules."

Kelly was right. If a prisoner called from jail, a very long message informed the person receiving the call that they were accepting a call from someone in county jail and would be charged for the call, or something to that affect. It wasn't like Ashley had ever had to make a call from jail, but she was familiar with the basic procedure.

"No," Ashley said exasperated with the whole situation. "I have thirty seven messages on my phone, and so far the first three are from Leslie. I don't think I can listen to them, Kelly."

Kelly wrapped her arms around Ashley and hugged her. Ashley hadn't thought she was so fragile, but she had underestimated her mental state. Leslie would be an albatross around her neck for some time to come. She looked at the future and saw the next few weeks filled with questions, innuendos, and a lot of self-doubt.

"So you think you can listen to the rest of them?" Kelly looked at Ashley, but the woman looking back at Kelly wasn't the strong, brave police officer she worked with, Ashley was an innocent woman who almost had her life jerked from her just a few days ago. "Come on, let's sit down and figure out what we have to do."

Chapter Thirty

Tyler dialed Kelly's number and waited. She had called the hospital earlier to let Ashley know she had been released, and was informed Ashley was already gone. She had felt compelled to tell Ashley of her release so Ashley didn't show up to her room only to find out Tyler had been discharged. Rubbing her lips she thought about the kiss she had shared with Ashley, if you could call it sharing. The whole experience left Tyler more unsettled than the shooting had.

"Hey, Sparky." Kelly's voice bubbled through the phone.

"Hey Kelly. What're you doing?" Tyler hoped Kelly would give her Ashley's phone number or at least pass a message to her.

"Oh," Kelly paused, looking at Ashley staring at the phone on the coffee table. How much could Kelly tell Tyler? Then, she continued, "Just taking a break. What's up?"

"Hey, I was wondering if you had Ashley's number. I got released from the hospital today, and oh, I don't know, I just wanted to let her know. I...well...I just thought if she needed someone to talk to, you know... that. Oh shoot, forget it. How's Michael?" Tyler made a quick subject change as she struggled with her feelings. It wasn't like her to be so indecisive about a woman, but Ashley was different.

Tyler heard the mouthpiece covered and mumbling

before Kelly came back on. "I'm with Ashley right now, but I can't stay." Kelly covered the phone again and Tyler heard more mumbling. "Do you think you can come over? I don't think she should be alone right now. She got a few messages…" Tyler heard Kelly stop mid-sentence and say something to Ashley. "She says you don't have to come over. It's no big deal."

"Ask her if she's eaten," Tyler requested.

More mumbling on the other end of the phone made Tyler smile. Clearly, they were having a heated discussion and Tyler wasn't sure if it was because of her or because Ashley felt she could take care of herself. If Tyler were guessing, it was the fact Ashley could take care of herself and was incensed that Kelly would assume differently.

"Thai is good. Bring enough for three and how about something to drink, too. She doesn't have anything here."

"You got it. See you in a few," Tyler said almost closing her phone. "Wait, wait. Where does she live?"

A quick mental note and Tyler was on her way. Grabbing her cane she walked to the phone and stopped. *Oh shit, the doctor hasn't cleared me for driving.* Pausing, she briefly considered calling Kelly back, but dashed the thought. She could handle her truck. It was her motorcycle the doctor said she couldn't drive, right?

She could hear the doctor's voice telling her she needed at least a week, if not two, of bed rest. 'A little walking, but take it easy. Your body has been through a traumatic event and it's not at a hundred percent. Heck, it isn't even at seventy five percent.' Tyler didn't know what that meant, but she felt good. Screw it. She felt better than she had in a week, and if she sat around she would go crazy. Besides, Thai sounded good.

Placing her order at a Thai restaurant close to Ashley's, she grabbed her jacket, two pillows from her bed and her keys, then hobbled her way to the door. Whatever was going on at Ashley's didn't sound good and Kelly was on shift tonight, so she wouldn't be able to stay too long with Ashley. So, Tyler would be Kelly's surrogate. She was okay with that. Besides it was a great excuse to see Ashley again, wasn't it?

Tyler looked at her truck, then to her car and back again. Biting her lip she changed her mind and tossed the pillows on the driver's seat of the car. While she loved her truck, and how powerful it made her feel, right now comfort overrode power. Sitting easily in the driver's seat, Tyler grunted then closed her eyes tightly, hoping the pain would subside enough so she could drive. If not, she had two choices, take a pain pill or call Kelly and beg off. Neither choice was an option, actually. Tyler wouldn't get a DUI and lose her career over a little pain and she really wanted to see Ashley, so she would gut it out. Starting the car, Tyler had one thought, *thank God it's an automatic.*

Chapter Thirty-one

The trip to the Thai restaurant stressed Tyler's leg more than she liked. But the smell of the food was a great payoff for the pain. She had tired of the hospital food quickly and was glad when her buddies had slipped in a couple of slices of pizza. Now, her mouth watered at the intoxicating aroma. A few more minutes and she would have a mouthful of goodness and she wouldn't stop until she was satisfied.

Looking down the street, Tyler spotted Kelly's cruiser. Pulling into the driveway, Tyler studied Ashley's house. It wasn't just in a good neighborhood, it was in one of the older, more established neighborhoods in the city. Nice, was all Tyler could think as she looked at the manicured lawn and hedges. This beat her average home, in her average working class neighborhood. An SUV, clearly needing a wash, sat in the driveway. Honking her horn, Tyler waited until she saw Kelly look out the front window and motioned for Kelly to come out.

"Wow, Kell, not exactly what I was expecting," Tyler said still admiring the house.

"Yeah, I was surprised the first time I saw it, too. Seems her grandfather left it to her in his will. Lucky girl, huh?" Kelly grabbed the food and the wine while Tyler grabbed her pillows and cane.

"Yeah, some people have all the luck." Tyler smiled, walking toward the beautiful home. She wondered what other surprises it held.

"Hey, who's this for?" Kelly said picking up the small bouquet of flowers and smiling.

Blushing, Tyler said, "Not for you, silly." Tyler grabbed the flowers and smiled, embarrassed that she had thought of Ashley that way. "I thought they would cheer Ashley up. That's all," Tyler said walking past Kelly.

"Uh huh."

"What? Didn't you take her flowers in the hospital?"

"Of course, she's my partner."

"Well, I didn't see any from you in my room and I'm your best friend." Tyler smirked at the stinging remark.

"Yeah, but you're a—" Kelly stammered.

"What?" Tyler asked, cutting off her friend.

"You know. You're like one of the guys, Ty. You know, one of the guys."

"Hmm," Tyler grunted walking into the house.

Tyler was startled by what she saw as she entered the brightly lit house. Ashley sat curled up on the couch. The brave woman she had seen at the hospital and the strong woman she had seen wearing her police uniform were both gone, replaced with a pale, fragile, scared imposter. Her heart ached for Ashley. Whatever Ashley was going through, Tyler wished she could make it go away. Tyler heard plates rattling and boxes opening in the kitchen as Kelly served up dinner. Unsure of what to say or do, Tyler limped over to Ashley and sat next to her, rubbing Ashley's leg.

"Hey," Tyler said softly. "It'll be okay, I promise." Tyler smiled, raised her eyebrows and shyly presented Ashley with the bouquet.

"Oh, Tyler, how sweet. They're beautiful."

The moment was short lived as Ashley looked up at Tyler and gave a weak smile, then looked at the phone on the table.

"She called me and taunted me while she shot at us," Ashley said pointing to the phone. "She just won't leave me alone, Tyler."

"Sure she will. She's in jail now. She can't hurt you anymore." Tyler still stroked the soft pajama clad leg and smiled. "I'm not going to let her hurt you again, Ashley, and neither will anyone else. Okay? You need to try and relax. I know it's hard, but you have to try."

Ashley nodded her head and then looked at Tyler. Tyler's heart melted as she studied Ashley's petite face. Her green eyes looked lost somewhere in the past. Tyler wished she could help Ashley find what was lost those many months ago when the abuse had started and give it back to her. Innocence wasn't something only the young had. It was something people like Ashley had, like the hope for a better tomorrow or the belief that they could always find the good in someone. That kind of innocence was beyond Tyler's reasoning. She had lost that years ago in a war on another continent. But seeing Ashley lose it was heartbreaking for Tyler. It made Tyler want to scoop Ashley up and cuddle her like a child and tell her everything was going to be fine. No matter what happened, it would be all right and Tyler would make sure of it.

"Here we go. Hmm, this smells great. Thanks, Tyler, for picking this up." Kelly set the plates down and went back to the kitchen. "What do you gals want to drink? Wine, soda or water."

"Make mine water, Kelly." Turning towards Ashley, Tyler whispered, "What would you like, Ashley?"

"Water's fine." Ashley sat up, groaning as sore muscles reminded her that staying in one spot too long was a no-no. "You know what? I think I'll have a glass of wine."

Tyler raised her eyebrows and wondered when the last time was that Ashley had any pain medication.

"When was the last time you had some pain medication?"

"When I left the hospital …" Reaching mindlessly for her cell phone and tapping the screen, she continued, "four hours ago."

"Would you rather have meds or wine?"

Ashley raised her eyebrows at Tyler and looked at her quizzically. "Really?"

"I'm just asking. You're in a weird place right now and," Tyler placed her hand on Ashley's arm and tried to sound understanding, "I just don't want you to mix alcohol and drugs. I'm not your mom, Ashley, just someone who cares."

"I know. You're right. Water's fine." Ashley patted Tyler's hand and smiled.

Tyler winked at Ashley, out of habit more than anything. But a smile was her reward so the infraction was worth it if Ashley relaxed. Pulling the coffee table closer to them, Tyler poked around her food. The aroma was delightful and Tyler was ready for her first real food since leaving the hospital. With the exception of the pizza that had been snuck in, Tyler had lived off stuff she never wanted to see again, gelatin being one of them. Kelly joined the group, passing out waters, sat down and started eating. Both women watched as Kelly inhaled the Thai food. When she was done she set the bowl down and exhaled.

"What?" Kelly questioned as both women stared with their mouths open. "I was hungry and I have to get back on duty. Besides, you know I love Thai." Kelly stood and took her bowl to the kitchen and yelled back at the two women, "You gals need anything before I go?"

Tyler looked at Ashley who was shaking her head, "No. I think we're good."

Coming out of the kitchen Kelly tossed a rag at Tyler, hitting her in the face, and sat back down.

"What was that for?"

"In case you make a mess, Sparky. I don't want you to have to get up too often, and I know what a messy eater you are." Kelly smiled at Tyler.

"Thanks, LEO," Tyler quipped right back.

"Well I'd love to sit and chit chat, but someone has to keep this city safe," Kelly said, smiling back at Tyler. "Okay, I can trust you to behave yourself, right?"

Tyler stared at Kelly and the innuendo she threw out like a bomb. She was going to have to have a long talk with Kelly, but now wasn't the time. So she let the comment slide, for now.

"Not to worry. I'm sure Ashley will be on her best behavior," Tyler said, redirecting the comment. Smiling at Ashley, she said, "Just kidding. We'll be fine. Thanks for asking."

"Okay, well, I'm off. If you need anything call me," Kelly said making a phone gesture and raising it to her face. "I'll be close by."

"Good night, Officer." Tyler said turning back to her food.

"Good night, Sparky." Kelly looked at Ashley and, in a softer tone, said, "Let me know if you need anything, Buddy. Anything. Okay?"

Smiling back, Ashley said, "I'll be fine. Don't worry. Be careful out there."

"Will do. Good night you two."

The door closed quietly leaving the two women in silence. The aroma of the food filtered through the front room and Tyler's mouth watered as she eyed the plate. Looking over at Ashley, she took Ashley's plate from the coffee table and handed it to her, along with a fork.

"You look like you could use a good meal," Tyler said picking up her own plate and settling back against the couch. The smells of lemon and cilantro made Tyler's stomach growl. She hadn't had Thai in a long time. Twirling her fork in the rice noodles she lifted it, losing some along the way, and filled her mouth. The flavors danced on her tongue as she closed her eyes and slowly chewed. Ecstasy, pure unadulterated ecstasy on the taste buds. Tyler blushed when she heard a moan escape her. Food was something she rarely took pleasure in, but the bland hospital food had left an impression on Tyler and not a good one.

Tyler looked over at Ashley in her embarrassment and saw her cock an eyebrow and smile. Clearly, Ashley was enjoying the display Tyler was putting on and all Tyler could do was smile back.

"Good, huh?"

"Sorry, I'm not usually a foodie, but this is so good." Tyler motioned with her fork towards Ashley's plate. "Try it."

Ashley twirled her fork in the noodles and slipped them in her mouth. Looking at the pursed lips, a surge of pleasure shot right through Tyler as she watched Ashley slowly chew and then snake her tongue out and lick sauce from her lips. A smile caressed Ashley's face and Tyler had to turn away to keep her composure. This was going to be an exercise in restraint if Tyler watched Ashley eat, so she focused on her own plate, moving to try something else that looked delicious.

A groan reached Tyler's ears and she tried not to turn and look at Ashley. She knew Ashley was having the same food orgasm she just had and didn't want to see it. The visuals in her head were enough to make Tyler come unglued.

"You're right, this is good. God, I haven't had a decent meal in weeks." Ashley moaned again stuffing more noodles in her mouth.

Without thinking Tyler looked over at Ashley, who was clearly enjoying her dinner, and watched as she made love to her food. Okay, at least that's what Tyler thought she was doing as Ashley savored each bite, licking her lips every time she finished a mouthful. This was harder than watching a porn movie when she was horny. Grabbing her water bottle, she practically drained it in one gulp. Anything to distract her from watching Ashley right now was a welcome diversion. *How could food be so sexy,* she wondered. Obviously, she had meals with other women, but Ashley made it seem so inviting or was she just imagining everything?

Finishing her food, she slowly stood and grabbed her plate and empty water bottle and walked towards the kitchen.

"Would you like more?" She said over her shoulder, not wanting to look at Ashley.

"Hmm, maybe. What do we have left?"

Tyler squeezed her eyes shut when she heard Ashley let out a little groan. *Oh God, this is torture,* she thought, spooning a smaller serving of food on her plate. She almost reconsidered any more food since this was the first real meal she had since leaving the hospital. She didn't want to get sick by over indulging.

"Everything," Tyler said trying not to look out at Ashley.

"No, I better not. I don't want to get sick, especially since I really haven't had a lot of solid foods yet. But you go ahead. I would hate to see it go to waste."

Tyler sighed in relief. Watching Ashley eat was pricking every nerve she had. The problem was Tyler liked the feeling. Oh, what was she doing here? All Tyler wanted to do was let Ashley know she had been released from the hospital, and instead Kelly had roped Tyler into bringing dinner over. At least that was how Tyler wanted to remember it. Now, she was here with a woman she found herself slowly falling for. It was troubling to Tyler how easily she found herself thinking about Ashley.

Walking back into the living room with her plate, she tried to avoid looking at Ashley as she finished her last bite. A delightful hum was coming from Ashley's side of the couch making it nearly impossible for Tyler to eat. Accepting she wasn't going to finish her dinner, she set her plate down and grabbed her new water bottle and settled back on the couch facing Ashley. Smiling, she sipped her water and just watched. She would readily accept defeat if it meant indulging her need for torture.

"What?" Ashley questioned, wiping her mouth and struggling to sit upright.

"Hmm, oh nothing," Tyler said reaching for Ashley's plate and napkin. "Let me get that for you."

"Thanks, I don't think I'm as mobile as I think I am." Ashley readjusted her position on the couch, facing Tyler.

Nothing was said as each woman studied the other. Each gazed at the other's face; one noticing the marks where a mic had exploded next to her face, the other admiring the strong jaw and purposeful eyes. The silence seemed to last forever.

Chapter Thirty-two

Ashley watched Tyler fidgeting with a thread on her sleeve. She had been on pins and needles ever since Tyler arrived. Hating herself, she wished Kelly had left earlier, leaving her and Tyler alone. Alone for what she wasn't sure, but she could feel herself warm when Tyler had caressed her leg earlier.

"I like your new haircut."

Tyler reflexively ran her fingers through her hair, the compliment making her blush.

"Do you do that often?" Ashley inquired.

"What?"

"Blush when someone pays you a compliment," Ashley said, smiling as the blush deepened.

"Not usually. No." Tyler cast her gaze down at her hands as she tried to figure out why she was blushing. Bedroom talk, as Tyler referred to it. She had heard plenty of compliments before, but usually from women who wanted something from her, like sex.

"I see," was all Ashley could say.

"So, how are the shoulder and ribs?"

Ashley smiled as Tyler tried to change the subject. "Sore, but I'll survive."

Ashley instinctively rubbed her sore shoulder and grimaced.

"I'm really glad you weren't seriously hurt. I mean...." Tyler said looking up at Ashley.

"I know what you mean," Ashley said, noticing how

uncomfortable Tyler was finishing her sentence. "How's your ass?" Ashley gave Tyler a mischievous grin and chuckled. "I'm sorry, I shouldn't have laughed. I'm sure it hurts like hell."

"It's okay. I like to see you smile, even if it's at my expense. It's good. I should be ready to go back to light duty in a week. The doctor said two weeks, but I can't sit around the house that long. I'll go crazy," Tyler said, still playing with a string that had come loose on her shirt.

"I know what you mean. My doctor said, 'let's wait a week and see how thing go'. So I have no idea when I'll be going back to work. Sooner rather than later, I hope."

The silence lingered long enough that it made Ashley uncomfortable. She had wanted to be alone with Tyler, but she couldn't figure out what to do now that she finally was. Trying to stretch out on the couch, Ashley groaned. A shooting pain splintered through her rib cage.

"Careful. Here, let me give you a hand," Tyler said moving off the sofa and standing next to Ashley. She felt Tyler slowly move her hands down her legs, trying to move them. Electricity shot right through her body at the touch.

Ashley tried to get herself off the couch, but was having little success. "Do you think you can help me up? I can't sit here any longer. I need to walk."

"Sure. Here let me grab your upper arm and—"

Ashley felt Tyler lift her off the couch, her body cradled tightly against Tyler's chest. Tyler didn't give as much as a grunt when she picked Ashley up. Surprised, Ashley found herself face to face with a smiling Tyler. Tyler's eyes were alluring, and Ashley felt herself get lost in Tyler's seductive gaze. A tongue slipped from

Tyler's lips, smoothed them and retreated back. Without thinking Ashley licked her own lips in response and bent closer to kiss Tyler. Soft, firm lips returned Ashley's kiss and waited. Pulling away from the kiss, Ashley looked first at Tyler's lips then her eyes. It was clear to Ashley that Tyler had enjoyed the kiss as much as she had.

"You can put me down now," Ashley whispered.

"What if I don't want to?" Tyler whispered back. "What if I want to stand right here and kiss you again?" Tyler smiled and cocked an eyebrow.

Ashley felt her body responding to the suggestion. Her nipples ached to be touched, her body craved the caresses that loving Tyler could give her. She could no longer deny the attraction she was feeling for Tyler. Ashley let herself get lost in the brown eyes that seemed to need her as well. She felt Tyler turn and slowly sit back down on the couch. Ashley was now firmly planted in her lap.

"Now what?" Tyler asked.

"What do you mean?" Ashley questioned staring back at Tyler. Lust oozed off of Tyler and hit Ashley in waves. She wasn't in the mood for talking, but she wasn't sure her body had the ability to make love, at least not the way she wanted to make love, with wild abandon. She was ready to shake the tendrils of Leslie from her mind and body and replace them with fresh memories of someone like Tyler.

"We could play twenty questions all night, Ashley, but I think you know what I mean. You kissed me, but I'm assuming you want something more than a little first base action. But, then again, I could be wrong. Am I?"

Ashley blushed at the statement and looked down. Before she could say anything, Tyler lifted her chin and pulled her in for another kiss. Ashley felt Tyler caress her face then weave her fingers into Ashley's hair and hold her closer. Tyler's tongue slid against Ashley's lips begging for entrance. Without thinking, Ashley relented and slid her own tongue against Tyler's. Someone let out a moan, fanning the flames further.

Tyler's hand slid down Ashley's injured shoulder, giving it a gentle squeeze and then moved closer to her breast, stopping short of the assumed target. Disappointed that it hadn't completed its journey, Ashley gently moved it over her breast and helped knead the hard peak of a nipple. Electricity shot through her body as she felt Tyler pinch the hardened tip. Her body responded again as her pussy clenched. She knew she was losing control, but she didn't care. She wanted this as much as Tyler did and her shoulder and ribs be damned, she was going to make love to this woman one way or the other. Breaking off the kiss, Ashley panted.

"I guess that answers your question," Ashley responded, moving her arm around Tyler's neck and pulling her down for another kiss.

"I guess it does, but we're a little further than first base. Do you want to stop?"

"Do you ask your other dates if they want to stop?" Ashley looked up at smiling eyes and knew the answer before Tyler could even give voice to it. "I didn't think so."

Before she could return for another kiss, Tyler's slender finger touched her lips and stopped her progress. "But they weren't injured. You are and I would hate to take advantage of you in this condition."

"I find it hard to believe you've never dealt with a woman that wanted you, Tyler. Besides, my ribs are injured, not my brain. So, I can assure you I know what I'm doing. But if you're in no condition," Ashley said trying to dislodge herself from Tyler's lap with no luck.

"Oh, my condition is just fine. Trust me."

Ashley felt Tyler pull her hips firmly into Tyler's lap. Ashley slid her arm back around Tyler's neck and smiled into a smoldering gaze that set Ashley's body on fire.

Standing, Tyler looked at Ashley and continued, "Still want to go for that walk?"

Chapter Thirty-three

Tyler felt like her skin was on fire where Ashley slid down her body. When their eyes met, Tyler knew what she wanted to hear and Ashley's eyes gave away her answer. Could she give Ashley what she wanted? Ashley's head rested on Tyler's chest for the briefest of moments while her fingers intertwined with Tyler's. Gently wrapping Ashley in an embrace, she kissed the top of Ashley's head, and then rested her cheek against her forehead. A long deep sigh escaped Tyler's lips as she tipped Ashley's chin up to meet her gaze. There were no words needed for the conversation their bodies were struggling with.

"A walk?"

Tyler watched as Ashley shook her head and gently led Tyler toward her bedroom. Tyler struggled with her emotions. On the one hand she ached for Ashley, on the other she worried that the accident might have clouded Ashley's judgment and how she saw Tyler. Tyler halted their progress and turned Ashley to face her.

"Tyler, I know what I want. Trust me," Ashley whispered, pulling Tyler.

"Ashley." The name died on Tyler's lips as Ashley placed a delicate kiss on the back of her hand. Her heart fluttered at the simple tenderness of Ashley's lips lingering on her hand. Another pull and Tyler found herself firmly inside Ashley's darkened bedroom. Without a clue of where to step, she was guided to the bed and instructed to sit. Tyler felt Ashley kneel between her legs and rest her head in Tyler's lap. Without thinking, Tyler ran her fingers through the soft locks of hair, finding comfort in the intimate act. Her mind tossed away all the reasons she shouldn't be doing this and focused on the one reason she wanted to, Ashley.

For once Jill didn't cloud her mind, pull at her guilt, or push every other woman out. This felt so right on so many levels and Tyler was at a loss to explain it. Jill's words from the hospital room came back to her. *She's a wonderful woman, Tyler.* Tyler looked down at Ashley and ran her fingers through her hair again.

Pulling the covers back, Tyler gently lifted Ashley up and sat her on the bed. This time, Tyler knelt in front of Ashley and brought Ashley's hands to her lips. When Ashley reached for Tyler's face, Tyler kissed the palm of her left hand and let her tongue gently make its way to the tip of a finger, sucking it into her mouth. A slow caress back and forth on the tip and Tyler heard Ashley moan. Tyler ached for Ashley, her body craved Ashley's touch and electricity surged through her when Ashley moaned again at the continued friction of Tyler's tongue against her finger.

"Tyler, you're killing me. Please…." the sentence died on Ashley's lips and she slipped another finger into Tyler's mouth.

The gentle sucking nearly drove Tyler crazy, feeling the charge down to her toes. She released Ashley's hand and moved above her. *Careful not to push too hard.* Tyler laid Ashley on the bed and slid up beside her, trying to protect Ashley's injured shoulder. Her long body cradled against Ashley's petite one. Ashley lifted her head and rested it on Tyler's shoulder, snuggling in closer. Tyler wrapped Ashley protectively in a strong embrace. The quiet of the room lent to the protective cocoon Tyler found herself in mentally. Tyler pulled on the legs of her jeans trying to ease the rough contact on her already stimulated clit. Shifting once more she tried twisting and spreading her legs in an attempt to ease her discomfort.

"Why don't you take your pants off?" Ashley asked, lifting her head up and looking at Tyler.

"I don't think that would be a good idea?" Tyler was sure her throaty response gave away how turned on she was.

"Tyler, I see women in their underwear all the time in the locker room," Ashley said, trying to sound dispassionate.

"That would be fine if I was wearing underwear, but my briefs were rubbing against the bandage and cutting into the stitches, so I opted to go without." Tyler blushed at the declaration.

All of a sudden Tyler felt awkward, almost shy at the revelation. She felt like a schoolgirl with her first girlfriend. The warmth of Ashley's body against hers and knowing there wasn't anything she would be able to do about it until she got home prolonged her agony. The gentle kisses and touching earlier were enough to drive her body straight over the edge she was teetering on. Perhaps she should go home. Her nerves were just about to snap and she knew the only thing that would help her currently sat in a drawer in her nightstand. It had been at least a week since her last orgasm. In fact, she remembered the shower quiet vividly now. She flinched when Ashley placed a hand on her stomach.

"I'm sorry. Does that hurt?" Ashley pulled her hand back and tucked it between their bodies.

The slow burn Tyler was going through showed no

signs of letting up so she needed to come clean, relatively speaking. "I'm sorry, Ashley. It isn't you, it's me." Tyler turned so she was facing Ashley and continued, "I really like you." Tyler grabbed Ashley's hand and brought it to her lips. "I mean, I really like you and I worry that you're going through some really heavy stuff right now and might be mistaking your feeling of being rescued for something else."

"Stop. I know what you're trying to say. I understand that you think that somehow what I feel for you is because you saved my life." Shaking her head, Ashley continued, "I'm not some delusional woman who falls for her rescuer. Not that you're not something to fall for, I mean." Ashley scrubbed her face and then ran her hand through her hair. Frustrated she continued, "Look, I'm not explaining this very well. Maybe it's the medication, maybe it's the stress of the situation, but I've been interested in you for a while. I don't wear my feelings on my sleeve or anything, but obviously Kelly warning me off you should have told *you* something."

"Okay," Tyler said waiting for Ashley to finish.

"Okay what?"

"Well, you obviously knew I was interested in you at the bar, otherwise you wouldn't have been so quick to shoot me down."

"Yeah, but were you interested in me for the night or...oh it doesn't matter."

Tyler watched in the darkness as Ashley retreated and surrendered emotionally. Moving closer to Ashley, Tyler's finger followed the contour of Ashley's face and then moved over her lips. A soft kiss replaced Tyler's fingers. Moving back Tyler studied Ashley's face.

"Will you stay? I don't think I want to be alone tonight." Ashley's request was barely a whisper as she moved closer to Tyler.

"Sure."

"Just one thing," Ashley said. "I don't like shoes on the bed and, since you're staying, there are some boxers in the second drawer on the right." Pointing in the direction of the dresser, Ashley continued, "You might as well get comfortable, right?"

Chapter Thirty-four

The silence in the house kept Ashley awake. The hospital had been full of activity, even in the dead of night. Nurses making rounds, checking vital signs, moving from room to room made for long nights. But now that Ashley was home and in her own bed she was wide awake. No activity meant no sleep. Lying around all day dozing on and off didn't help her insomnia and now, lying next to Tyler made things worse. The slow, deep breaths of her bedmate were a noise she hadn't heard in a long time. If she remembered correctly, it took a few weeks to get used to having Leslie in her bed. But listening to Tyler's breathing wasn't the problem. The fact that she laid almost spread eagle on the bed was.

Tyler had tossed the covers off herself and onto Ashley sometime in the night. Sweating, Ashley woke up to find herself pinned under a pile of blankets and a leg. Trying not to move too much, she slid Tyler's leg off, expending what little energy she had. Now, she needed to go to the bathroom and take more medication or the night would drag on forever as the pain of wresting with the blankets took its toll. Looking over at Tyler, Ashley noticed that the t-shirt she wore rode up and exposed the soft skin of Tyler's stomach. Looking further down Tyler's body, Ashley couldn't help but notice how tight the boxers fit Tyler. Ashley let out a deep breath trying to calm the butterflies that had quickly taken up residence.

A touch, just one little caress along Tyler's taut stomach would be enough to satisfy her. At least, that's what she hoped kicking the blankets to the floor.

Ashley's fingertips touched the taut muscles first. Feathery light, she moved them across Tyler's stomach and watched as a slight contraction made the muscles twitch. Biting her lip, she looked back to Tyler's face, the sleeping expression hadn't changed. But the t-shirt gave a hint to Tyler's body responding when Ashley noticed firm nipples peaked under the fabric. Her gaze lowered back to where she was pulling her hand back across Tyler's stomach. Goose bumps covered Tyler's stomach this time. Before Ashley could move her hand away, Tyler captured and held it to her stomach.

"Two can play that game you know?" Tyler whispered into Ashley's ear.

"I'm sorry, Tyler. I saw you laying there and I just…." Ashley said, thankful Tyler couldn't see her blushing.

Ashley tried to pull her hand back, but Tyler had it firmly in her grasp. Looking at Tyler, she felt as if she was being devoured by the smoldering gaze. Pushed to her back, Tyler moved to kiss her neck. The touch made Ashley flush and sent a surge of electricity straight through her body to her clit. Without realizing it, the buttons to her pajamas were quickly opened and Ashley felt Tyler's hand roaming over her stomach. Ashley's head spun as touches were replaced with kisses and little nips on her skin. Ashley threaded her fingers into Tyler's hair and moaned as Tyler moved lower.

"Do you want me to stop?" Tyler asked so seductively that Ashley didn't think she could eke out a response if she wanted to, so she shook her head.

"Sure?"

Ashley knew she was being given an out, but she just couldn't find it in herself to say yes. Closing her eyes, she laid her head back on the pillow and waited. She felt Tyler's breasts slide up her body. Opening her eyes, she stared into understanding brown eyes that made her heart beat faster. There was no way she would turn this woman down and she knew it. Ashley felt protected as Tyler settle on her elbows keeping most of her weight off of Ashley's body. The butterflies rumbled around in her again as she moved to kiss Tyler's soft lips.

Ashley felt Tyler moving to her left side and mold her body against Ashley's. Ashley's body throbbed as Tyler slid a thigh between her legs and gently slid it over her hard clit. Turning towards Tyler, she groaned as Tyler pulled her hip into the motion and ground harder on Ashley. Begging for release Ashley lifted her hips up and craved deeper contact, feeling the start of an orgasm tremble lower in her body. A spike went through her when Tyler's lips grabbed her nipple and gently tugged on it. Rolling the tip of her tongue over Ashley's nipple served its purpose as Ashley started to come. Each stroke of Tyler's thigh against her clit drew Ashley faster and faster into the orgasm. Closing her eyes she threw her head back and gasped as she peaked. Slow shudders ebbed through Ashley's body as Tyler continued to stroke her clit with her fingers. Working the hard nub faster, Tyler moved up and licked Ashley's neck before she placed a kiss on it. A low whisper in Ashley's ear pulled her further into the moment.

"That's it. Spread your legs for me. I want to feel your wetness all over my fingers." Ashley's nerves fired all at once as Tyler continued, "Oh, you're really wet Ash. I bet you taste good, too."

Ashley never had someone talk to her during

sex and she was almost ready to jump out of her skin the more Tyler talked. She could hear Tyler's breathing speed up as she worked her fingers deeper into Ashley. She never came more than once during sex, so she wasn't sure how much more she could take as Tyler whispered into her ear again.

"Oh, I can feel your muscles tightening around my fingers. You're so close, just let it come, Ash. Just let it come."

Ashley felt the pressure of Tyler's fingers curling up into her vagina and stroking her. Each stroke went a little deeper as Tyler worked Ashley's wet pussy. A tremor started to build and before Ashley could do anything her body rocked back and forth on Tyler's hand. Her muscles tightened then released with each spasm of her orgasm. Grabbing Tyler's wrist, she stopped the movement and let the orgasm roll through her body.

"Oh fuck," Ashley said, forcing Tyler's hand deeper inside.

Ashley felt empty the minute Tyler pulled her hand from her body. A warm feeling replaced it when Tyler wrapped her arms around Ashley, gently pulling Ashley on top of her. Laying her head on Tyler's chest, she listened to Tyler's heart beat against her ear. Tears rolled down her cheek and she tried to wipe them before they fell on Tyler's chest, but she wasn't able to stop them once they started. Ashley didn't know why she was crying and could only hope that Tyler wouldn't notice. Controlling her emotions were usually her strong suit and she had learned to keep them well hidden at all times, but it was like someone had released the flood gates and she couldn't stop crying.

"Hey. Why the tears? Are you okay? Oh god, I'm so sorry. I shouldn't have pushed you." The regret in Tyler's voice only made Ashley cry harder. "I don't know what came over me."

"It's okay. It's not you, really." Ashley rolled off of Tyler and wiped her eyes with her pajamas. "That was the most amazing thing I've ever experienced, Tyler. I don't know why I'm crying, honestly." Ashley covered her eyes with her arm too embarrassed to look at Tyler. "Maybe it's just the buildup of all those emotions coming to a head and sex was the release."

Ashley looked up at Tyler's face filled with concern. She felt so protected when she was with Tyler. Something about tonight gave Ashley the strength to let go of her emotions and be open with Tyler.

Tyler pulled Ashley back against her chest into a tight embrace. A grunt escaped Ashley's lips when her ribs made their presence known. The pain was shooting, but she didn't want to leave the tight embrace. The pounding orgasm made her injuries throb as well. Now she needed to get up and take something for the pain and quick. Before she could say anything Tyler was up, picking up the blankets off the floor and looking at Ashley smiling.

"Where are your pain meds?" Tyler inquired, pulling on the legs of the tight boxers.

Ashley felt her heart skip a beat as she looked at Tyler's messy hair, hard nipples and the way too small boxers she was wearing. Her life wasn't perfect, but if this kept up it was getting damn close.

Chapter Thirty-five

If someone had told Tyler that being shot would lead to the best thing in her life she wouldn't have just called them crazy, she probably would have laughed. But, here she was sitting in a coffee shop with Ashley, talking about nothing in particular, and people watching. The last few days had passed in a blur of sex, crying, talking and more sex. While Ashley had a hard time taking care of Tyler sexually, Ashley, on the other hand, had let Tyler sooth her, hold her, and protect her.

Tyler had accompanied Ashley to the station where Ashley had given a more thorough statement of the events leading up to the shooting. Kelly had taken Ashley's phone the night of Ashley's release from the hospital. She had given it to the detectives who were handling the investigation. While Tyler had little to tell, she knew Ashley would have to come clean on everything that included Leslie, from the abuse to the shooting. Tyler didn't like to think of the questions the detectives would ask Ashley about her relationship with Leslie, but it couldn't be helped. An officer involved shooting, regardless of whether the officer did the shooting, or an officer was shot brought in the big guns. At least that's what Kelly had told Tyler. Her heart ached for Ashley as she came out of the interrogation room, the remnants of tears covering her face, looking defeated. Wrapping her arms around Ashley, Tyler reminded her that she wasn't responsible for Leslie's actions.

Tyler watched Ashley stir her coffee with cool dispassion, knowing today had been the roughest day for Ashley as the district attorney questioned her about the abuse. The trial was moving closer and Tyler knew it would be hard for Ashley, since Ashley wanted to attend.

Another minute passed and Ashley asked, "So, why did you stop being a paramedic?"

Tyler dropped the spoon on the table and looked up at Ashley. "Why?"

"Yeah, why did you go back to being a firefighter?"

"Well—" Tyler scanned the crowded coffee shop, hoping to recognize someone she knew to avoid the question.

"Look, if it's too personal, you don't have to answer. I was just wondering what causes someone to go from saving lives to running into burning buildings, risking their own instead."

Tyler looked at Ashley. Her eyes were so green, like someplace Tyler always wanted to get lost in lately. Remembering the day Jill died made her hands shake. Clasping them together, she stuck them between her thighs hoping to stop the tremor.

"I happened to switch shifts with another firefighter so he could get married. I wasn't supposed to be on duty that day." Slowly, Tyler retold the story of what had happened the day Jill died. Never looking at Ashley, she only watched the swirling coffee in her cup. Finishing she looked up at Ashley who had tears threatening to drop and her heart ached. Ashley gave her a reassuring smile and then wiped at her eyes.

"Tyler, I'm sorry I asked," Ashley said, covering

Tyler's hands. The warm comfort made Tyler smile. Things had changed for Tyler. Before she wouldn't have been able to share the story with anyone and now she was telling Ashley everything.

Tyler acknowledged the comment with a weak smile and continued, "When Jill was shot, my mom was my rock. She got me through the first couple of weeks." Tyler's eyes, now vacant, looked at something only visible to her. Her fingers rubbed little patterns on the table as she thought about those days. Tyler was quickly lost in her nightmare. She explained how she didn't think she needed to see a shrink, but the department had mandated it since it was her wife. She told Ashley how she had lied her way through the whole session and every session after that. She'd do anything to get through that hour of hell, once a week. She hadn't thought about that moment lately. Now that she had started, she couldn't seem to stop herself from telling Ashley everything. For some reason, Ashley made it easy to talk about the past. Tyler looked into her eager eyes as she thought about Jill and her mom.

"Two weeks later, I was on duty when a head-on collision with fatalities was called in. My squad rolled on it," Tyler said, her mouth dry. "When we got there, the two vehicles were totaled. We were told it was now an extraction, but we had to make sure."

Tyler took a deep breath and bit her top lip, then continued, "As I was walking to one of the cars, I noticed a woman's purse about a yard from the vehicle. It a…" Tyler swallowed hard and took another deep breath before continuing. "For some reason I picked up the purse and opened it. Sitting right on top were my mom's reading glasses in a case I had bought for her when I went to Hawaii."

"Oh Tyler."

Tyler felt Ashley stroke her hand, trying to comfort her.

In a trance-like state, she continued her story, "I dropped everything, the purse, the med kit, my helmet and ran to the car, but it was too late." Tears clouded her vision and she wiped them with the back of her hand. "The car was on its top and I dropped to my knees, praying it wasn't my mom. There had to be a mistake, there just had to be."

Tyler rubbed her lips wondering how far she would be able to go.

"Tyler, you don't have to say anymore. I think I understand," Ashley said, reaching across the table and grasping both her hands.

"No, you wanted to know why I'm not a paramedic. Now you'll know." Determined to finish her story Tyler started again, "I looked in the vehicle and there she was. She looked like she was sleeping, but with cuts and bruises. I gently shook her, nothing. I reached for a pulse, nothing. She was gone. By the time I stood up my dad was there."

"How did your dad get there so quick?"

"He's the Fire Chief. He was already on his way. Standard procedure," Tyler said, shrugging her shoulders and swallowing hard again. "She was my best friend, after Jill. I couldn't believe it. It damn near killed my dad. We had to hold him back—keep him from seeing her like that."

"Oh Tyler, I'm so sorry," Ashley whispered.

Tyler didn't hear Ashley, too lost in her misery. She continued, "My mom and I were supposed to go to Hawaii the following day for a vacation, get way from everything. My mom and Jill loved Hawaii, now they're both gone."

Her memories brought her world crashing down on her and she wasn't sure she could handle it again. Ashley's strong arms wrapped around Tyler and rocked her back and forth. The soothing motion reminded Tyler of how her mom would rock her to sleep when she was little.

"Sometimes it's okay to let someone else shoulder your pain, Tyler," Ashley whispered, rocking Tyler.

Tyler felt the warmth of Ashley's breath on her face as she closed her eyes and cried. She had been strong for so long that it felt good to let go. Remembering where they were Tyler wiped her eyes and cleared her throat. Patting Ashley's arm she turned and placed a light kiss on her check and patted her lap for Ashley to sit.

"Really, Tyler? Here in front of everyone?"

Tyler liked pushing Ashley's comfort zone. She was used to being out and seen with women. It didn't really faze her when someone stared. Most people were smart enough not to try and take on the six foot woman. But every once in a while someone, usually a guy, had a comment that made Tyler shake her head. Most of them had to do with being the center of a chick sandwich or the possibility that they would need a man's help with something. Tyler just attributed them to repressed adolescence and moved on. She was sure Ashley, however, might blush at the comments.

She watched as Ashley opted for the seat next to hers, letting her hand rest on Tyler's thigh, an easy compromise Tyler didn't mind. Tyler went back to her favorite pastime lately, studying Ashley. The simplest things made Tyler's heart jump. The way her lips formed when she sucked on the straw in the mocha-something or other. The way she fingered her hair when she daydreamed or the way she looked after they made love. That lost in the moment look drove Tyler crazy and put her back in that mood all over again.

"Tyler?" Ashley said, running her fingers down the inside seam of Tyler's jeans.

"Huh?" Tyler felt her body tighten at the contact. Stopping Ashley's hand before it could do any more damage, Tyler looked up and found her frowning. "What's wrong?"

"I'm going to go see Leslie," Ashley said flatly.

"What?" Tyler tried to comprehend the statement before she said anything else.

"I think I need to face her. If I wait until court…I don't know what I'll do if she taunts me there and I know she will." Ashley stirred her drink trying not to look at Tyler.

"Well, we just won't look at her, that's all," Tyler said pulling Ashley's hand back into hers. "I don't think it's a good idea, Ash. I mean, she isn't right in the head and who knows what she'll say."

"Yeah, well how much more damage can she do, Tyler? I mean honestly. Besides, I need to know why?"

Ashley's question lingered for a moment as Tyler wondered the same thing more than once since the shooting. But a confrontation? What would Leslie say to Ashley knowing that everything was taped in the jail? Thinking about what she wanted to say, Tyler studied Ashley. Tyler's heart would break if Leslie said something to hurt Ashley and she knew that was a very real possibility. Tyler realized at that moment she was falling fast and hard for Ashley and she would hurt anyone who hurt Ashley.

"Ashley, what is it you think she'll tell you? This is crazy," Tyler said sliding her hand along Ashley's arm, trying to offer some reassurance she wasn't quite sure she felt.

"That's just it, Tyler. The D.A. told me she is pleading temporary insanity."

The fear in Ashley's eyes was palpable. The thought that Leslie was playing the insanity card was unbelievable. Even more unbelievable was that it was a real possibility a jury might find Leslie insane and put her in a State institution and not prison. Tyler had seen juries do strange things lately and this wasn't beyond reason.

"There's no way, Ashley. There's just no way that the D.A. is going to plead her out like that." Tyler refused to believe that with everything that had happened to them, the district attorney would do such a thing.

"She's not, but she said that Leslie's lawyer is working all the angles. The phone messages, the way she set everything up at the building, Leslie even had some stupid card or something in her car addressed to me."

"A card?"

"Yeah, it seems she got an anniversary card and wrote something about our supposed 'wedding anniversary'. I don't know, Tyler. It's just too weird and Leslie is just smart enough to have planned for every possibility."

Ashley scrubbed her face in frustration and then gave Tyler a weak smile.

"Ashley, she's a basket case, but she isn't your basket case to deal with," Tyler said stroking the back of Ashley's hand. She was hoping she was being supportive, but resolute in the fact that Ashley would only be hurt in an exchange with Leslie.

"Maybe she'll screw up and say something, Tyler. Maybe I can get her to admit to planning out the shooting."

Tyler felt like she needed to come clean before Ashley made any rash decision as far as Leslie was concerned. Seeing Leslie wasn't a deal breaker, and Ashley had to deal with what happened on her own terms, but Tyler wanted to protect Ashley. Being open was difficult for Tyler, but if she wanted to stay on the new path she had created, she needed to let Ashley know how she felt.

"Ashley," Tyler said studying their intertwined fingers. "I'm…a…well, I just want to say that…I…" Tyler felt her throat constrict and a lump form that she couldn't swallow down. This was harder than she expected, but Ashley's sudden proclamation that she wanted to see Leslie made Tyler wince in pain for her lover. "I just, "Tyler whispered rolling her eyes, and shaking her head. *Fuck, this is harder than I thought.*

"What's wrong, Tyler?" Ashley said running her fingers through Tyler's hair, pulling her head forward so that their foreheads touched. "Are you okay?"

"Ashley, these last few days have been wonderful and well, I'm falling for you." Tyler closed her eyes and waited.

"Tyler," Ashley whispered in Tyler's ear, "if you haven't noticed, I'm more than kind of falling for you, but I didn't want to say anything. With the shooting and all. I mean, well you know, the sex and everything, I just thought—"

"What," Tyler said, pulling back from the warm caress of Ashley's voice in her ear. "That you were just a conquest?" Tyler's voice trembled low giving away her fear of rejection.

Ashley blushed, then looked around the coffee shop. "No, not at all. I just thought I was moving too fast in my thought process."

"I'm sorry." Tyler paused briefly before she continued, "Look, if you want to see Leslie, I just want you to know you don't have to do this alone. I'm here for you and I want to be there when you see her."

Tyler felt a warm caress down her face as Ashley leaned in to kiss her. The ever present ache between Tyler's legs flared again and it was all she could do to keep it at a low roar. Tyler picked up Ashley's hand and kissed it, letting her lips linger. Laying Ashley's hand on her thigh she felt the familiar caress along the inside seam of her pant leg again. Smiling, she stopped the caress and moved closer to whisper in Ashley's ear.

"If you don't stop, I won't be responsible for actions and two can play this game, Ash," Tyler said, the warning sending another surge through her body.

Chapter Thirty-six

The stark white linoleum and steel of the jail made for a cold, unwelcoming environment. The glass walled partition between the prisoner and the visitor, while thick enough, wouldn't be enough in Ashley's mind to protect her from Leslie. Ashley looked at the clock on the wall and wished she could turn around and forget this crazy idea. What had possessed her to think she wanted to confront Leslie? Her heart was beating out of her chest as she watched each second tick by. It had been hard convincing Tyler she needed to do this alone, but Tyler had finally agreed. The compromise was Tyler would wait at Ashley's for Mongrel to be dropped off. Smiling to herself, Ashley was surprised how easily Tyler was starting to fit into her life.

When she had asked to see Leslie, everyone was against it. In fact, no one thought Leslie would even agree to the meeting. But Ashley knew Leslie. She was banking on Leslie's arrogance. Leslie would want to gloat, to taunt her, and to try to convince Ashley that it was all a big misunderstanding and that Lesley still loved her. Was Ashley ready for it? She wasn't sure, but she would show Leslie she was the one in control. Ashley wouldn't let Leslie victimize her any more.

Taking her place at the window, Ashley sat ramrod straight, her eyes focused on the door through which Leslie would arrive. Briefly, Ashley saw the uniform of a deputy sheriff pass in front of the sliver of a window then look through it. The slide of the lock grinding against the doorjamb sent a chill through Ashley as she watched a handcuffed Leslie step through. The over-sized orange jumpsuit Leslie wore hung on her, making her look frail and weak. But Ashley knew looks were deceiving when it came to Leslie.

The smirk on Leslie's face when she sat down told Ashley everything she needed to know about Leslie's attitude. What she wouldn't give to reach through that glass and smack it off her face. Winking at Ashley, Leslie made a motion for Ashley to pick up the phone on the wall next to her. The hair on the back of Ashley's neck stood as she picked up the receiver and pressed it to her ear. Steeling herself, she focused on Leslie's eyes and waited.

"Hey, beautiful, you look good." Leslie's low tenor assaulted Ashley's ear. "I'm glad you came. I've been worried about you."

That smirk, if Ashley could only smack that smirk off Leslie's face. Well, two could play whatever game Leslie decided to play today. Ashley would play along, for a little while at least.

"Hello, Leslie." The cool words oozed through the phone, but had no effect on Leslie's demeanor. Ashley waited though. She knew Leslie wouldn't be able to resist baiting her.

The way Leslie slowly closed her eyes and then let her gaze roam over Ashley almost made her want to throw up. It was the same old Leslie, trying her slow seduction, only this time the glass wall between them made her next predictable move impossible. Ashley's gaze never wavered, she didn't drop her eyes and only grunted in disgust at Leslie's attempt at seducing her.

"They tell me you were shot, Baby. Are you okay?"

Leslie softened her voice trying to pull Ashley in. "When I get out of here I'm gonna take care of whoever did that to you. I got your back, Babe."

Ashley hated it when she called her babe, or baby, and Leslie knew it. Watching Leslie was an exercise in restraint. It was all she could do not to go into a rage. The arrogance was rolling off Leslie as she continued to smirk at Ashley.

"I'm fine." Ashley's tone reflected the same sickening sweet one Leslie used. "Why'd you do it, Leslie?"

Leslie's eyebrows knotted briefly then relaxed as she licked her lips. Ashley recognized the slight signs of Leslie being uncomfortable. Yet, Leslie continued as if she didn't hear Ashley.

"Did you get the card I got for you? It was in my truck when these bozos arrested me." Leslie threw her head towards the guard standing behind her. Smiling, Leslie put her hand on the glass and waited. Ashley knew that Leslie was trying to make some kind of connection with Ashley and it made her want to retch.

Still staring at her, Ashley raised an eyebrow and said it again, "So why did you do it, Leslie?" Each word emphasized with Leslie's name drawn out in a menacing tone.

"Do what, baby?"

"Why did you do it, Leslie?"

"I don't know what you're talking about here, Hun."

"Why, Leslie?"

"Ashley, come on. You're going to have to give me a hint on what you're talking about."

"Why, Leslie?" Ashley's slow menacing tone was starting to peel back Leslie's cool veneer.

"Look, Ashley, I don't know what's going on or what game you're playing, but it's getting old," Leslie said, staring back at Ashley.

Ashley wanted to smile. She knew Leslie was getting pissed by the way she sneered. Ignoring Leslie's attempts to engage her was pushing Leslie closer to the edge. When Leslie got mad, this was the start of the slow burn coming to a full flame.

"Just tell me why, Leslie."

Each time, Leslie's composure cracked just a little more as she realized she had lost her grip on Ashley. Finally, Leslie had had enough and when Ashley next repeated that same question, Leslie lost control. The explosion just under the surface started right in front of Ashley as she watched Leslie move closer to the glass and glare at Ashley.

Just barely a whisper, Leslie said, "'Cause you deserved it, you fucking cunt. And that woman who tried to save you, your girlfriend, I gave her a little something to remember me by, too." Spit covered the window in front of Ashley. If evil had a face, it was Leslie personified.

Ashley smiled. She had Leslie. There was no denying what Leslie said. Now she only hoped that the recorders at the jail didn't malfunction. Moving closer to the glass, Ashley kissed it briefly and smiled again. Mouthing 'thank you' she set the receiver back on the cradle and stood. She knew she shouldn't have taunted Leslie, but relief flooded her when Leslie couldn't control her ego. Ashley wasn't going to be a victim anymore and Leslie was going away for a long, long time.

Leslie jumped up and slammed her head against the glass. "You fucking bitch, I'm gonna get out of here and when I do, I'm gonna ..." The words died on her lips as two deputy sheriffs rushed Leslie and pulled her away from the glass and out the door she had come in.

Stepping back from the window, Ashley stood and tried to watch through the slim window in the door. It was clear Leslie was out of control behind it. Screaming and yelling filtered through the heavy barrier, but Leslie wasn't a threat to Ashley anymore, so she wasn't scared. In fact, sitting across from Leslie gave Ashley a power she couldn't describe, but the idea of facing your demons came to mind. She had come to confront and instead had taken back the power she thought Leslie had over her. Never again would Ashley fear anyone, never again.

Chapter Thirty-seven

The waiting was killing Tyler. She had offered to go with Ashley to the County jail and wait, but Ashley had turned her down, instead asking her to wait for her mother to bring Mongrel home. The meeting between the two women had been interesting, Ashley's mom sizing up Tyler, and Tyler wishing she could crawl under a rock. There was nothing worse than meeting the parent of someone you were sleeping with and a parent always knew when you were sleeping with their daughter.

"Good morning, Mrs. Henderson?" Tyler questioned, looking first at her then down at the dog on her left. "Hey, Mongrel," Tyler said, squatting down to pet the obedient pup.

"I'm sorry, have we met?" Mrs. Henderson asked, her gaze appraising Tyler.

"Oh, I'm sorry. I'm Tyler Jackson. I was the firefighter that helped Ashley out at the shooting." Tyler extended her hand and waited.

Tyler noticed the slight hesitation in Mrs. Henderson as she took Tyler's hand and offered a meek handshake. It was going to take some time to break through the shell Mrs. Henderson had erected around herself and Tyler expected no less from someone who almost lost her daughter. Still waiting at the door, Mrs. Henderson cleared her throat and raised an eyebrow.

"You're the firefighter who saved my daughter."

Tyler smiled briefly, "I was just doing my job Ma'am."

"Well, I would say you went above and beyond your job. Thank you." The sincerity evident in Mrs. Henderson's voice.

The two women stared briefly at each other, each knowing something more needed to be said, but neither was comfortable with the other to express those feelings, yet. The silent lingered for a moment more before Tyler broke it.

"Oh, please, come in. I'm sorry." Tyler swept her arm wide as she moved out of the door way.

"Where's Ashley?" Mrs. Henderson inquired looking towards the bedrooms.

"Oh, she's not here. She had to run some errands and asked if I could wait for Mongrel." Tyler's hand rested on the dog's head scratching him. "Would you like to come in and wait?"

"No thanks. I've got some things I need to take care of. Just tell her that her mother stopped by and to call me. Thanks."

With that, the experience of meeting Ashley's mom was over and it didn't go well if Tyler thought about it too long. Looking down at Mongrel, Tyler shrugged her shoulders and closed the door. When she turned she watched Mongrel go from room to room, sniffing and looking.

"She's not here big guy, really." Tyler followed the dog into Ashley's room and watched as he jumped on the king size bed and sniffed around. "I bet you really missed her, huh?"

Mongrel stopped at Ashley's pillow, sniffed again and promptly laid down on Ashley's side of the bed with his head on Ashley's pillow. He looked up at Tyler, as if to let her know he wasn't going anywhere. Smiling at the dog's antics, Tyler walked over, sat on the bed and started petting the oversized security blanket. Obviously, he was used to sleeping on the bed or he wouldn't have just made himself at home, so who was Tyler to tell him to get off. It wasn't her house or her rules. She would let Ashley deal with him when she got home. Hopefully, she hadn't made a mistake letting him stay on the bed.

###

Standing taller, Ashley felt a calm cascade through her body. The heaviness in her shoulders was gone as Ashley had a bounce in her step while walking to her house. Looking around she noticed her SUV needed a wash, and her flower garden needed tending. Both were things she hadn't thought about doing just in case Leslie accidentally drove by. Ashley took a deep breath and suddenly realized she could live again, like a normal person. On duty her badge afforded her strength and protection, but now she no longer had to hide behind the badge. She had finally faced her demons, well one demon to be exact, and won. To say she felt free was an understatement. She felt liberated from the heavy burden of waiting for Leslie to show up at her door. The constant fear of accidentally, or purposely, seeing Leslie was over. Visiting the jail had a side benefit she hadn't expected and given Ashley the closure she now knew she needed. She would never forget how powerless Leslie looked in handcuffs. It helped solidify the fact that she was out of Ashley's life for good. Ashley knew court was still on the horizon, but hopefully Leslie's outburst at the jail would kill any option of an insanity defense.

Opening the door, Ashley expected to be greeted

by Mongrel, but nothing, not a sound. Tossing her purse on the bar she continued through the house until she came to the door of her bedroom. There, on the bed, lay her dog and her girlfriend, sleeping. Did she just think of Tyler as her girlfriend? Remembering Tyler's revelation at the coffee shop gave Ashley a nice jolt, her body throbbing as she remembered the way they had made love that afternoon. If she was lucky she would get a replay of those events now.

Mongrel popped his head off the pillow, his tail slapping the bed.

"Come here, boy." Ashley said, kneeling down to pet him.

She was surprised his excitement didn't wake up Tyler, but Tyler had warned her she was a heavy sleeper. *Interesting for a firefighter*, Ashley thought. Walking back through the house, she opened the French doors to the backyard and let Mongrel out to do his business. He'd find his way back in through the doggie door she had just taken the cover off of. After washing her hands she walked back into the bedroom and started to take her clothes off, tossing them indiscriminately on the floor. Naked, she slid along Tyler and wrapped a leg over her hip. Tyler's warm hand caressed her thigh as Ashley slid her hand under Tyler's t-shirt. Slipping her fingers under the band of Tyler's bra she heard Tyler groan when she squeezed the taut nipple.

"Well this is a nice way to wake up. Can you be my alarm clock every day?" Tyler asked, the husky tone making Ashley's pussy clench.

"Well, that depends," Ashley said, rubbing her groin against Tyler's tight ass.

"On what?" Tyler questioned, wishing she had a mint.

"What's in it for me?"

"Hmm, I see. We're working on the barter system, huh?"

"Maybe." Ashley smiled pinching the nipple a tad harder, making Tyler jump. "I like negotiating a deal that's beneficial to both sides. Besides …" Ashley slid her tongue along Tyler's ear and then went for the spot on Tyler's neck knowing it would take her over the edge, instantly. Ashley's teeth grazed the spot before she started sucking on Tyler's neck causing goose bumps to cover Tyler's arms. Tyler's reactions were so visceral that Ashley had to smile. Tyler could never hide how her body reacted to Ashley's touch. She was an open book Ashley loved to read, over and over again. She moved to the other breast and squeezed and pulled the hard nipple as she continued, "I think I'm in a better position to negotiate than you are, wouldn't you agree."

Her hand moved down inside Tyler's pants and cupped her pussy. Ashley's finger slipped between Tyler's wetness before it was pulled across Tyler's hard clit. Ashley felt Tyler rock against her hand each time she stroked her. This was going to be fast and hard if Ashley had anything to say about it. Catching Tyler sleeping was her undoing, but Ashley couldn't think of a better way to celebrate her liberation than a hot romp between the sheets.

"Ash, let me undo my pants."

Tyler was panting with each stroke across her clit and Ashley wasn't sure she wanted to let Tyler stop her.

"In a minute Ty. You're so close, I can smell you."

Ashley buried her nose in Tyler's hair and took a deep breath. Tyler had her own scent that drove Ashley wild, and when she was excited, Tyler had something about the way she smelled that was uniquely Tyler.

Ashley would have a hard time explaining exactly what it was, but she knew when Tyler was in the throes of coming.

"Oh fuck, Ash."

"Hmm, yes," Ashley said, drawing out the last word.

Slipping two fingers inside Tyler, Ashley had little room to work her whole hand in and out so she gently worked her two fingers deeper, then slowly pulled them to Tyler's opening, then thrust them deep again. With just enough room, Ashley's palm slapped against Tyler's clit, each thrust making Tyler gasp at the contact.

"Ty?"

"Huh?'

"I want you to reach up and squeeze your nipples for me."

Ashley licked Tyler's neck and started working on it with her teeth, gently nibbling the bugling muscle. Tyler's body was like a bow under tension, ready to snap any minute given the right amount of pull. Ashley could feel her own pussy clench watching Tyler squeeze and pull on her nipples through her t-shirt. The sight of another woman touching herself was a turn on for Ashley and watching Tyler's body respond to her touches was making her wet.

Ashley gasped when she felt Tyler's hand reach around and grab her clit. Tyler pulled away just enough to get her hand between their bodies and masturbate Ashley.

"You thought I was too far gone, didn't you?" Tyler's husky voice vibrated with each stroke from Ashley.

Tyler's finger was flicking Ashley's clit as she tried to concentrate on what she was doing to Tyler. Pushing her pussy against Tyler's hand she trapped it, preventing it from any further movement. She was on a mission and Tyler was trying to derail her and take control, but she was in control now and making Tyler come was her focus.

Ashley released her hold on Tyler's neck long enough to tease her. "Is this making you wet, Lover?"

"You know the answer to that. Can't you feel how wet I am?"

Ashley could feel Tyler's wetness dripping into her palm as she continued. Suddenly, Tyler's muscles tightened around Ashley's fingers and spasmed. Tyler tried to force herself further on Ashley's hand groaning with each thrust.

"Deeper, deeper Ash. Fuck."

Tyler's moaning jolted Ashley into action cupping Tyler's pussy and pushing her clit against Tyler's rock hard ass. The friction from Tyler's jeans would rub her raw, but she didn't care. She just wanted to come. She could feel her body tense as she started to orgasm and spiral out of control. Hoping to intensify her orgasm, Ashley rubbed her nipples against Tyler's t-shirt, making her body jerk with each stroke against Tyler's back. She had lost the battle to be in control, but the war wasn't over as she felt Tyler jerk each time she rubbed Ashley's sensitive clit. Tyler stopped her hand and forced Ashley's fingers deeper.

"Just hold them right there. Fuck."

Ashley held Tyler tighter, the last of her orgasm spreading throughout her body. She could feel Tyler's body shudder one last time before she released Ashley's hand then pulled it from her pants.

"Off."

"What?"

"Off," Tyler said pulling at the waist band of her jeans. "I feel like they're cutting me in half and my clit is rubbing against the seam. Shit."

Ashley was only too happy to help Tyler rid herself of her jeans. The night was young still and she hadn't had enough.

Chapter Thirty-eight

Pulling the towel tighter around her body, Tyler watched Ashley wipe the last drops of water from her body. Smiling, Tyler could feel contentment worm its way through her soul. She hadn't felt this good in a long time and she liked the way Ashley made her feel when she was around.

"Hey, Sexy, you hungry?" Ashley said sauntering towards Tyler.

Scooping Ashley up, Tyler kissed the bruised lips and slid her tongue over them. Ashley's towel was a deterrent that Tyler wanted gone, so she snaked a hand beneath Ashley, stood and let it fall to the floor.

"Hey! That was sneaky, You," Ashley said playfully slapping at Tyler's shoulder.

"I know. If you're nice I'll teach you all my tricks."

"Careful, you're still wounded."

"You think so?" Tyler picked Ashley up higher and pulled Ashley's legs around her waist. Cupping her ass Tyler slid Ashley's clit across her towel hoping the friction did what she wanted. She watched as Ashley closed her eyes and let her head roll back enjoying the friction against her body. The movement gave Tyler easy access to Ashley's neck and she took advantage of the moment. Kissing Ashley's neck Tyler could feel her throbbing pulse beneath her lips. With every up swing, Tyler licked a nipple. Not content with just a lick Tyler walked Ashley to the bed and laid her down.

"Don't remove your legs," Tyler commanded as she caressed Ashley's breasts, thumbing the nipples into hard points.

Palming the generous breasts Tyler slid her palms over the tips. She was starting to ache as she watched Ashley close her eyes and moan. Tyler caressed the soft, warm skin, sending a flood of warmth throughout her body. Tyler never got enough of touching Ashley. Her soft skin against Tyler's often made her feel like she was on fire. Each caress pushed Tyler closer and closer to the edge of losing control. Tyler liked her sex a little rougher, but Ashley wasn't in a place where Tyler thought she could go. Tyler bent over Ashley, rolling her tongue around a nipple, her other hand still torturing the other. Tyler felt Ashley weave her fingers through her hair and pull her head back, then grab one of her nipples and gently pinch it.

"Tyler?"

"Huh," Tyler felt Ashley's gentle grinds against her hips.

"Nightstand," Ashley said motioning with her head. "Inside."

Tyler felt Ashley release her hair as she leaned over and pulled open the drawer in the nightstand. Raising her eyebrows she looked back at Ashley and smiled. *Who knew,* Tyler thought pulling the harness and dildo from the drawer. Watching Ashley blush as she opened the box, Tyler let a slow, sensual smile ease across her face. She was somewhere she never thought she would be, with a woman she never imagined would have such a wild side to her.

"You sure?" Tyler asked, tossing the box to the floor and fingering the flesh colored dildo.

"Oh yeah," Ashley said reaching up to stroke the

cock. "I've been waiting for the right woman and well, you're the right woman."

Tyler almost melted when Ashley slid her tongue along her upper lip and gently bit her lower lip. Sensuality oozed off Ashley. Tyler pulled herself out of Ashley's embrace, stood and stepped into the harness pulling it up to her waist. The corset harness settled on her hips and before she could pull the straps, cinching herself in, Ashley grabbed the straps and pulled forcing Tyler's hips to her face. The sexy grin Ashley gave Tyler had mischief written all over it. Dropping her head Ashley flicked her tongue out across the tip of the dildo then looked up at Tyler. A jolt went through Tyler and her nipples responded to the brief contact Ashley's lips made with the dildo.

"I need to wash this thing, Ash." Reasoning washed through Tyler.

"I already did," Ashley said, seductively.

Tyler felt her knees weaken when Ashley stroked the phallus. Each stroke hit Tyler's erect clit making her body jerk. She knew she wouldn't last if Ashley kept this up, but before she could stop Ashley, she wrapped her lips around the tip and slowly moved down the dildo.

"Ash." Tyler could barely get out the word as she watched Ashley come back up to the tip, sliding her tongue around it again.

Tyler closed her eyes and rolled her head back as she felt Ashley stroke the rubber again. She felt a wet finger slide between the folds of her pussy and stroke her wetness, begging to be let in. Spreading her legs further Tyler let Ashley slide into her. Looking back down at Ashley, she smiled before Ashley descended on the dick one more time. Tyler felt like it was connected to her body, each stroke making her clit throb.

"Tyler, open your eyes and look at me," Ashley said softly.

Tyler hadn't realized she wasn't looking at Ashley, perhaps because the image of Ashley going down on the dildo was seared into her brain, a visual that would stay with Tyler forever. Looking again she found Ashley on her back beckoning to her, her legs and arms open to Tyler.

Lowering herself to the bed Tyler grabbed Ashley's legs and wrapped them around her waist. She felt Ashley run her hands over her breasts when Tyler got close enough. Holding the phallus Tyler gently brought the tip to Ashley's wet pussy and rolled it around her opening. Wanting to make the moment last, she hesitated watching it lay just outside of Ashley. Looking up at Ashley's face, Tyler watched intently as she slowly eased it inside of Ashley. Tyler's pussy clenched again when Ashley closed her eyes and moaned. Leaning down she kissed Ashley's lips and thrust her tongue inside. Ashley's legs hooked behind Tyler and pulled Tyler deeper inside. Once inside Tyler rolled her hips, gently moving the harness so the dildo slid back and forth in the warmth that enveloped it.

"Tyler, I want you to fuck me, not treat me like a virgin on our first night."

Tyler leaned back to look in Ashley's eyes and flashed her a roguish smile. "Well, now that I know what you want," Tyler said, pulling the harness back and sliding into her a bit harder. Keeping that tempo she watched Ashley lift her hips in anticipation of each stroke.

"That's it, just like that," Ashley said, breathlessly.

Grabbing Ashley's hips Tyler positioned the harness so that every stroked sent a charge through her own body and before she knew it an orgasm started coursing through her. Tyler blushed as she caught Ashley watching her come. Wave after wave washed over Tyler, her orgasms making her body tighten. Suddenly, she found herself rolled over and on her back, Ashley still firmly ensconced on the dick. Grabbing Ashley's ass and pulling her down with each thrust of her hips, she heard Ashley's orgasm before she felt it, a low growl slipping past Ashley's lips. Rocking back and forth on her hips, Ashley's body shook through the orgasm. Tyler couldn't resist kneading the soft pliant breasts in front of her as Ashley continued to shudder on her hips. Rolling Ashley over and resting her arms on either side of Ashley's head, Tyler looked down into fathomless depths of green. A soft kiss, a gentle breath and Tyler felt Ashley wrap her arms around her.

Pulling her hips to one side she slipped free of Ashley's warmth. She'd never loved someone that way and it felt amazing. An orgasm without touching, she knew it could be done, but she didn't think she was capable. Now she marveled at the thought. Lying on her side, she pulled Ashley close and tossed a cover over them. A soft chuckle drifted to her ears as she looked down at Ashley who tossed her head to the tenting of the cover.

"I probably should take it off, huh?" Tyler asked, slipping the harness down her legs and kicking it to the side. She didn't want to move, to lose the contact with Ashley's warm body. Red soft hair splayed across her chest as Ashley moved lower licking a nipple. Reaching up she wiped at the sheen of sweat that covered her forehead. *Lesbian sex in the past was not this strenuous, but add an enhancement and it changed the game,* thought Tyler.

Tyler watched Ashley's shallow breaths become long deep breaths, sleep having claimed her. Tyler ran her fingers through the soft hair and remembered they hadn't even talked about what happened at the jail. Later, she thought. Later.

Chapter Thirty-nine

The gavel echoed throughout the courtroom. Hours of silence finally ended as everyone in the room had listened intently to the prosecution's case. Ashley rarely looked over at Leslie sitting at the defendant's table. She'd seen Leslie walk in, dressed in a business suit looking more like her corporate self than the criminal she really was. She looked away when Leslie searched her out in the crowded gallery. The brief eye contact and a wink made Ashley want to gag. Clearly Leslie was still as cocky as ever. Ashley felt Tyler squeeze her hand when Leslie winked in their direction.

"It's okay," Tyler whispered.

Ashley patted Tyler's leg and smiled up at her. She felt Kelly pat her leg and whisper something, but she missed it. Her support system was firmly entrenched around her. Her mother sat next to Kelly, Tyler sat next to her and an assortment of officers had come to lend their support throughout the opening of the trial. Today was especially grueling since both she and Tyler had testified. She had been warned ahead of time that her testimony would probably last several days for the prosecution and it was a good bet that the defense would probably be a long cross-examination, too.

Sitting on the stand Ashley did her best not to look at Leslie and focused on the D.A. Some of the questions had been preemptive to squash anything the defense might try to twist. But she was under no illusions, they would ask anyway so she prepared herself for the onslaught. At least she would get a break due to the long holiday weekend.

"You ready," Tyler asked, pulling Ashley to her feet.

"Yep. Take me out of here, Handsome." Ashley crinkled her nose and regretted the comment as soon as she said it.

"Handsome, huh?" Tyler pulled Ashley into a hug.

"Handsome. Way to go stud?" Mike slapped Tyler on the back as he walked by.

"Sorry," Ashley said visibly cringing then giggling.

"Cute."

Ashley enjoyed the banter with Tyler and she knew Tyler gave as good as she got. Sliding her arm through her mother's as she walked up Ashley kissed her on the check.

"Had enough, Mom?'

"Oh, maybe. Why didn't you tell me, Honey?"

Ashley shook her head and shrugged her shoulders. "I didn't want you involved, Mom. Besides, it didn't last that long." Ashley was embarrassed now that her mother finally knew the truth about Leslie. Would she have told her mother anyway? Probably not. Leslie would have used her mother against her.

"I'm just sorry you had to go through all of that alone, Honey." Ashley's mom patted her hand and then hugged her waist.

"Well, I won't have to go through anything like that ever again." Ashley grabbed Tyler's hand and smiled at her.

"Well, you just better make sure she doesn't," Mrs. Henderson said in Tyler's direction.

"Mom!"

"What?"

Ashley heard Kelly laughing behind her and turned to face her partner. "And just what are you laughing about?"

"Looks like Tyler has her work cut out for her. Right, Handsome?"

"Excuse me, Ashley and Tyler. Can I talk to you for a second?"

Everyone stopped and turned at the sound of the district attorney's voice echoing down the hallway.

"Assistant DA Walker," Ashley said knowing something was wrong.

"Can I see you both in private?"

Ashley looked at Tyler and nodded, "We'll catch up with you guys at the restaurant."

By the time everyone had looked at each other and shrugged, Ashley and Tyler were taken to a room off the corridor.

"What's going on?" Ashley said, grabbing Tyler's hand for support.

"They want to make a deal."

"What? They can't do that, can they?" Tyler questioned the D.A.

"They can and they did. You guys were very sympathetic on the witness stand. They know they run a risk letting it go to the jury. Look, I just wanted to give you a head's up. We're weighing our options. With what happened in the jail, they took the insanity plea off the table. They're trying to shave some time off their client's sentence and plead her out."

Ashley felt sick to her stomach. Would the D.A. make a deal to close the case and move on or would they finish what they started? The strain of the last few days showed on Ashley's face and she just wanted this over so she could move on with her life. One way or the other she needed some type of closure. Looking at Tyler she smiled weakly and shook her head.

"I can't speak for Tyler, but do what you have to do."

"We just want to get on with our lives. It's been weeks and…" Tyler looked down at Ashley and patted her hand. "Do what you have to do."

"I was hoping you were going to say that. Leslie is going down for a long, long time. Life won't be long enough as far as I'm concerned. I'll call you when I have something to report. If you don't hear from me, I'll see you in court next week."

With that the D.A. was gone and Ashley and Tyler were left alone. Ashley felt Tyler wrap her in a warm embrace and squeeze, holding her tight. Ashley wrapped her arms around the one thing that had kept her grounded all this time, Tyler.

"Hey, you okay?" Tyler lifted Ashley's chin and smiled.

"Yeah. I think its setting in that all of this might finally be over. It feels like a bad nightmare and I'm finally waking up." Ashley felt Tyler stiffen. "Hey, hold on there. I didn't mean you. You're the only good thing that's come out of all of this."

Ashley backed up and looked down at their intertwined hands, and then brought Tyler's hand up and kissed it. While this chapter in her life was ending Tyler wasn't part of that ending. She was part of Ashley's new beginning and Ashley wasn't about to let Tyler walk out of her life so easily. Ashley cupped Tyler's face and kissed the pouting mouth.

"I love you, Ty." Ashley batted her eyes trying to stop the tears from forming. "I don't know if you feel the same way, but I need you to know. Now that the trial might end and things are getting back to normal, you don't have to stay. I mean—"

"I'm not going anywhere, Ash. I don't know when it happened, but I fell for you a long time ago. Maybe it was the strong woman who rejected me in the bar or the vulnerable one who needed protecting after the shooting, I don't know. But you're an amazing woman and I want to spend the rest of my life with you. I won't promise I don't come with some baggage, but it isn't a whole suite of luggage."

Ashley looked down and sighed, then chuckled at Tyler's joke and waited. She knew what she wanted to hear, but she had already heard what she needed to hear. Tyler wasn't going anywhere and Ashley knew she wouldn't force Tyler to say what she couldn't. Ashley heard Tyler clear her throat and continue.

"I love you, Ashley Henderson. I want to spend the rest of my life with you and when you're ready, really ready, I hope you'll do me the honor of marrying me some day."

As much as Ashley tried, she couldn't hold back the tears. She felt Tyler tilt her chin and kiss her, a slow seductive kiss that only Tyler could give. It set her skin on fire and made her body ache all over. Finally pulling back, Ashley's smoldering gaze gave way to a broad smile.

"Why don't we go home and finalize the deal, Handsome?"

"Oh, more bartering?"

"Oh no, we have a deal. I just need to tweak it a bit," Ashley said slapping Tyler's ass as they walked out.

Ashley felt herself pulled along the corridor. The only thing that would make this moment complete would be a setting sun, a naked body next to her, and the sound of waves hitting the sand. She knew it sounded cliché, but wasn't all romance at some point in time?

About the Author

Award winning author Isabella, lives in California with her wife and three sons. In June 2011, Isabella's first novel, Always Faithful, won a GCLS award in the Traditional Contemporary Romance category. She was also a finalist in the International Book Awards and an Honorable Mention in the 2010 Rainbow awards

She is a member of Gold Crown Literary Society, Romance Writers of America. She has written several short stories, and is now working on her next novel, Executive Disclosure due out in February 2012.

Other Titles Available at Sapphire Books

Always Faithful - By Isabella ISBN - 978-09828608-0-9

Major Nichol "Nic" Caldwell is the only survivor of her helicopter crash in Iraq. She is left alone to wonder why she and she alone. Survivor's guilt has nothing on the young Major as she is forced to deal with the scars, both physical and mental, left from her ordeal overseas. Before the accident, she couldn't think of doing anything else in her life.

Claire Monroe is your average military wife, with a loving husband and a little girl. She is used to the time apart from her husband. In fact, it was one of the reasons she married him. Then, one day, her life is turned upside down when she gets a visit from the Marine Corps.

Can these two women come to terms with the past and finally find happiness, or will their shared sense of honor keep them apart?

Scarlet Masquerade - By Jett Abbott ISBN - 978-0982860816

What do you say to the woman you thought died over a century ago? Will time heal all wounds or does it just allow them to fester and grow? A.J. Locke has lived over two centuries and works like a demon, both figuratively and literally. As the owner of a successful pharmaceutical company that specializes in blood research, she has changed the way she can live her life. Wanting for nothing, she has smartly compartmentalized her life so that when she needs to, she can pick up and start all over again, which happens every twenty years or so.

Clarissa Graham is a university professor who has lived an obscure life teaching English literature. She has made it a point to stay off the radar and never become involved with anything that resembles her past life. She keeps her personal life separate from her professional one, and in doing so she is able to keep her secrets to herself. Suddenly, her life is turned upside down when someone tries to kill her. She finds herself in the middle of an assassination plot with no idea who wants her dead.